WHILE THE EMPEROR SLEPT

DECIMUS JULIUS VIRILIS

BOOK TWO

B. R. STATEHAM

Published 2023 by Next Chapter

Edited by Charity Rabbiosi

Cover art by Lordan June Pinote

CHAPTER ONE

The crowd was in a festive mood. The mass of Roman citizenry and others stood and mingled around casually, waiting for the first of the day's races to begin, the ambient noise of the large gathering a clash of voices, dialects, and language. Here and there vendors moved through the crowds selling their goods. Spicy foods, their various aromas strong enough to entice even the dead back to life, filled the air. But there was also watered down wines, and cheap trinkets by the hundreds to choose from. Today's races in the Hippodrome held the promise of being quite exciting. Phillipus The Greek, the number one driver of the Reds, would be racing against his fellow countryman, Titus Magnus, the Green's best driver, in the fourth race of the day. It promised to be a hard fought battle. Neither Phillipus nor Titus could tolerate the other. Both promised bloody mayhem if one saw the other ever again in a race they participated in.

There was a growing sense of anticipation in the milling throng. For several days there had been the buzz of whispered excitement vibrating through Rome concerning the rivalry between Phillipus the Greek and Titus Magnus. The vast wooden oval of the hippodrome almost groaned audibly from the weight of the crowds that had come to witness the battle. But the crowd seemed docile enough. Perhaps it had something to do with a large contingent of purple clad soldiers of the Praetorian Guards moving quietly through the crowd in groups of two, eyeing the crowd and looking formidable in the process. There was nothing like Roman soldiery, especially those now dressed in purple, which could put a dampener on a potentially rowdy crowd.

Apparently, the rumor was true. Caesar was coming to observe the races from his color canopied box. It was said the old man had a passion for the sport. Whenever he graced his presence at such a sporting event the presence of his newly created Praetorian Guards were obvious and intentional. As the old saying went, *Better to nip trouble in the bud than to quell a full-fledged riot.* Caesar was a master at finding trouble and nipping it in the bud long before it became a problem for him.

He was too. And, with a thin smile of a sneer barely pulling his lips back, it made sense. They were related. He and the *Augustus*. Distant cousins. The Julii family were a large clan which ran all through the ranks of Roman society. Patrician and Plebian, one could find a Julii kinsman hovering within hailing distance here in Rome. And as the gods knew... if there was trouble to be had, the odds were a Julii was either the instigator of the problem, or the recipient. In this case he firmly believed he was the latter.

His name was Decimus Julius Virilis. And he could feel it in his bones. Almost sniff it in the air. Someone wanted to kill him. Someone in this crowd. Someone close and waiting for the right moment.

The thin sneer of an amused smile stayed on his lips as he

gazed at the crowd, standing with his two comrades, and waited for the attack to come. Others, politicians or tradesman, might have sloughed off the feeling of imminent danger with a shrug of the shoulders, or a wave of a hand. Or, if guilty of some deed hidden from the world, perhaps their guilt would make them weak in the knees with beads of sweat beginning to pop up across their brow like unwanted weeds. But he was neither politician nor coward. Neither worried nor unwary.

He could sense it in his bones. Danger, imminent danger, was pressing down upon him, waiting for the right moment to strike. Twenty-five years serving in the legions of Rome gave him this sixth sense. Twenty-five some odd years as an officer working up through the ranks of the army hammered into his soul this ability to sense trouble coming long before it materialized. Giving him an advantage over others in many instances. Knowing it was coming, he was prepared for it. A fight was coming. An enemy was close at hand. Forewarned and ready, he stood in the middle of the milling masses with his two loyal followers beside him, ex-legionnaires themselves, and calmly waited for the action to begin.

The two were dressed in the plain, functional clothes of a Roman freeman. Hard looking men. Tanned and weather beaten. Reminding onlookers of dried strips of leather that had, over the years, endured much and survived all. Both were holding plain looking plates of cheap pottery in one hand, intent on consuming the foul smelling piles of some Germanic dish as rapidly as possible. Sour kraut and sausage. He was quite familiar with the dish. Five years of serving as the primus pilum of the *IV Macadonica*, a legion based in the land of the Teutones, introduced him to the delicacy.

Decimus stood between the two dressed in an off-white toga which had a fine purple hem, distinct but subdued, prominently displayed in the cloth. A patrician. A Roman nobleman.

An older man with a high sloping forehead, a receding hairline, and dark, piercing brown eyes.

A soldier. Unquestionably. And a veteran.

He had the commanding presence of a Roman officer. It was obvious. Especially for a Roman. Almost every male milling about in the crowd had at one time or the other, served his time as a legionnaire. The Dalmatian revolts of 8 A.D. were not that long ago. Prior to that was the revolt in the forest of Germany to quell. And before that ... not that long ago ... were the wars fought against fellow Romans. The long wars Caesar fought to subdue the radical Marcus Antonius and his fabled mistress, Cleopatra.

Yes, this middle-aged patrician was a Roman officer. One who saw action and knew hardships. One who knew how to command men and expected to be obeyed. Dressed in civilian clothes he was now. But that meant little. For this kind of man, a soldier was a soldier. There was no other way of life.

"Observed anyone who looks suspicious?"

The patrician's voice was soft but filled with a resonating quality of quiet authority and confidence. Soothing to one's ear for now. But promising a harsh reality if aroused to anger.

The smaller of the three men nodded gently, a hand coming up to form a gesture or two toward the patrician in the process. Both patrician and the other freeman watched the little man's hand and nodded as if they knew exactly what he was silently saying to them.

"I did not see him. Describe him quickly," he said quietly.

More hand gestures.

A small man. My size. With curly blond hair and a dirty face. He was dressed like a Greek peasant. He kept moving through the crowd some distance from us. First, he would be in front of us. And then to our rear. But always close enough to observe us, tribune. I last saw him standing to our left. Over by the fountain.

"Humph," grunted the taller of the two freemen. A dark complexioned figure from the deserts of perhaps Libya or Morocco. "Your old friend, Menelaus, coming back to haunt us again, tribune?"

The patrician's dark eyes looked into the face of his second companion for a moment or two thoughtfully before finally, shaking his head.

"Menelaus is an old, old man by now. Too old and too sick to have any desire to seek revenge. Besides, there are no better spies and assassins than a Greek. Anyone could have hired this creature to keep us in view. Until we have more information it is useless for us to conjecture over."

The small man's hands flew into action again.

Our orders, tribune. Do we capture this man alive? Or do we quietly dispatch him to his just rewards?

The patrician smiled. The wicked, cruel smile of a man who knew how to hunt. And hunt not just any query. But hunt the ultimate prey.

"We spread out. Each of us will stay within sight of the other. One of you will sit in the stands above me. The other to one side. If this Greek spy is seen, rub your nose with the index finger of your right hand as a sign. If he has accomplices in the crowd working with him, the signal will be the index finger of your left hand. We will encircle him and try to catch him. If he sees us and flees, perhaps we can follow him and see where he leads us."

Both freemen nodded before disappearing into the growing crowd as if they had been nothing more than smoke from a burning vizier blowing away in the wind. The tribune's smile widened minutely on his thin lips. It was like old times. Working the streets again in a foreign city playing the spy. A spy hunting a spy. It was an exciting game. A deadly game. One that he so much enjoyed and sorely missed.

The crowd began moving. Above, high on the walls of the stadium, trumpeters told the crowd the races were soon to begin. He made his presence conspicuous, nevertheless his eyes roamed the crowd casually yet alertly. He wanted visual contact with this talented blond-haired spy. But as he and the crowd filed into the Hippodrome he saw no one that fit Gnaeus' description. He was not surprised. If this man was as good as Gnaeus suggested, he doubted he would get much, if any, of a glimpse. Yet he remained vigilant. There was a question which remained to be answered. Was this spy here just to keep watch on him? Or was he here to assassinate him?

An assassination attempt made sense. He had enemies. Many enemies. One did not serve in the legions as long as he had in various roles and not make enemies. Especially if one considered the many special 'detached duties' assignments he had been given over the years. Spying on allies as well as enemies were some of the special assignments. Others were more deadly. Far more deadly. And secretive. Not the kind one bragged about in the open. Not if one wanted to live quietly in retirement in Rome for their remaining years unmolested.

But if the Greek was spying, keeping tabs on his whereabouts, then a whole new set of questions came to mind. Who? Why? Why take the trouble to spy on an old soldier who had recently retired from the army and was, for all practical purpose, unemployed and uninvolved. He led a quiet life. He rarely accepted invitations to social gatherings. He kept himself out of sight and out of mind from those in Rome who still wielded power. With the reputation he had it was better for him to remain sight unseen for as long as possible.

But if Gnaeus was right, and he was seldom wrong in these matters, someone had taken interest in him. That did not bode well for his long-term safety or quality of life while here in the city. It would be best to find out who, and for what reason, this newfound interest had been generated over him.

He appeared to be interested in the races. The first two races pitted some of the up and coming chariot drives of each of the six more renowned racing associations in four and six chariot sprints. Teams draped in the colors of their various racing teams paraded around the long, narrow track below before each race, giving time for the crowds to place their bets. He made it a show of betting on the Reds in every race. Each time he laid a wager he would stand up from his seat. Each time he stood, his eyes played across the crowd around him.

Twice he thought he saw just the suggestion of blond hair in the crowd. Never a face. Just the movement of a body and blond hair submerging deep into the standing crowd and disappearing from view. A casual glance toward Gnaeus found his old companion in the wars eyeing the crowd but seeing nothing. On one wager he stood up and turned to face the crowd behind him. Three rows up, sitting directly behind him was the long, darkly tanned face of Hakim, his other companion. He too made no gesture indicating anything amiss had been observed.

Below in the dirt young drivers were driving their chariots recklessly in an effort to make a reputation. The sounds of thunderous crashes and splintering wood came all too often. With each mishap the crowd leapt to their feet and roared in delight. When they did, he *felt* more than saw bodies moving through the crowd. Bodies inching closer and closer to him in a patient stalking of predator toward prey. When the attack came, not unsurprisingly, it came from a totally unexpected direction.

There was, below, the resounding collision of three teams of horses and chariots crashing into each other. Horses screamed in terror. Splinters and chunks of various chariots flew into the air. Bodies of drivers, thrown from their chariots, hurled through the air before tumbling across the stadium's thick sand. The crowd went wild. Everyone came to their feet. For several long seconds the crowd roared and cheered and booed all at the same time. And then, to his right, a fight broke out between partisan groups sitting too close together for comfort. Four burly looking men dressed in the colors of the Greens began pushing around five men dressed in blue. Fists flew. The fight pulled in additional participants. Pandemonium broke out in the stands.

The crowd was packed tight in the seats around him. As he watched the fight to his right grow in intensity, followed by loud cheers and jeers from those surrounding the spectacle near him, behind him he felt bodies moving suddenly to one side in an unnatural fashion. Someone was pushing through the crowd behind him. Half turning, he caught the glimpse of blond hair directly behind. More importantly he glimpsed the long narrow iron blade of a dagger held low and partially covered by a cheap tunic appear beside the assassin's waist. It flashed forward with astonishing speed straight for his lower back. A deep wound to his liver would be fatal.

His right arm swept around him in a swift, hard move. His forearm caught the assassin's knife hand at the wrist and knocked the deadly blade to one side. Rotating around, his left hand came up and reached for the assassin's shoulder while his right arm moved, allowing him to grasp the man's right forearm firmly with an iron grip. But the assassin was good. He twisted his shoulder away from the tribune's attempt to grab it and used a foot to kick hard at the tribune's right leg. The assassin's foot caught the tribune just above his knee with a powerful blow.

The pain was excruciating. His hand fell away from the assassin's knife hand. He staggered backward and bumped into someone directly behind him. Angrily, the man yelled out something unintelligible and shoved the tribune off him. The violent push helped the tribune to regain his footing. But all for naught. The assassin was gone. Like the ghost he was, he had slipped somehow deep into the sea of faces and disappeared altogether.

When the brawl in the stands was finally subdued after a squad of Praetorian Guards descended onto the menagerie of fisticuffs with bludgeons and iron bars, the crowd quickly settled back into their seats. But the tribune, his right leg throbbing in pain, slowly withdrew from his seat. As he ascended the steps to the cause walk he was joined by Gnaeus and Hakim. Neither had seen a thing. To their dismay they had not even seen the attack on the tribune.

The long walk back to the tribune's small house was a trek of pain filled with grim silence.

CHAPTER TWO

He sat the silver goblet of wine onto the polished marble surface of the table beside him and stared off into the distance. Something bothered him. Nagged at him deep in his mind. Something about the morning's attempt on his life. His leg throbbed from the kick the young assassin had so expertly administered to him in making his escape. But that was not the problem. There was something else ... something *else* which worried his mind like a dog worrying a legionnaire's worn out leather sandal.

The assassin had been very skilled. Very young and very skilled. And incredibly fast. He knew if it had not been for that small disturbance of the crowd behind him he would never have been in time to turn and ward off the killing blow from the man's knife. But the odd movement of the crowd had warned him just in time.

Hmmm...

Perhaps that was it. The odd movement of the crowd. Perhaps that was what bothered him the most. A skilled assassin with superb reflexes and excellent training. One who knew how to move within a crowd, sight unseen, even while others were aware of his general presence and were looking for him to make his presence known, making the mistake of warning his prey before the blow fell. Warning his prey by unnecessarily jostling the crowd as he stepped up to strike the killing blow.

It was as if ... as if the assassin *wanted* to warn him of his presence.

Decimus frowned and lifted himself off the marble bench and turned to face the wide, long marbled bath. His mind rumbled in dissatisfaction and worry. He did not like incongruities in any portion of his life. He did not like questions running through his mind which had no concrete answers that would resolve the conundrum. This morning's assassination attempt had been foiled by a simple mistake. A rookie mistake from a killer who clearly knew his trade consummately.

Why? Why the obvious slip of professionalism?

Or was it a mistake?

Was it, possibly, something else? Perhaps, if one was willing to wildly speculate, it could be construed as a subtle *invitation* being offered. An invitation by, so far, parties unknown. Parties who would, when they were ready, identify themselves soon enough.

Or could it have been a *warning*? A warning from some important person who found it too dangerous to warn him through normal channels? If so, subtle but powerful sources were at work beneath the tranquility of Rome's usual raucous daily life. Either way, it did not matter. Whether *invitation* or *warning*, forces unknown were mysteriously circulating around his shoulders like some growing maelstrom. As it stood at the moment, his only recourse was to wait. To wait and see what came next.

With a shrug from a shoulder he slipped off the short toga

and took the first tentative step into the hot bubbling waters of the bath. Behind him his servant, the pepper-haired Gnaeus, eyed his master ruefully and then bent down and retrieved the short robe from the marbled floor. In the light of a hundred candles filling the bath with a soft warm light, the man descending into the water eyed the black marble columns of the private bath. He noted the rich drapes which hung from the marbled ceiling, felt the warmth of the marble floors he stood on and nodded to himself in pleasure. Yes. The pain in his right knee still ached. But the warm waters of the bath would go a long way in the healing process.

The *Baths of Juno Primus*, with its marbled columned porch and impressive water fountains at the base of its portico, was the newest public baths in Rome. It sat three blocks away from the gigantic *Balisca Julius*, the elegant and impressively enclosed public forum and administrative building just completed in the heart of the city. The baths, rumored to have been built with donations from the Imperator himself, were equally impressive. It may have been true. He knew Gaius Octavius. An old man now known as Gaius Octavius Caesar, *the Augustus*. He knew the other Caesar was that kind of person. Julius Caesar had a passion for spending money lavishly on grand architecture. Octavius inherited the family trait. Both had a passion for building. Building large, grand structures out of the finest marble. Each dreamed of converting, in one lifetime, a once dreary, almost rural, city called Rome into a world class megalopolis.

Smiling, Decimus Julius Virilis stepped into the warm clear waters of the steaming bath and lowered himself onto a marble bench. Closing his eyes, he stretched arms on either side of the bath and leaned back, heaving a sigh of relief.

He sat in the water and allowed his senses to wonder. Vaguely, in other parts of the large bathhouse, he heard the voices of men mumbling or the splashing of water. Somewhere a woman's voice, probably that of a serving girl, was laughing merrily. Somewhere else the tinkling of goblets clinking together told him men were enjoying their wine. The baths were a giant complex filled with senators, generals, politicians. The rich and elite of Rome's rather complex society. In such a place like this one would find the most noble and the most carnal. Without question cabals were being hatched. Dark secrets were being revealed. Roman politics thrived behind the closed doors of each large bathing pool reserved for one patron or another. Chin deep in the artificially warm waters of these baths there was no conceivable plot, no scandalous terror, men of power and wealth could not converse in with conspiratorial whispers which had not been discussed a hundred times before.

His mind ran through, for the hundredth time, the little incident earlier that morning. A very talented Greek spy/assassin. A master at blending in and out of large crowds like some human chameleon. Who was his master? Why had he been selected for assassination? What dark, diabolical cabal of intrigue was beginning to move quietly yet savagely here in the heart of Rome?

He would not lie to himself. This morning's little game had stimulated his mind greatly. It felt good to be in action again. Yet it irritated him as well. A brief respite from the drudgery and boredom of an active life condemned to return to the retirement of civilian life lay ahead of him. Unless, somehow, miraculously, his fortune was about to turn, and some new danger would soon crop up its ugly head and offer a return back into the life he so clearly loved.

Sighing, he gently pushed the cacophony of noise from his mind, allowing the heat of the water to seep into aching muscles and a tired body. The scented water was like the hands of a trained masseuse. He felt himself slipping away into an ocean of sensual delight. He was an average size man in height. But the numerous scars which tattooed his flesh in a bizarre matrix of randomness, along with the amazing display of muscles he yet retained, would have indicated to any onlooker this man was anything but remotely average.

Twenty-five years soldiering in one of the many legions loyal to Octavius Caesar had a way of hardening a man's body ... a man's soul. From Hispania to Aegypt; from Illyrium to Gaul. One legion after another. Fighting. Fighting Gauls. Fighting Spaniards. Fighting Romans. Hundreds of skirmishes. Several pitched battles. Stepping over friends and foes alike lying on the ground dead, sword dripping with blood in one hand and shield in the other. Battle fields littered with the dead. The dying. And those who had miraculously survived through no fault of their own.

Twenty-five years.

Watching fool politicians appointed to command riding prancing horses, banners and Eagles rising in the sunshine, with men shouting and hammering their shields with the swords eager for battle, only to, months later, see the same legion either victorious and lusty or defeated and disgraced. Or worse ... decimated and barely clinging in existence.

Twenty-five years.

Rising up through the ranks. First as a simple legionnaire in the tenth cohort ... essentially the raw recruits of a legion. Proving himself as both a leader and as a fighter. Attaining on the battlefield the promotion to centurion and assigned again to a tenth cohort as its commander. Years of slugging through summer heat and winter's cold. Through rain and snow. Facing an almost unlimited number of Rome's enemies. Facing rampaging war elephants. Facing armor clad Parthian cataphract cavalry with their deadly lances and stinging composite bows. Facing Greek spears stacked up in their compact, vaunted, phalanxes. Facing naked, blue painted Celtic madmen wielding gigantic two-handed swords taller than a man. But eventually ... with a little luck at surviving defeats as well as victories, along with the acumen of using his own natural abilities ... his star kept rising. Rising eventually to *primus pilum,* or First Spear: the top-ranking centurion commanding the First Cohort in a Roman legion. And finally, from there, to being promoted to a tribune and given the rank of *Praefectus Castorum.* The highest rank a professional soldier could attain. Third in command of a Roman legion. The soldier's soldier a legion's twenty or so tribunes and eighty or so centurions came to with their problems. The soldier expected to maintain discipline in the army. To feed the army. To provide the arms. To mold thousands of disparate individual souls into one efficient killing machine.

But no more. No more.

A lifetime of soldiering was enough. With what few years of good health remained to him he would enjoy as a free man. He had accepted all the accolades, all the honors bestowed on him by noblemen and commoner. He no longer served anyone. No longer took orders from anyone. No longer felt *obligated* to anyone. It was a strange feeling. A dichotomy of emotions. On one hand was the feeling of joy ... immense joy of finally, *finally* being in command of his own fate. On the other hand was this feeling of extreme loss. An odd emptiness hanging just below his consciousness. As if something critical was missing. An order given and yet to be obeyed. Frowning, he inhaled the hot humid air of the baths and opened his eyes.

What was he going to do with himself? The need to be gainfully employed was of no concern. Retiring from the position of *Praefectus Castorum* meant he left the service of the Imperator as a wealthy man. Almost fifteen years of being first a centurion and then a tribune meant, among other things, being involved in the handling of his men's savings. Yes, most of the men he commanded spent their wages on women and drink as fast as they could. But a number of men in any legion had learned to save some money back. To throw it into the cohort's banking system in the hopes that, if the army was successful and cities or provinces were plundered, their meager savings would grow.

The final three years of his army life had been a considerable financial boon. As *Praefectus Castorum,* his staff had been in charge of the entire legion's savings. Several thousand sesterces worth. If an officer was astute in his men's investments, a sizeable profit could be had by all. And if a legion was fortunate to be favored by its commander, or legate, for exceptional service, the reward would be even greater.

He was not called *The Lucky* for nothing. Lucky in war. Lucky in investing. Lucky in being related to the richest man in the empire. Gaius Octavius Caesar. Money was of no concern to him. He would live comfortably for the rest of his life.

But what to *do*? What exercise to entertain and stimulate his mind? He needed a challenge. A goal ... a ... *puzzle* ... to keep his wits about him. Without some challenge for the gray matter in his skull to dwell on, life was nothing but a series of boring mannerisms to endure.

Closing his eyes again, he idly heard his servant Gnaeus pouring wine in a large goblet for him. And then ... a brief silence. An odd silence. An out of place silence. Softly followed by just the lightest whisper of heavy cloth rubbing across the leather scabbard of a sheathed gladius.

He didn't move or show any outward gesture he was aware of a new presence behind him. Resting in the water of the bath he appeared to be asleep. But every nerve in his body was tingling with delight! He heard the soft tread of three distinct sets of sandals. With one of the three, strangely, without question an old man. Opening eyes slowly he noticed the colors around him ... the blue of the water, the black of the marble columns, the white of the marble bath walls ... seemed to be a hundred times more intense! For the first time in *weeks* he felt alive. And when he heard that distinct shuffling of feet and the odd hissing of someone finding it difficult to breathe, he almost laughed out loud.

"Greetings, cousin," he said quietly, coming to a standing position and turning to face his unannounced guests. "I see the weight of the empire has yet to dim the light in your eyes. Still the wily old fox you've always been, I suspect."

Three looked down at him as he stood in the bath. Two of them were big men dressed in the distinct cuirass and greaves of the Praetorian Guards. Around their shoulders were short capes of the royal purple trimmed in silver thread. Underneath their left arms were their brightly polished bronze helms. At their waists lay the short blades of the Roman gladius; the double-edged weapon had carved out a vast empire for the City of Rome and its people.

Between the two was an old man slightly stooped over and dressed in a dark, wine-red toga. Around his shoulders and covering the curls of his white hair was a plain cloak and hood of purple linen. There was no mistaking this man.

"Good evening, Decimus Julius Virilis," Caesar *Augustus* said, an amused smile spreading across thin lips. "I see you still, after today's little tussle at the races this morning, retain all your limbs and most of your senses."

"No thanks to you, Imperator," Decimus laughed, making his way out of the bath completely unconcerned about his nakedness and men armed standing before him. "You've tried to kill me at least a hundred times."

"One of my few failures I'm sure," replied the old man, chuckling.

"Am I mistaken to assume your presence among us unannounced is related in some fashion to this morning's festivities?"

The old man's eyes, bright and alive, looked upon his distant cousin with mirth and pleasure. They had known each other for years, ever since Decimus, as a boy of fourteen, ran away from home and joined his first legion. A legion he happened to be commanding in Greece facing Mark Anthony so many years ago. Nodding approvingly, the old man moved closer to the younger man, took him gently by one arm and squeezed it affectionately.

"I am in need of your services, cousin. An old enemy of ours has decided to lift itself out of the grave and return from the dead. An enemy who, if it is allowed to refresh itself and grow among the living, will surely threaten the work you and I have accomplished in the last thirty years. The empire is indeed threatened, my faithful cousin. The peace of Rome might soon shatter into irreparable shards of broken dreams if we allow this poison to gather strength. I confess, I am reluctant to come to you and ask you for your assistance. You have stood by our side so faithfully all your life. I had no intentions of interrupting the peace you have so deservedly won. But I have nowhere else to go. No one better suited to track this danger down and destroy it."

Decimus smiled. The eloquence of Octavius was still radiantly apparent, even now in his advanced age. His cousin's oratory could move entire armies, even nations, to accomplish great deeds. His words had moved him, often, to tears of joy over the decades he had served him. Nothing had changed.

"I am yours to command, Caesar. Who is this ancient foe I must track down and return to the grave?"

CHAPTER THREE

To his right the waters of the Tyrrhenian Sea seemed to lift up and fill the late afternoon sky with a soft blue haze from horizon to horizon. Sails, white and wine red from several large cargo ships, moved with an elegant ease as they headed for the port of Ostia. Sea gulls circled and wove through the partially cloudy skies above them. The Roman countryside that slid down to the sea was a lush verdant green. To him it looked like the vast gardens of a royal estate as he rode down the rough trail toward their destination.

The sun was out and deliciously warm. The panoramic view of the countryside pleasing to the eye.

One would think, if one only trusted his eyes and nothing more, the world was beautiful and peaceful, and tranquility was the order of the day. But he knew better. He knew the true nature of the world. Life was an illusion. Beauty only a mask to hide the darkness and pain from our eyes.

Reining in his powerful mare he turned and looked at the small entourage behind him. Gnaeus looked decidedly ill at ease sitting on a horse. In his opinion a good Roman soldier never road a horse. But, dressed in the garb of a Roman legionnaire, he remained silent and stoic. With the plain conical helm of a legionnaire partially hiding the thick mass of pepper and salt colored hair, the simple off-white linen undergarment underneath the typical lamellar armor of a Roman cavalryman, Gnaeus reined in his horse expertly and eyed Decimus with an unreadable mask for a face.

A humorous smile, barely visible, played across the tribune's lips before turning his head and looking at the two other men who reined in on either side of Gnaeus. One was thin framed with the hooked nose of a scowling hawk. Like Gnaeus, he too was dressed in the typical armor and uniform of a cavalryman. And like his servant, a man whom Decimus had known for years in the army. A specialist in his own right. A man who knew how to find things. Anything. Find it and retrieve it without making any raucous noise about it. Some said Rufus was a thief. A pick pocket. A purse snatcher. He knew Rufus for what he truly was. A man with a very special talent any commander of a legion would require sooner or later.

Or a man now in his newly appointed position.

The third cavalryman was very much different. He was a tall man with thick arms and powerful thighs. He rode his horse with the ease of someone who had lived all his life around horses. He was dark complexion with jet black eyes and a small mouth. There seemed to be an aloofness ... a sense of otherness ... that separated him from the rest of them. Indeed he was this stranger. He was not Roman born. He was a foreigner. A tribesman from the deserts of Numidia. Or Libya. Perhaps even Morocco. Yet he too, like the others, was a man whom he had known and trusted for years.

"Hassad ... that way," he said lifting an arm and pointing toward the south. "Check the surrounding countryside for any tracks. Make a full circle around the crime scene. You will find us there when you return."

The black-eyed hunter from the desert nodded and urged his horse on. He moved out rapidly and soon disappeared into a copse of trees hugging a small hill. Decimus, waiting until the rider was well out of sight, grunted and turned his horse toward the southwest and heeled its flanks.

With the two riding abreast and slightly behind him, the newest tribune of Rome's *Cohortes Urbanae* topped a small grassy knoll and began descending rapidly down upon the odd scene below.

After the civil wars, after Octavius' arch rival, Mark Anthony, had been dispatched to Hades, Octavius returned to begin rebuilding both the city of Rome and the empire. In Rome, after decades of neglect and civil strife, he found a city dominated by powerful underworld gangs. Gangs, bought and paid for by powerful patrician families of Rome had carved out their own private empires within the city. To fight the tenacious tentacles of organized crime, Caesar created two organizations and gave them the specific tasks to accomplish. Together they were to bring crime under control and provide some measure of safety for the citizens from the ever-constant fear of the city burning to the ground in one gigantic conflagration. One was the old *Vigiles Urbani.* The other was the *Cohortes Urbanae.*

The vigiles were the firefighters and beat cops of the city. The city-watch. A carry over idea, greatly expanded, from the numerous privately funded fire brigades and neighborhood watches that littered the city during Julius Caesar's time. The Imperator collected the various units into one unit, assembled them along the lines of a Roman legion, and established taxes to pay for them. Most of the men were ex-slaves commanded by Roman citizens—usually retired officers from the army. They worked during the night looking for fires and chasing down common hoodlums. They were effective if not, occasionally, a bit brutal.

The *Cohortes Urbana* acted more like the homicide division of a city's police force. They investigated violent crime, organized crime, political shenanigans. They too were organized along the lines of a Roman legion. But unlike the vigiles using ex-slaves as their manpower, only free Roman citizens could join the cohorts. Better paid and equipped compared to their vigiles cousins, the Urban Cohorts could, if the need arose, actually be pulled from the city's streets and used in military operations.

The Imperator commissioned Decimus with the rank of tribune in the Urban Cohorts. A tribune minus the normal eight hundred or so men most tribunes in the army, or the Vigiles, or the Urbanae, would command. His orders, straight from the quill of Octavius himself, decreed he was on detached service answerable only to the Imperator.

His assignment was simple. Find, and bring to justice those whom the Imperator thought were of a particular dangerous threat to the newly acquired peace of the empire.

Like this case.

Reining up in front of a mixed bag of vigiles and urban cohort soldiers standing around the destruction of what once had been a large wagon, he nodded to the centurion in charge and then slipped from his horse, throwing back the edge of his scarlet and purple trimmed short riding cloak in the process.

"Hail, tribune!" the young officer said, snapping to attention and saluting.

"At ease, son. And be so kind as to inform me of this situation."

In the thick grass were several large dark stains where people had died violent deaths. The bodies were gone but the visual evidence was ample to the trained eyed to conclude no one had survived the attack. A quick sweep of the ground suggested to Decimus at least four people were dead. The litter of several wooden trunks smashed to pieces with their contents strewn all over the side, even the ripped out bottoms of the wagons themselves mixed in with the other flotsam, indicated someone must have been in search of something important.

"Night before last the servant of a merchant in Ostia brought word there had been a series of murders ... a massacre as they described it ... just outside the port. I sent two men out on horses to ascertain the truth. As you can see the information was correct."

He saw Rufus nod his head toward his master and drift off toward the sea to begin his assigned task. Gnaeus, scowling as always, silently moved away in a different direction and began looking at the signs left behind in the dirt and grass. Decimus nodded, turned, and strode to one particularly large dark stain in the grass and knelt down. The young centurion behind him followed respectfully yet watched the two servants of the tribune curiously.

"The bodies?"

"In Ostia, sir. In the morgue of the vigiles' barracks."

"Any survivors?" he asked as he used an index finger to trace the outline of a particularly large partial print of distinctive shoe sole in the dust of the narrow trail beside the grass.

"None that we know of. When I arrived I found four bodies. Two men of rank it would seem and two servants. And, of course, the scene which greets you now."

"Identification of any of the men?"

"None. No signet rings. No personnel scrolls. Nothing of monetary value left behind."

"Are you sure, centurion, of the veracity of your men? Are you sure no one in your command decided to claim a small prize of his own? Say the first two men who came out and discovered this scene?"

He stood up and turned to face the younger man. A hot flash of anger swept across the centurion's face but quickly subsided. The officer was of a famous plebian family. A very famous, and *rich*, family. Rarely had anyone doubted his veracity.

But standing before him was a tribune with a high sloping forehead and a thin swipe of grayish/blond curly hair covering the upper regions of his cranium. The man also had the deep, experienced, weather-beaten face of a man who had seen much in life; like that perhaps of an old soldier. Certainly the man exhibited the confident, almost arrogant, gate of a Roman officer. And there was the way the tribune gripped his ivory tipped baton, the symbol of rank for any high-ranking Roman officer, which cautioned him. Not just an ordinary soldier. But someone who was used to command.

A man not to be trifled with.

Frowning, he turned and barked loudly two names.

From the huddled group of Vigiles, two men stepped forward and came to attention in front of the centurion. Decimus, eyeing the two freedmen, slapped hands behind his back and stepped very close to the men. He circled them, inspecting them closely. Glancing down into the dust of the wagon ruts, he noticed the prints of their sandals they had just imprinted into the dirt.

"You," he said, using the long wooden baton of authority he gripped in one hand and slapped the man forcefully on the man's biceps. "Your name."

"Gallus, sir."

"You and this man beside you discovered the bodies last night when you rode out from Ostia?"

"Yes, sir."

Decimus nodded, hands gripping the baton behind his back, head down and staring at the ground thoughtfully. He walked slowly around the two men and stopped directly in front of the one who called himself Gallus.

"Centurion, what is the punishment for a vigilii who is convicted of thievery?"

The rough looking plank of an ex-slave visibly paled. As did the man standing beside him. Decimus eyed the centurion for a second or two before turning his attention back to the two standing in front of him.

"Ten lashes with the whip, sir. And garnishment of one month's wages. Of course, if the theft is large enough, perhaps he might become a contestant at the next set of gladiatorial games."

The white-faced Gallus groaned softly, and his knees almost buckled. The centurion, angry, exploded in rage.

"By the gods, Gallus! You filthy liar. I'll personally peel the flesh off your back with a cat'o nine tails if you don't confess to your crimes now. Do you understand me!"

"Sir! I ... we ... it was just a little thing! Nothing expensive ... really!"

Decimus turned his head and watched the forever scowling Gnaeus trotting up toward him carrying something white and thin between the forefinger and thumb of his right hand. The tribune nodded and smiled grimly. He extended a hand, palm up, toward his servant. The bushy haired man gently deposited the grim piece of evidence into the tribune's hand.

The centurion, watching closely, did not see what was deposited into the older officer's hand. But he felt relatively certain it was something which would not go well for the undersized oaf named Gallus.

"Let me paint you a picture of what happened last night, soldier. Interrupt me whenever I stray from the truth," the tribune began in a pleasant, conversational tone as he stood directly in front of the now pasty white Gallus.

The young centurion strode up to stand by the balding yet dominating force of Decimus Julius Virilis and turned crimson faced in rage when his eyes fell upon the severed ring finger. Slapping the small baton all centurions gripped angrily against the side of his bare leg, he turned and gave his man a dark, murderous look.

Decimus, snarling back a dangerous smirk, zeroed in on the man in front of him. "You and your companion arrived last night just as it began to lightly rain. You found this site as it appears today. You found four dead bodies, clothes and furniture scattered all over the field, along with the two wagons completely dismantled and strewn about. There was no gold. No jewelry. Nothing. Except for one small item ... "

Lifting the severed finger in his palm he delicately put it directly under the ex-slaves flaring nostrils and continued.

"You found a rather large fat man with a small signet ring on a finger. A ring which would not come off because the man's fingers were swollen. No, no ... don't deny it. It was a signet ring. To be precise, I suspect it was a signet *key* ring. A key that was supposed to open a small jewelry box or some other small wooden chest. See the circular discoloration on the flesh? Yes? Clear evidence the man wore a ring. Now look closely at the finger. It is a man's middle finger. The finger a man of some importance would decorate with a signet key ring. So tell me, Gallus. Did you find the wooden box the ring you removed from the dead hand of Spurius Lavinus last night?"

"I ... uh ... we found what ... what was left of the box, tribune."

"We ... !" exploded the man standing beside him, wheeling around and stepping away from his comrade. "I told you not to cut off that finger! It was a trifling ring! It wasn't worth a penny!"

"Silence!" The centurion, baton in hand, backhanded the man across the face viciously. The man staggered to the side, holding his face with one hand, but came back to full attention. For one second, the young officer thought about clubbing the man again. But he contained his anger and turned to face the tribune.

"My sincerest, most humble, apologies sir. I assure you when these two return to their barracks they will be severely dealt with."

Decimus shook his head negatively and placed a hand on the officer's arm.

"Severity in punishment will not correct evils committed, centurion. Discipline them you must. Preferably in front of their comrades for all to take note for those who cannot restrain themselves from petty theft. But measure the punishment to the quality of the crime. Otherwise you will generate more animosity than compliance among your men.

Besides, I believe this man. I suspect they did indeed find the small jewelry box already destroyed and its contents missing when they arrived."

Turning back to the ex-slave the balding, darkly tanned tribune lifted a hand up and told the man to give him the ring. The man fumbled the ring out of a small leather pouch and dropped it into Decimus' hand.

"Sir, if I may ask a question?"

Decimus smiled, turning from the two ex-slaves and motioned them to leave at the same time.

"You're wondering how I knew so quickly this nasty little deed had taken place last night. Yes?"

"Sir!" the centurion nodded, surprised, and wondering if the older officer could read his mind. "I mean ... how?"

Decimus half turned toward the young officer and smiled fatherly as he lifted a finger up and motioned him to follow his actions. Kneeling in front of the stain on the grass beside the dust of the wagon trail he waited for the centurion to kneel beside him and then pointed toward a set of tracks in the recently dried soil.

"There are two sets of footprints. Here and here," he said, using the tip of his own baton to point to one and then the other set of tracks. "Look closely. The vigilies and the urban cohorts issue to their men the exact type of sandals as the army does for their men. They have a distinctive pattern on the soles of the leather. Notice one set is that of someone wearing such footwear and the other isn't?"

Once pointed out, it was obvious for anyone to see plainly written in the soil. With the addition of the military soled sandal extruding from underneath it, mud. As if Gallus had knelt in the rain to do his dastardly deed.

"Precisely." Decimus nodded, smiling with quiet pleasure as the younger officer saw the evidence without the need to point it out to him. "A slight rain producing just enough mud to generate such a track. But not enough to wash away the other. Meaning?"

"The murderer must have committed his dead prior to the rain last night. He dispatched his victim, found the small jewelry box in question, destroyed it and found what he was looking for, in the process disregarding the dead man's signet ring. The rain began just a little after midnight. So ... that means the massacre must have taken place sometime before. When my men arrived, the ground was muddy. Their tracks are deeper into the soil."

"Very good," the older man said, coming to his feet. "Remember this small lesson, young man. Every living creature uses their gift of sight to see the world around us. Our eyes give us this wondrous sense of vision. We see ... but very few of us observe. For an officer such as yourself, the difference between seeing and observing could be all the difference in the world in keeping you and your men alive."

"But ... but how did you know in the beginning the dead man would have a signet key ring? And this blood stain? How did you know this was the precise stain to look at and not the other three?"

Decimus laughed casually and glanced at Gnaeus who had come up to stand beside him. The scowl on his servant's face softened a bit but did not go away as he eyed the young centurion.

"As to the knowledge of the key ring, I confess I came owning such knowledge already. I've been asked to look into this case and to bring it to a swift conclusion. I was informed the patrician involved was carrying a small wooden box engraved in ivory with a set of papers in it that were important. Important to several groups of people. That box and those papers are my task to find and obtain, as well as to bring to justice those who killed Spurius Lavinus and his men.

As to knowing to look at this stain and not the others? I took a chance and guessed. Over the years I have observed men in powerful positions and how they react in a number of extreme situations. Experience, in other words, centurion. Drawing on my experience in similar situations led me to believe a man of Spurius' position would have placed him in the lead wagon. He would be the first to step down from the wagon if confronted by ruffians. I knew the man, centurion. I know how arrogant and supremely confident he was toward those he considered his inferiors. I'm sure Spurius thought he could bluster his way through this confrontation and continue on with his journey. Unfortunately, he sorely misread the situation and paid for it dearly."

"Spurius Lavinus?" the young centurion echoed, frowning. "I don't recall hearing this name before. Who was he?"

"An old, old, old villain my boy. Very old ... and very dangerous," Decimus answered softly.

"Yet it appears, tribune, someone even older and more dangerous found your man first. I assume this may be the opening gambit for a far more complex crime wave to begin?"

Decimus Julius Virilis glanced at the young centurion and frowned.

Indeed so, my boy. Indeed so.

CHAPTER FOUR

"Quintus Flavius, you look like the dead rat a cat just drug into his master's house. And drinking wine this early in the morning? Something serious must have taken place."

The jovial, somewhat loud words came from a small man with a thin chest and a very tanned complexion, a mass of curly salt and pepper hair atop his head. A large grin spread wide on his lips; the grin twisted the long streak of white scar tissue that decorated the right side of his face. With hands on his hips, he chuckled in amusement the moment the taller, more elegantly dressed centurion approached from across the busy intersection, plumed helm underneath his armpit. He reached for the simple wooden stool tucked underneath the table in front of the small wine shop.

"I am, Hesod. More than you think. But my thanks to you for meeting me here today. Come, sit. Let me buy you a bottle of the best."

Hesod, the Scarred One as he was called, observed the

younger man for a moment, the wide grin on his dark face not changing, but shook his head in surprise.

"You? The son of an old legion mate of mine? Buy me the best of the best? Hmmm ... methinks something is amiss here, young friend. Tell me. For what dastardly deed must I do to repay for such kindness?"

"Sit, Hesod Sit. Payment will be simple enough. Let me pluck from you memories while serving in the empire's legions some information you might possess."

Kicking a wooden stool out from under the table, the curly haired ex-legionnaire sat himself down just as a fat waiter bearing a dusty bottle of wine and two large glasses came loping out of the darkness of his establishment's interior. He bowed slightly toward the centurion.

The small wine shop was but a few blocks away from the barracks which housed the city's legion contingent and the urban cohort. The street was not one of the main thoroughfares of the city. Nevertheless, pedestrian traffic was moderately heavy, along with the constant rumble of wooden carts drawn by oxen lumbering back and forth across the cobble stone streets. This was not Rome where wheeled traffic could traverse through the streets only at night. This was Ostia. A port city. Commerce took precedent over all other considerations.

Eyeing the older man across from him, Quintus Flavius poured a large measure of wine into Hesod's cup before measuring out half as much for himself. Setting the bottle down on the table between them, the centurion reached for his cup and lifted it in salute toward the older man.

"To friendships, Hesod. And to family ... and loyalty."

"As you say, my boy. As you say." The older man nodded, then tossed the wine down his throat with one flick of his wrist before looking at the younger man again with narrowed eyes.

"Now quit running around the bush, Quintus Flavius. Tell me why we are here at this ungodly time in the morning."

The centurion of the urban cohort lowered his glass of wine, frowned, and glanced toward the massive brick edifice for the city's barracks which was quite visible even from this distance.

"I have been pulled from my duties and placed on temporary assignment. I am to assist in the investigation of a murder involving a Roman senator. I will be under the command of a tribune freshly commissioned by the Imperator himself. A man, I suspect, you might know. An old soldier who calls himself Decimus Julius Virilis."

The smile on the older man's face wavered and then disappeared altogether. So did the man's usually dark complexion. Color in the man's cheeks paled visibly. Reaching for the bottle of wine, he looked quickly over his shoulder and then back at the bottle and filled his glass to the very rim. Setting the bottle aside, he reached for the glass, lifted it partially to his lips, and paused.

"You are to assist Decimus Julius Virilis in an investigation? A murder of a politician?"

Quintus Flavius leaned on an elbow braced on the table and nodded before propping his chin on a clenched fist. The sudden mood swing from this old family friend caught him both by surprise and activated his curiosity at the same time. Apparently he had been correct. Hesod indeed knew this tribune from the past. Watching intently, the older man remained quiet and waited for more to be revealed.

"Quintus, my boy. Is there any way you can wiggle yourself out of this assignment? Perhaps come down with a near fatal sickness which would require you to be bed ridden for the next several weeks?"

Still resting his chin on his fist, the centurion shook his

head *no*. The older man, frowning, drank his wine and sat the empty glass down in front of him. He glanced to his right and then behind him again.

"Run from this man, Quintus Flavius. I jest not. Run from this man. He is possessed. He sees into a man's soul and knows what he thinks even before the thought is formed. At night, alone in his tent, I have heard him speaking to the gods! Aye, I know Decimus Julius Virilis. Served with him twice in two separate legions. He is Janus come among us. The two-faced god. On one hand he can be the most benign of men. Brilliant in handling his command. A genius at commanding a legion. He is inspiring. You *believe* you can do *anything* when he is leading. I've seen generals defer to him on countless occasions. I've been with him in combat when we were outnumbered three to one and win. He can be the friendliest of companions. The most jovial of all!

But, at odd times either day or night, something comes over him. A darkness. A miasma. He becomes ... possessed. He stalks the wilds alone. He speaks in tongues. He has this way of looking at you which makes you feel as if his eyes are boring straight into your soul. He knows when you are telling the truth and when you lie. And when angry ... when angry ... "

The old man never finished the thought. A soldier walked past their table, catching the older man's attention and silencing him as swiftly as if someone had pushed a knife into his heart. Quintus, impressed with the man's intenseness, sat back in his chair and reached for the bottle of wine.

"Hesod, this man ... you make him sound fascinating."

"Quintus Flavius, son of my old friend. I beg you. Beg you! Do not get caught up in this man's web of deception. He comes from the depths of Hades!"

Another off-duty soldier strolled past the table. And something strange happened. Hesod, the old soldier and survivor, eyed the second as he had the first and panicked. Leaping from his chair, he half turned, as if to say something to the centurion but hesitated, glanced to his left furtively, then quickly strode away with a swift, firm step.

Amazed, Quintus Flavius watched the old man disappear around the corner of a building. Impressed with the man's sudden complete change in personality, he poured himself another glass of wine and drank the delicious fluid while his mind replayed the conversation just completed. What would make a hardened, cynical old soldier like that become almost terrified at the mere mention of a man's name? What did he mean when he said this tribune was the two-headed god, Janus? Or that this tribune could speak to the gods? And what about this dark miasma that would come over the man suddenly and without warning? Did it portend ill tidings? Did it make the man become a monster?

Who was Decimus Julius Virilis? Why would the Imperator himself commission him as a tribune in the Urban Cohort? Absent mindedly pouring himself another glass of wine, he sat comfortably on the rough wooden chair, an elbow resting on the table top, staring off into infinity.

What kind of man was both capable of inspiring undying confidence in a man and at the same time, undying terror? He had been told, and often by relatives and various tutors in his youth, there was no race of man in the entire world more superstitious than the Romans. Roman folklore and Roman history was rife with instance after instance where some incident as innocuous as a flock of geese flying overhead profoundly influenced a Roman in one fashion or another. The gods, it seemed, loved to play terrible tricks on Romans in general. Signs, like reading the entrails of a goat's intestines, or the clap of thunder in a cloudless sky, if interpreted wrongly, portended grave disaster soon to befall. Narrowing his eyes thoughtfully, he wondered what odd eccentricities this tribune may have exhibited which had so deeply impressed Hesod. Curious, a quick smile played across the centurion's lips as he glanced at the glass of wine in his hand and quickly tossed it down before standing up and flipping a coin onto the table.

Duty called. He had to report to his new commander. Curiously he found himself half anticipating, half dreading the encounter.

Standing on the second floor of the administrative building housing Ostia's *Praetor Urbanae*, Decimus Julius Virilis, with hands behind his back, stood in the marbled columned doorway leading out onto the second-floor balcony and stared in silence at the artificial harbor constructed in the river's mouth. Dressed in an off-white toga trimmed in purple, his thinning hair combed back and thus emphasizing his high sloping forehead, the hard, experienced old army veteran looked the very picture of a competent officer.

Ostia, the port lying in the mouth of the Tiber, was the mouth which fed the city of Rome. From Egypt, from North Africa, from Sicily, came the tons and tons of grain Rome needed to keep the masses satisfied. A critical job for any public official to maintain. Disturb the flow of grain from Ostia to Rome and you disturbed the tranquility of the empire. This stark reality had been vividly burned into the memories of every politician who rose to power. It was of such vital importance a politician could use it as a tool to make his rise in politics more smooth and more rapid. Or, by manipulating it from afar, use it to destroy his rival.

Narrowing his eyes thoughtfully, Decimus turned his head and gazed upon the large structure of the city's new coliseum. Under construction, the edifice was in the heart of the city, and when finished, promised to exhibit gladiatorial and other games with three or more thousand fans cheering them on. Right now the D-shaped structure was veiled in a wall of flimsy looking wooden scaffolding littered with slaves and stone masons. Scaffolding and bricks towered over the city, undoubtedly giving the lucky worker standing at the very top of the wooden exoskeleton surrounding the edifice a magnificent view of the sea and the harbor.

Shaking his head, deep in thought, he turned and started walking slowly down the balcony of the long administrative building of the city, staring out over red clay tile roofs of its many buildings, but in truth seeing hardly any of it.

Who killed Spurius Lavinus?

And question number two: Who knew Caesar would soon ask me to look into this affair before *the Imperator approached me?*

Two seemingly innocuous questions. But each one filled with vast, and quite frankly, disturbing possibilities. Spurius Lavinus came from an old, old and half-forgotten patrician family some said was as old as Rome itself. A family of ancient wealth and an almost rabid desire *not* to reveal themselves to those who wished to throw their fates into the mortally dangerous game of Roman politics. But that was not to say they secretly dabbled into the enticing sport of the empire's machinations. The Lavinii preferred to hover in the background. Like a puppeteer, they preferred to back potential candidates, plucking the strings of those who wished to rule in a subtle fashion that would assure them personal wealth and sacred anonymity. The Caesars of the world pranced and strutted about like actors on a grand stage in order to obtain power, and once power obtained, to hold onto it for as long as they could. Gaius Julius Caesar played the game all his life. His successes were astonishing. His death from the hands of those he both had manipulated and assisted in their political lives steeped in legend.

Now Caesar Augustus, the current Julii member leading the family, was close to death from old age, and knowing it, struggled to retain the power of being declared permanent *Imperator* of the empire. The old man declared he wished to hand the power over to his adopted son, Tiberius, upon his death. There were rumors that Caesar and Tiberius had finally reconciled their many differences and mistakes each had heaped upon the other. It was no secret Octavius Caesar wished to regain and revive the love he once had for his adopted son. Once the two had been very close. The Imperator made it clear there was to be no question of a transfer of power to his adopted son after his death. Tiberius was to be his successor. No questioning of that decision was allowed.

But before his death, Caesar, called *the Augustus,* wanted to make sure the transition of power would happen smoothly and quietly. Many who knew the old man suspected Caesar intended to hunt down and silence those who might wish to disturb Tiberius' reign. Others suggested, in soft conspiratorial whispers, it was not so much *Caesar* who wished to get rid of those who may contest Tiberius when the younger Caesar came to power, as it was Caesar's wife, and Tiberius' mother, Livia Drusilla. The regal woman who sat beside Caesar on the throne had a backbone of steel just as strong and just as cold when it came to controlling and manipulating imperial power. It was said even the gods sitting on Mt. Olympus could not help the person who seriously thought about harming her only son. It was rumored even the magnificent Jupiter winced in pain when Livia Drusilla spoke to him in her prayers.

So again, the question had to be asked.

Was Spurius the weapon being forged to oppose the transition of imperial power? Or was the elderly patrician somehow a tool being used by the imperial family to hunt those who were the enemies of Tiberius?

Who killed Spurius Lavinus? And why? And who knew of my presence in this case even before I did?

When Caesar quietly slipped into the bath house to converse with him, the old man told him Lavinus possessed a document which, if revealed to the public, would ignite a civil war. Gaius Octavius would not reveal exactly what was inflammatory in the document. Nor did he hint in any way whether Spurius Lavinus was ally or foe when it came to the Julii family. The only thing Caesar told Decimus was that the information contained within those letters clearly revealed something about the death of Julius Caesar. That revelation, if thrown into the public forum for all to see, would make the civil wars of the last fifty years so recently brought to a conclusion, nothing but a minor skirmish in comparison for what would come.

The death of Julius Caesar in 44 B.C., more than fifty years earlier, was still a vivid memory in the minds of most Romans. Especially vivid in the minds of most patrician families. The civil wars and political intrigues which followed the first Caesar's murder nearly ripped apart the empire. Intrigues and old hatreds were still nourished in the hearts of those patrician families who had chosen the wrong sides in the struggles for power that ensued. Revenge was an oil lamp which refused to flicker out. In some places it still burned with a fiery brilliance.

The assassination of Julius Caesar was an act of bravado so insane, so horrific, it plunged the empire into a maelstrom of murder, retribution and finally, into a civil war that ripped Roman society asunder. In essence, those loyal to Caesar raised armies to seek out and fall upon those who assassinated their beloved leader with a vengeance. Vast swaths of the empire were divided up and fell into the camps of each contesting party.

Yet everyone knew ... once that Pandora's Box of civil war was opened, in the end, only one man would be left standing who would take on the mantel of imperial rule. After years of struggle, after a number of victories and defeats; after a series of treacheries and deceits, in the end, the man who survived and claimed the title of imperator was Gaius Octavius Caesar.

For thirty some odd years after the last battle fought, Caesar had consolidated his power and ruled the empire effectively and efficiently. The empire was outwardly safe and secure. Yet it was a facade. Nothing more than a canard. Underneath this tranquility old hatreds and old grudges simmered. Simmered, yet remained in check and hidden because a strong hand ruled in Rome with ruthless determination. For that facade to remain intact deeds had to be committed which guaranteed potential enemies of the public good were cut down ruthlessly. The current Caesar was, by no one's imagination, a saintly man. Like his forebearers, he too possessed a devious political mind that cherished the desire to maintain and hold political dominion over his opponents.

It boiled down, for many, including Decimus Julius Virilis, a simple choice. Which murderous politician would be the most beneficial to the empire? A choice he had made early in his career. One that, sometimes, he regretted. But one that he would not deny nor withdraw from.

So who killed Spurius Lavinus? Why now, so close to Caesar's coming death, even steal these letters at all? Who would benefit from them? How many players were involved in this dangerous game? Apparently the game was afoot. But what was this game? And ... even more curiously ... who had originally written this set of scurrilous lies?

Questions.

Questions to be answered. And now ... and now ... a murder to be solved along with a document to be destroyed. Gaius Octavius had been quite clear in his orders to him. *Find the letters. Find them before they slipped into the hands of those who could use it to most harm the empire. Destroy the missives with your own hands. You, personally, allow no other to view the vile scroll.*

So be it.

The Imperator had given him an order. A chore, deliciously complex, and filled with uncertainty. A conundrum which, if he was honest with himself, he reveled at the thought of beginning. It was just the odious task, the devious device, the pugnacious puzzle his wildly heated mind needed to tackle. He allowed himself a smirk of amusement, standing at the railing at the far end of the balcony and looking out toward the harbor again, as he heard the soft gait which was distinctly his servant Gaius' footfall behind him. Turning, he smiled at the mute ex-legionnaire and tilted his head slightly to one side inquisitively.

"You have found Atia Graccia?"

The darkly tanned, swarthy but powerful built little man nodded his head and grinned.

"Is she home?"

Again a nod.

"In mourning?"

Another nod.

"Ah. Alone?"

For an answer the servant pulled out a small slate and a piece of chalk. Quickly he scribbled two names on the slate and handed it to Decimus. Taking the slate, he read the names and lifted one eyebrow with interest.

"Very good," he said, handing the slate back to his servant and nodding. "I suspect the game is at hand, old friend. The foxes have come out of their dens to console their mistress. Who watches her house now?"

For an answer Gnaeus raised a hand high over his head. Decimus smiled and nodded. Hassad now watched the house of Spurius Lavinus. In a few hours his other faithful servant, Rufus, would take over. If, as he suspected, some form of intrigue began to unfold in the house of Atia Graccia, he would be kept informed.

Behind him another set of footfalls came to his ears. Turning toward the youthful officer, his eyes began twinkling in mirth.

"Ah, I see our heroic centurion, Quintus Flavius, has just been informed of his re-assignment."

The centurion, plumed helm underneath his right armpit, still dressed in the uniform and armor of an *Urbanae* officer, came marching down the columned arcade of the balcony with a powerful stride and a severe scowl on his face. It was obvious he was a mixture of irritation and curiosity. Part of the young man's mind did not want to be here. But a larger portion of the man's personality did. Decimus' smile widened. Curiosity was a powerful tool. A man with an active imagination was like a cat naturally inclined to explore any dark cavity it came upon. Imagination was what made the human what he was. With a one-sided sly grin stretching his thin lips he watched in amusement the man's approach.

"Tribune. I have been reassigned to your, uh... command. At your insistence I am told. I was first told this was to be but a temporary assignment. But I was just informed this assignment is permanent. Of course I am greatly humbled by this honor. To be reassigned to serve underneath such a distinguished officer as yourself, sir, is indeed something a junior officer like myself would and should leap at. Nevertheless, I have come to ask this duty be assigned to another officer."

Decimus' smile did not waver as he listened to the centurion's words fully before shaking his head *no*. Silencing the youth with an upraised hand before he could lodge a protest, he stepped around the young officer and started walked back up the shaded balcony with the young officer falling in step beside him.

"I know you are close to your wedding day, Quintus. I am sincerely sorry for this imposition which draws you into the chase. But your Imperator needs you. I need you. The job we must do together is so important it momentarily outweighs the importance of your pending nuptials."

"But ... but ..." and then the realization hit the centurion, the older officer *already knew* he was about to be married. "How ... how?"

Decimus Julius Virilis chuckled bemusedly as he turned his head and smiled fondly at the young man. With the silent Gnaeus following mutely behind them and a wide grin of brash amusement on his face, the older officer raised a hand and pointed to the small golden chain hanging around his neck and partially tucked into the centurion's uniform.

"I noticed the little pendant yesterday while we examined the crime scene, young man. A small portrait from your betrothed, no doubt. I also noticed how impatient you seemed to me when the investigation began. Suggesting to me that other things were on your mind more pressing that what at first appeared to be a run of the mill murder. I also noticed that distinctive aroma of perfume ... something Egyptian, isn't it? ... Yesterday. Again the whiff of the same perfume, only stronger this time.

Noting your age, noting the social status your family holds in the ranks of the nobility, and noticing the lack of a betrothal ring on the appropriate finger, it seemed to me a safe guess that you were not married. To confirm my suspicions, I made some inquires. You are to be congratulated. The young lady who will soon be your bride comes from family much beloved by Caesar himself. But for now, your nuptials must be postponed. This murder investigation takes precedent over all other matters."

Speechless, the centurion glanced first at the grinning servant following them and then at the old tribune beside him and just stared in disbelief. Decimus, observing the lad's incredulity, carried on.

"Did I not point out to you the idea that most of us see but we do not observe? A simple process of looking at someone and taking the time to evaluate how the person is dressed, what may or may not be lacking in his choice of attire, the stains on his clothing, the marking of his shoes etcetera, can tell us a wealth of information. Observe, young man. Observe the environment around you. Your eyes ... your senses ... are gifts from the gods who have given you all the instruments you need to decipher the mysteries which surround us. Use them to the fullest extent. Now, with that in mind—" He reached inside a small leather pouch and withdrew an odd looking, roughly hewn pewter ring. "What can you tell me about this?"

Quintus Flavius took the odd shaped ring from the tribune's hand and inspected it closely. And frowned in displeasure.

"Ah. See the symbol of a sail filled with wind on the small roundel beside the key lock? And engraved on the inside of the ring the line, *Maris secreta tenemus.* 'We keep the secrets of the sea.' An old evil, tribune. A very old evil supposedly stamped out and exterminated when the first Caesar cleared the seas of pirates. May I ask how you came to possess such a relic?"

The tribune turned his head to his old servant, lifting an eyebrow expectantly. Expressively the mute, dressed in the short toga of a servant, shrugged and lifted a hand to make a silent gesture saying, *Maybe so. Maybe not.*

The tribune nodded, the cynic's thin smile on his lips widening.

"Given to me by the Imperator himself, centurion. One of two made that were a matching pair. One I already possessed when I found you and your men earlier today. The second one plucked from a severed finger. The two represent a puzzle of immense importance. Two pieces of a puzzle that must be quickly solved. Done so quietly and swiftly before harm comes to those who wish to remain free of spurious accusations."

The young officer of the Urbani lingered his gaze on the older man for a moment then shifted his eyes back to the ring.

Maris secreta tenemus.

Yes. The sea keeps its secrets. Secrets forgotten by the living. With some especially dark ones which should forever be forgotten.

CHAPTER FIVE

"I have your first assignment, Quintus Flavius," the balding tribune said as they stood in one of the many narrow streets that bisected the bustling port city. "There is a ship's captain by the name of Caius Septimus. I want you to find him and question him. You will not find him receptive to any of your inquiries."

Decimus, Quintus Flavius, Gnaeus, and Rufus stood in a tight knot of men in the intersection of two streets crashing into each other. Around them the bustle of the city street moved back and forth with no one paying them the slightest heed. Vendors pushed their wheel carts slowly down the street hawking their wares. Children of all ages played in the streets. Old men huddled in small groups here and there in deep shades and solved the problems of the empire with caustic candor.

The three men encircled the tribune and paid full attention to every word. Some men wandered through their lifetimes forever being the follower. Some, through the strength of their personality and charisma, trained themselves to become a leader. And some just led. Instinctively. Naturally.

"Take Rufus with you. Expect trouble. Deal with it forcefully. Understood?"

"Yes, tribune."

The answer came with ease. With ease and outwardly without a care that trouble was expected. Quintus Flavius was tall for a Roman and well-shaped. His arms rippled with muscle, and he moved with the grace of an athlete. Throwing a rakish, dimple-infested grin at the tribune, he turned and started moving away but halted when Decimus spoke.

"You have not inquired as to what it is you should ask this ship's captain, centurion."

There was that flash of an arrogant grin as a breeze ruffled the young man's dark hair roguishly.

"I think I know what you want. I have a few questions of my own I would like answered. This sea urchin and I have had our run ins before. I am acquainted with the man's good-natured buffoonery."

Decimus nodded and watched the centurion and Rufus turn and begin striding purposefully down the middle of the street heading for the wharves. Turning eventually to go their own way, he saw Gnaeus looking up at him with that irritating sly grin on his weathered face.

"Don't say it. I know what you are thinking. You think I've put too much faith into the boy's ability. Hardly, my old friend. This is a test. The first of many which will tell me if my first impressions are accurate. So be quiet and lead on. We have much to do today."

Gnaeus, mute as ever, nevertheless was very eloquent with a shrug and a tilt of his head and, of course, with the book that was the man's facial expressions. The silent ex-legionnaire had no tongue, thanks to the sharp knife of a German tribesman from north of the Alps. But missing a tongue did not mute the man's intelligence or astute observations. Nor keep him from being both loyal and sarcastic toward his old commander.

Decimus, a look of a wily old fox burning brightly in his eyes, watched with an amused smirk on his thin lips as his servant turned and started loping down the street in front of him and thought he wouldn't have it any other way.

CHAPTER SIX

"So, they call you Rufus, eh? From what parts of the empire do you hail from?"

Rufus, roughhewn and recalcitrant, kept his eyes on the younger man in front of him with an unreadable face. The man was, like the mute Gnaeus, an ex-legionnaire who had survived wars, famines, mutinies, battles and everything else in between. Someone who, from hard experience, knew how to size up a man in a very short amount of time. A man who had served with the tribune for years.

He knew men who could lead into battle. He knew men who thought they could lead others into battle. He knew cowards. Knew heroes. Knew traitors. Reluctantly he found himself warming up to this handsome young centurion. There was a panache, an arrogant joviality and confidence in the man's gait he found satisfying and familiar. The young man reminded him much of the tribune. A younger tribune many years past.

"From Gaul, centurion. Far to the north of the Alps. In a little village not too far from the lands of the Cherusci."

Quintus Flavius looked over his shoulder at the man following him and nodded silently. The Cherusci. A German tribe who, led by a Romanized German chieftain by the name of Arminius, had slaughtered three of Rome's finest legions along with six cohorts of auxilia, in a dark forest called Teutoburg. Among the dead was their commander, Publius Quinctillius Varus. A kinsman to Caesar Augustus. Fifteen thousand men butchered or enslaved. Also captured by the Cherusci were three Roman eagles, the sacred emblems all legions mounted on their standards to represent the power and glory of Rome. It was the loss of the eagles, and ripping open the northern front of the empire, which humiliated the Imperator the most.

Turning his head, the curly haired centurion kept striding purposefully down the street. Yet he was not ready to refrain from asking questions. With an impish grin on his face, he glanced back at the man again.

"How long have you served with the tribune?"

"Ten years. Ten years and three legions."

"And you still serve him loyally?"

"For ten years I was on his personal staff. Along with Gnaeus. Joined his staff when he was *pilus pilum* in the *I Hispania.* Left the army with him when he retired from the *IXth Brundisi.*"

Leading the way, the centurion turned onto a different street and the Tiber River opened up before them. A river filled with hundreds of various vessels from dozens of different countries. The city streets were heavier with traffic both on foot and with oxen pulling carts. But Quintus Flavius pushed on resolutely.

Rufus, however, spotted the two scruffy looking seamen who peeled themselves from the wall of a local pub and blended into the crowd to begin following them. Lifting a hand casually to his waist he felt the weight of the heavy Spanish blade of a dagger hidden in the folds of his loose-fitting blouse and said nothing as he followed the young man in front of him.

"Over there is the piss hole of a tavern called, *The Gray Dolphin.*" Quintus Flavius nodded his head to the right. "That's where we will find our quarry. But before we saunter over and have a glass or two of the goat piss they call wine, we first must take care of a little business."

He followed the centurion across a small city square and then turned abruptly down an alley. The alley was very narrow and dark. On either side of them, the stone walls of a warehouse rose up two or more floors above, blocking out the sun. The rough cobble stone street beneath their sandals was muddy and in need of some repair. It was very dark in the deep shadow that filled the alley. A perfect place for a trap to be set.

"Stand in that doorway and don't move or make a sound. When the fun begins just watch and do nothing unless you see someone trying to kill me. At that point I would be most grateful if you would come to my rescue."

The centurion flashed that impish kid's grin at the unreadable leather mask of Rufus and stepped into the black hole of a door entrance disappearing into nothingness. Rufus, surprised and impressed, glanced behind him at a similar door and took a step back as well. Barely ten seconds later the two ruffians he had seen moved into the alley at a brisk pace.

Both men looked like seamen fresh off a long voyage. Darkly tanned, weather beaten, dressed in the typical common garb of a sailor, the two seemed intent on hurrying through the alley. They moved like men who were confident in their abilities to track someone and did not in the least suspect a young centurion nor an old legionnaire had spotted them. Halfway down the alley they encountered a rude surprise.

Quintus Flavius waited for the first man to pass. But the

moment he did, a hand shot out of the darkness of the doorway and grabbed the second seaman by the scruff of his neck. Violently jerking the man toward him, he slammed a fist into the man's nose and then used a knee to smash into the man's testicles. The man dropped to his knees, groaning in agony, both hands clutching his manhood, blood pouring out of his nose. Using the sole of his *caliga*, the heavy leather sandal strapped to his right foot, the centurion kicked the man in the chest and sent him rolling out of the blackened door entrance and straight into the legs of the first seaman who had walked past the doorway.

Reaching down with one hand, Quintus Flavius lifted the first seamen from out of the scrum the two men had created on the cobblestone street and drew his right fist back for another blow. But the first seaman came up with a gleaming blade of cold steel in one hand and slashed outward and straight at the centurion's chest.

The young officer twisted his chest to one side just as the blade scraped across his leather cuirass. Clasping the knife man's fist by the wrist the centurion twisted down and inside with such violence that he screamed in agony, dropped the knife, and fell to his knees.

"Yield! I yield, centurion! I yield!" the man yelped between clenched teeth.

Quintus Flavius let go of the man's wrist and kicked him out into what little light there was in the alley. Quickly, the little man rolled to one side, got to his feet, and scampered out of the alley as fast as he could. That's when Rufus stepped out directly in front of him and stopped him in his tracks. Bracketed between Rufus and the centurion, the little man stepped back and raised his hands up toward his shoulders.

"We meant you no harm, centurion. None. Our orders were to follow and observe. Nothing more."

"Follow and observe," Quintus Flavius echoed curiously, a dimpled grin on his handsome face but his eyes bright and menacing. "Who's orders, good fellow? And be quick with an answer or I'll break an arm or two just for the sport of it!"

"I ... we ... we can't ..." the man said, color draining from his face and shaking his head *no*. But it changed the moment the smile left Quintus' face and the look of death filled the void. "Wait! Wait! It was Caius! Caius Lucius! He's ... he's the one who told us to follow you!"

The look of murder on the centurion's face began to fade. Frowning, puzzled, he began to form a question on his lips, but the voice of Rufus stopped him.

"Take your comrade and leave, spy. Return to your master and tell him exactly what happened. Now!"

The man didn't hesitate. Leaping around the centurion, he roughly hauled his still suffering partner to his feet. He half pushed and half carried him out of the alley and they splashed into bright sunlight before disappearing altogether. Quintus, for his part, kept silent and watched the two men disappear before turning to look curiously at Rufus.

"My apologies, centurion. But before you make a bad situation worse, I had to step in and stop you."

"A bad situation worse?" the centurion repeated, looking even more puzzled. "Explain."

"This Caius Lucius they mentioned as their employer. I know the man. The tribune and this man have talked often. Caius Lucius is the private secretary to Caesar Augustus. He employs a network of spies all across Italy. What the man said about being assigned to watch and observe is the truth."

"Watch and observe *us*? Why?"

Rufus shrugged simply and elegantly before speaking.

"The Imperator has enemies, centurion. Sometimes it is hard to know what is behind a smiling man's face. Or what lurks in a loyal servant's heart. The Imperator is a cautious man."

Quintus Flavius stood in the deep shadow of the alley and stared at the old soldier. For a moment or two he thought about the man's words ... and then suddenly burst into that boyish grin.

"The tribune seems to find himself in a most precarious position, Rufus. An interesting one to be sure. Quite interesting. One I find oddly stimulating. So be it. Come! Let us go to the Inn of the Gray Dolphin and have a chat with a certain sea captain."

CHAPTER SEVEN

A little more than three miles east of the city's walls, Decimus and the evocatively silent Gnaeus stood underneath a large Poplar tree and eyed the walled compound that once belonged to the deceased, Spurius Lavinus. The villa sat off the main road leading to Rome, the *Via Ostiense*, in the midst of a stand of Poplar trees. The villa and its surrounding buildings were extensive. The Lavinii were very rich. Very old. Very powerful. Unlike the *plebian* families who controlled Ostia, the *patrician* Spurius Lavinus did not live in the city. The power he had coveted, as did his entire family, rested in Rome. Ostia was a city. Rome was an empire.

Behind the heavy looking walls of the estate, the large villa rose two floors above the walls. The walls were plastered smooth with a pink hue added to the plaster. The tile roof of the villa was a light green tinged with yellow. It was, the old tribune thought to himself, a most pleasing eyeful to behold. The villa and its surrounding walls were shaded on three of its four sides by the towering trees of the grove. None of the trees had limbs overlapping the walls. Here and there along the walls his sharp, hawkish eyes caught the sight of movement. Armed guards dressed in helm and holding spears moved along the walls constantly.

The heavy timbered arching gate leading into the estate looked massive and almost impregnable. In front and to the right of the gate was a brick-constructed gatehouse. Even from the distance he could see men, several men, lounging inside. A half smirk played across the tribune's thin lips as he walked back to the black mare he had ridden out of the city and stood idly chewing grass beneath the trees.

"I believe our friends expect us, Gnaeus. I suspect we will receive a cool reception."

The mute frowned, eyed the villa a second more, and nodded in agreement as he turned to walk back to his mount. Leaping up onto the bare back of his steed he made a few gestures to the tribune and lifted an eyebrow questioningly.

"A trap?" Decimus echoed, the half-smile widening a hair as he shook his head *no* and mounted his mare. "Not today, old friend. Atia Graccia has undoubtedly heard Octavius has employed us to look into this affair. She may or may not be involved in this conspiracy. Her husband had a bad habit of being circumspect when it came to talking about politics in front of his wife. Either way I will lay a fat wager on the table with the assertion that our presence is expected and under no circumstance would she allow any harm to come to us. Not yet at least."

With this he kicked the flanks of the mare and shot out of the dark shade of the stand of trees into the sunlight and aimed the mare straight for the main gate of the villa. Gnaeus caught up with the tribune and together they road up to the gate and announced themselves. The gates were immediately opened without a word being said. Gnaeus, impressed his master was correct ... again ... could only shake his head in amazement and grin.

Servants waited from them at the front entrance and led them instantly through the house and out into the gardened atrium. Several large beds of flowers, bright and colorful, intermixed with small but exquisite Greek statuary filled the atrium. In the center of the wide space, where two paved walks intersected, a large statue of Mars carved in dark marble, helm off and held upside down in his left hand while his right gripped the sword of a Roman gladius upraised in victory over his head, stood towering almost to the roof of the villa. Around the base of the statue were three men and one woman. The men wore frowns. The woman sat on a marble bench, hands clasped in her lap, her long blond hair falling well past her shoulders. She was not frowning. Nor was she a widow grieving for the loss of her husband.

Two of the men standing flanking the marble bench wore the tradition Roman toga of a *patrician*. In fact they were. Roman senators. One of them was the frowning stoic face of Atia Graccia's father, Felix Gracchus. The other, with an arrogant smirk on his handsome face, was a Julii; Tertius Julius Romanus.

"Greetings, Madame," Decimus said, bowing his head slightly in respect. "The Imperator bids me to express to you his sincerest condolences for your recent loss. And, by his decree, to look into his untimely demise."

"I thank Caesar for his concerns, tribune. Perhaps your swift arrival will indeed bring justice."

"Ha!" coughed the tall, gaunt, bald figure of Tertius Julius arrogantly. "My distant kin is eloquent in his words, tribune. But what is his real purpose for sending the famous Decimus Julius Virilis so promptly?"

"We have met before, senator?" the high forehead figure of the tribune inquired politely.

"Not personally, tribune. But your reputation proceeds you," Tertius Julius said, eyes flaring in anger. "Dare I say it? Your presence here may be more accusatory than in condolence. Whom does the Imperator suspect killed our beloved kinsmen?"

"Silence, Tertius!" Atia Gracchia snapped, holding a hand up to hinder any further comment from the man standing behind her, anger on her face like a black cloud before clearing and looked up at Decimus. "You must forgive my cousin's surly ways, tribune. The death of my husband has severely affected him. As it has all of us."

"There is no need of an apology, Madame. In times of grief we all experience a loss of reserve. Let me assure you, the murder of your husband comes as much a surprise to Caesar Augustus as it came to you. But I must confess. I was not sent originally to investigate a murder. Another situation has arisen. One that compels the Imperator to act on the matter directly."

Atia Graccia boiled inside with anger and fury. She sat on the marbled bench outwardly composed and looking like the grieving widow. But to Decimus' keen eyes it was obvious her composure was a facade. The way she kept twisting a jeweled ring on one finger constantly. The way one heel of her foot kept tapping the cobblestone of the garden walk. The set of her lips compressed to just a thin slash of flesh across her lovely face.

She was not the grieving widow. She was a boiling volcano ready to explode. The question which needed answered was obvious. Anger instead of grief over the murder of her husband? Or had something else more important than the loss of a husband arisen which solicited such behavior?

"Please, tribune. Sit beside me and tell me how this dire assignment given to you involved my husband."

Glancing first at Tertius Julius and then at the father of Atia, he paused for a moment. Both men were dressed in the expensive regalia of a Roman senator. But curiously the silent Felix Graccus' sandals had the tell-tale, but obvious, markings of recently standing in a salt marsh. Dried salt crystals embedded in the straps of the man's sandals were clearly visible. There were also flecks of dead grass and dried mud.

And there was another tell-tale curiosity capturing the tribune's attention. On the voluminous sleeve of the man's right arm were the blue/black blotches of small ink mark stains. Fresh ones. Very small. Hardly visible. But there and obvious to someone who knew what they were.

Decimus bowed slightly and acceded to the woman's invitation. Sitting himself down on the bench beside the still beautiful woman he turned his attention to her. Atia Graccia was considered a rare beauty in her youth. It was rumored even Caesar Augustus, a man who often spoke of piety and propriety, but was equally known in years past, as someone who oft slipped from bed to bed with both married and unmarried women, had wooed her. If rumors were true or not only the Imperator would reveal. But there was no doubting the woman beside him was still very beautiful. And a renowned intellect in her own right.

"There," she said, offering the facade of a cold smile toward him as he sat down beside her. "Now, continue with your revelations, tribune. You were saying?"

"Perhaps in a more private setting, my dear."

"Nonsense," she snapped pleasantly, waving a dismissive hand in front of her. "My father is my closest confidant. My cousin involved in all of the family affairs. What you say to me can be said in front of them as well."

"Very well." Decimus nodded as he watched her closely. "I admit it is something of a delicate nature. News which, I must insist, does not leave this lovely garden in any form whatsoever since it could, and most assuredly would, have severe recriminations upon the imperial reign."

The flash of interest that momentarily flared in Atia Graccia's eyes was unmistakable. More puzzlement than knowledge. Indicating that what he was going to say could possibly be fresh news to her.

"A few weeks past, a set of documents were stolen from the private residence of a certain dignitary. A set of scrolls apparently written some time back before Caesar accepted the crown of Imperator. I am not privy to what news these scrolls had upon its pages. But I have been informed whatever it was it is of vital necessity that they ... all of them, I am not even sure how many there are ... must be retrieved as soon as possible."

"I am to assume Caesar thought my husband possessed these stolen items?"

Her hands could not be still. Nor the vibrating motion of one heel *tap, tap, tapping* the stones beneath her feet. Her face was a mask. A mask of neutrality beginning to crumble and reveal her true emotions.

"Perhaps. Perhaps not," the tribune said softly, shrugging gently. "All I can say is there is evidence suggesting the scrolls were to be delivered to your husband. As to whether they arrived I cannot say yet."

"These documents," Felix Graccus' deep voice broke the silence softly from above his daughter's golden head. "Could they be the reason why Spurius was so cruelly cut down?"

"Very likely," Decimus said, frowning, as he looked up at the white-haired senator. "As you well know, senator, someone who possesses secrets that might potentially embarrass the ruling family always carry a certain element of danger with them."

"Who was the author of these scrolls?" Atia asked, her voice dangerously soft and barely under control. "Why does the Imperator believe my husband was soon to receive them?"

"Alas, I do not have that information. As to why the Imperator believed your husband was somehow involved in this conspiracy I cannot say. That was not revealed to me either."

"What *do* you know, tribune?" Tertius Julius asked caustically, folding arms across his chest and glaring at Decimus.

"What I know for sure is that Caesar gave me a command. A command I intend to obey. But I would add that if any of you can provide any information to me it would go a long way in reducing the Imperator's scrutiny on this family."

The look Atia Graccia shot back at Decimus was filled with fear, anger, curiosity and intrigue. She hesitated, glanced down at her lap, then started to say something but stopped when her father laid a hand on her shoulder.

"Tribune, the three of us are at a loss for words concerning this issue. None of us know about these scrolls you mention. Nor would we as a matter of course. Spurius was not a man to reveal secrets. I doubt he would have said anything about them to any of us."

In Atia Graccia's eyes were conflicting emotions screaming to be released. But the woman was strong. Resilient. She kept her lips pressed tightly together and said nothing. Decimus said nothing but nodded in silence and came slowly to his feet. Stepping away from the marble bench and the woman sitting on it he turned to face all three.

"Our conversations concerning the scrolls will remain among the three of us only. Unfortunately, my duties require that I dig further into this matter. So do not be surprised that I might come calling on each of you individually with additional questions."

"Are you threatening a Roman senator, tribune?" Tertius Julius growled, coming to his full height, his face reddening.

"I do not threaten, senator. I merely express the Imperator's wishes. I am sure, however, if you believe I have in any way threatened you, Caesar would be very attentive in hearing your complaints."

Tertius Julius glowed like a threatening volcano. But his jaw set, his lips compressed, his hands rolled up into fists. Seeing the senator was not going to speak further, Decimus looked down at Atia Graccia and nodded.

"Again, I bring you both my own, and the Imperator's, condolences my lady. If your husband was an innocent bystander, I assure you all those who participated in this heinous crime will be brought to justice. Until we meet again, Madame, may the gods smile upon you and your house with favor."

With silent Gnaeus leading the way, Decimus withdrew from the atrium and made their way through the house and out the front door. Mounting their horses, they rode out of the open gate, passed the armed guards, and into the middle afternoon burning sun. Riding until they put some distance between them and the villa, Decimus pulled his horse toward Ostia but turned to look back at the villa.

"A nest of vipers, old friend. Vipers who are angry and ready to strike. But the question is— strike at whom?"

The silent legionnaire gestured a few motions with his hands and then waited for an answer.

"I agree, Gnaeus. Our Tertius Julius seems to be the most poisonous of the lot. He needs to be watched. But do not let outward looks fool you. My suspicions fall more on Atia's father at the moment. You did notice his sandals? He had recently been to one of the nearby salt marches. Why? And he, sometime after this journey into the marshes, sat down and wrote extensively about something. But very recently, my friend. Very recently. There were ink stains on the tips of his fingers he tried to scrub off not too long ago. There was also a small drop of ink on the lower hem of his toga. Still wet. I would be most eager to know what compelled him to journey into the marshes. Even more to read what had to be set down on a scroll."

The curly haired, darkly tanned, Gnaeus nodded and made a few more gestures. Decimus frowned and shook his head.

"Assuming that a courier is about to leave the villa by horse and hurry away with these scrolls is an astute assumption, Gnaeus. But to accost the courier and relieve him of the scrolls? I think not. Better to follow the courier and see where he scampers to. That will be your job, my friend. Find Rufus and question him. See if he observed the arrival of Felix Gracchus. Ask in what direction he came from. If, as I suspect, he came from the east there is a strong possibility he might have come directly from the marshes to the north and east of the Ostia. If so, tell him to journey in that direction and see if he can pick up the scent.

But you, my friend, are to follow anyone who might look like a courier leaving the villa. Discreetly, of course. They may be anticipating such a move on our part so you must be careful. Follow and observe. If I am correct this courier will head immediately for Rome. As soon as you discover where in Rome he goes, send word to me in Ostia and we will join you immediately."

Gnaeus flashed an evil looking grin, nodded and threw a hand up in a wave as he kicked the flanks of his horse. Decimus watched his loyal servant for some seconds ride down the paved road before turning his attention back toward Ostia. A little ways up the Appia Ostiense he saw a detachment of legionnaires, at least a century's worth, marching in the strict Roman discipline of an experienced legion, eagles and pennants held high, their baggage train pulled by two large oxen following them. Urging his horse on, he decided to attach himself to the unit and ride with them back to the city.

No would-be assassin would dare attack him surrounded by more than a hundred well trained legionnaires. Unless ...

A grim smile of amusement played across the tribune's lips as he touched the flanks of his horse with his heels and galloped away.

CHAPTER EIGHT

He stood in the middle of the apartment, hands locked behind his back, head down, a contrite look of unease on his handsome young face. One sandaled foot kept moving around in a small circle as he stared hard at the bare wooden floor and waited for the triad he knew was coming to commence.

The apartment was on the second floor of a large barracks in the middle of the *castrum*, the Roman fort, that occupied the eastern wall of the city. It was a spacious set of apartments, bright and breezy, which overlooked the parade grounds and practice yards in three directions. Outside underneath the hot Latin sun came the sounds of soldiers grunting and a harsh centurion voice barking as he pushed his troops through a series of exercises.

To Decimus Julius Virilis' ears the sounds were comforting, even pleasing, to hear. After so many years of soldering it seemed natural that he and his men, again, were sitting in an officer's barracks listening to the daily minutia of legion life. But, sitting behind a wide table, a lead goblet of wine sitting on the table in front of him, the high domed forehead of the balding tribune watched the young centurion in front of him and tried to look displeased. He found he could not. A thin smile crept across his narrow lips and dissolved any form of disapproval from his face permanently.

"So, my young ruffian. You say you noticed two suspicious lugs following you through the streets of the city and decided on your own to confront them. You did, and as I understand it, on your own volition broke the arm of one man and seriously harmed the other *before* you found out they were agents working for Caesar Augustus. Have I encapsulated your words sufficiently and accurately described the incident?"

Quintus Flavius, his cheeks turning red with embarrassment, continued to stand at attention and stare at some vague point on a wall across the room. Nodding silently, he prepared himself for the fabled anger of Decimus Julius Virilis to fall upon him like the wrath of some ancient god. Instead, something totally unexpected happened. Decimus' smile widened. The man standing in front of the table was powerfully built, young, and as strong as a bull. There was a natural ease about the youth he found pleasing to observe. Young, sometimes impulsive, yet at the same time decisive and confident in himself, Quintus Flavius was the kind of junior officer he looked for to lead men in his cohort. The kind of young man he could use even now.

Coming to his feet, Decimus reached for the large stone wine far sitting on the table to his right and then slid an empty lead goblet closer before lifting the bottle and pouring a liberal portion wine. Walking around the table with the wine, he chuckled softly and handed the goblet to the young man.

"Hmmm. I suspect Caius Lucius will be very displeased with both you and with his two agents. But my distant cousin will undoubtedly find it amusing. Just between you and me,

Caesar has a fondness for big lugs like you who act first and ask questions later. I think that's why he took to me so early in my career despite being distantly related to him."

Surprised, with relief clearly written on his face, Quintus Flavius took the goblet of wine from the tribune and grinned in immense relief. The tribune motioned to him to join him at the table. Following the older man to the table, he pulled a well-crafted wooden chair back and sat down after the tribune settled into a chair.

"Not that I won't have to write a letter of apology and send it to his secretary, mind you. Caius Lucius is a sensitive soul easily pricked with insult. Actually, he's a pain in the ass, to be honest. But he is a loyal servant to Caesar and does have some talent in running the Imperator's household. Including the Imperator's private spy network." The tribune paused as he lifted the wine cup to his lips and narrowed his eyes speculatively. "Still ... we have learned something interesting from this today."

"We have?" the century gulped, lowering his wine and looking at the tribune confusedly.

"We've learned Caesar is worried about this little affair, Quintus. So much so he has issued orders to Caius to have agents deployed to watch all the key players."

"So you believe spies are watching Atia Graccia, her father, and this Tertius Julius?"

Decimus nodded. "From afar. Keeping their distance while we openly investigate. Knowing how efficient our Caius is, I believe there is a warren of agents somewhere in the city being used, with many of them looking for our sea captain you found missing earlier today."

Quintus Flavius' youthful face looked thoughtful as he nodded. He took of sip of wine, lowered the goblet and started to form a question on his lips. But the soft laughter coming from the tribune sitting beside him made him pause.

"You are like a young pup worrying a worn out leather shoe, my boy. I know what bothers you. It is clearly written on your face. You wonder what does this sea captain, Caius Septimus, have in common with the mysterious scroll and how was I aware of this creature from the beginning? Yes?"

The centurion grinned and nodded.

"Caesar informed me. His spies informed him these scrolls we seek were handed to Caius Septimus three months ago while the captain and his ship visited Cyprus. From there the ship went to Greece, then to Sicily, and finally here to Ostia."

"Hmmm," the young man hummed. "He left Cyprus with the scrolls, but that does not mean he brought them here. He could have handed them off to someone either in Greece of Sicily."

"He could have indeed," said the thoughtful looking Decimus. "But likely not. The contents of these letters only matter to a few souls here in Ostia and Rome. The most damage it can do is here. Therefore, it must be here."

"These letters ..." the centurion began, meeting the tribune's gaze.

"Documents rumored to have been written by Mark Antonius himself detailing the exact plans of the death of Julius Caesar. Written, mind you, not as a person outraged over his friend's death reporting the crime and the results of his investigation. But written as a fellow conspirator. The one who *planned* Caesar's death."

Quintus Flavius stared at the tribune in confusion. The events the tribune was talking about happened fifty years earlier. But even today the repercussions of the event were still felt. Mark Antonius as the ringleader behind Julius Caesar's death? Impossible! Anthony was Caesar's closest friend and trusted confidant. He was the one who vowed revenge against those who had assassinated his beloved master.

Julius Caesar was assassinated in 44 B.C. At the time of his death Octavius Caesar, the nephew to Julius, was barely eighteen years old. Upon reading the elder Caesar's will, Octavius inherited Caesar's fortunes and became legally, Caesar's son. A move which infuriated Marcus Antonius. What followed after Caesar's death were dark years of treachery, murder, open battles and a civil war. In the end, when the last battle was fought and decided, with Marcus Antonius taking his own life, and after the death of the Egyptian Queen Cleopatra, once the mistress of Julius Caesar and afterwards, the love and fellow conspirator with Marcus Antonius, the wars ceased, and the empire found stability.

Under the rule of Octavius. Crowned *Augustus* by a grateful Senate.

But now, in the year 10 C.E., this was old news. Old fears. Fears which should no longer be dreaded. Yet, eyeing the tribune sitting with him at the table, Quintus Flavius found himself lifting an eyebrow thoughtfully. Obviously something was amiss. Something had not been revealed. There was more to this tale he had yet to hear.

Decimus observed the young centurion in mild amusement. It was as if he could see the cogs in the lad's brain clicking, one by one, and found himself coming to a surprising conclusion. He lifted his wine and waited for the young officer to finally see what remained.

"Again, these scrolls," Quintus began slowly, cautiously. "You say they revealed names? Names of those who conspired to kill Caesar. Perhaps there is a name of a person who does not want to be revealed? Yet lives after so much time has passed?"

The smile on Decimus' lips widened. Setting the goblet of wine on the table he nodded and folded arms across his chest.

"There have always been rumors, my boy. Dark rumors. Bad enough that it may be true Marcus Antonius may have recorded Caesar's murder. But other rumors more insidious, more damming, have been whispered. One in particular most dangerous. A rumor, that if true ... almost guarantees the empire being plunged into another bloodbath."

"And that would be what, tribune?"

The older man eyed his young protégé thoughtfully for a moment mentally debating whether to tell the young officer or not. To tell him meant to seriously put the man's life in jeopardy. Yet not telling him might do the same thing. On one hand, he could be killed for knowing too much. On the other, he could feel an assassin's blade for knowing too little. Either way the young man's life depended on what he said next.

"Caesar," he began slowly, quietly, with eyes watching Quintus carefully. "May have conspired to kill Caesar."

CHAPTER NINE

Quintus, startled, started to say something but the door to the apartment swept open and in hurried the tall form of Hassad. The darkly tanned horseman from the sands of Africa looked exhausted. His plain clothes were caked with mud and salt, his feet caked in sweat and grime.

"Hassad," the tribune said coming to his feet and walking around the table to grip the arm of the exhausted ex-legionnaire. "Here. Sit and drink some wine. Eat something and rest first."

The tall African sat and gulped down a goblet of wine. But, pushing away the food offered to him by Decimus, he shook his head and began his report.

"I found two fishermen who witnessed a most unusual sight the other night near the salt marches. A boat, heavy in the water, with a guide holding a torch over his head, rowed up the Tiber early in the morning and went ashore near the marshes.

Six men disembarked and followed the guide with the torch into the swamp. Hours later only four returned to the boat. The four pushed off from the shore and began rowing rapidly down river."

Decimus poured more wine into Hassad's goblet and told him quietly to drink. Hassad used both hands to hurriedly down the second goblet of wine noisily. When finished, he lowered the glass and wiped his lips with the back of an arm.

"A fisherman recognized one of the men. Caius Septimus. But the sea captain was not one of the men who returned to the boat hours later. After I talked to the fisherman, I hired them to take me over to the exact spot they saw the boat disembark its passengers. Their trail was easy to follow. Tribune, you must come. You must come and see what I have found."

The African tried to rise but exhaustion forced him to collapse back into the chair. Decimus, concern clearly written on his craggy face, laid a hand on the legionnaire's shoulder and told him softly to relax. Glancing at the centurion, he nodded toward the door.

"We must find this place. You and I," he said and then turned his attention back to the horseman. "Hassad, these fishermen ... can they row us to this spot again?"

"Yes, tribune. I told them we would return shortly. They are down at the river waiting for us. Please, let me go with you."

"You will stay here and rest, old friend. Rufus will be back soon. The two of you stay here until our return."

Decimus walked across the room, threw open a heavy looking chest and withdrew a sword belt and sheathed gladius and two long hunting knives. Slipping out of his sandals, he found a pair of soft leather boots. Already dressed in the short, comfortable Greek chiton, to this he added a dark red cloak.

"We chase our elusive opponents, Quintus Flavius. We must go well prepared for any surprises tonight, eh? Arm yourself. I do hope you know how to use a blade in combat."

The taller, wider centurion grinned boyishly as he strapped

a sword belt around his waist and slid a large knife in the belt behind his back. Glancing at the young officer, Decimus smiled. The fight earlier in the day with two of the Imperator's agents convinced him the centurion would be quite capable with a gladius in hand. Which was comforting to know. In these perilous times such skill would undoubtedly come in handy.

CHAPTER TEN

Three men waited for them sitting in a long fisherman's boat filled with nets and a stowed away sailing mast. Each of the three stood up and nodded as first the centurion, and then the tribune, leapt into the vessel and told them to shove away and begin the journey. Rough looking men, dressed in attire peasants would wear; unshaven and scowling. One of the men, the oldest of the lot, silently indicated to Decimus and Quintus Flavius to sit before stepping back to take up the tiller and steer the boat to one side of the opposite flowing stream and into smoother water. The remaining two took up oars and began rowing.

Decimus, sitting himself, observed the two men in front of him plying with the oars. Silently he watched as the men worked the oars laboriously, grunting and straining to stroke in unison against the current of the river. He glanced at the thick wad of nets lying on the floor of the boat and noted they were as dry as brittle grass. And half turning to look out at the river bank slowly slipping by, felt the wind on the back of his neck blowing from the sea inward onto the shore.

Surely better time would be made by raising the mast and using sail instead of rowing against the current? A fisherman was like any other man. Why labor unnecessarily in an arduous chore especially when there was an easier, and more efficient, way to accomplish the same deed? Unless, of course, you did not know *how* to raise a mast and set a sail.

Turning his head slightly to his left, the balding tribune noticed a dark blotch making an oddly shaped stain on the bulwark. He noticed something else. Hardly perceptible. Easily overlooked by a casual glance. But there nevertheless and quite telling to one who half suspected something of this nature being present.

"Centurion," he began, speaking in classical Greek. "Are you familiar with the Greek writer Homer and his masterpieces, The Iliad and The Odyssey?"

Startled, Quintus Flavius turned and looked at the man sitting beside him and grinned apologetically.

"Forgive me, tribune. But my training in Greek is not nearly as complete as obviously yours has been. I shamefully admit I have not read Homer's two classics."

"Ah. Upon our return I will loan you the books," Decimus continued in classical Greek. "No cultured soul should endure this world's treachery without first delving into the pleasures of Homer. You will find Homer has a splendid way with a witty phrase and an astute eye on how both gods and man mask their evil intents with smiles on their faces."

The young centurion almost frowned but stopped himself as he looked into the smiling face of the older man beside him. After a second or two his gaze fell on the man sitting in the stern holding the boat's tiller in one hand.

"Tell me, tribune," Quintus Flavius began in a conversational tone, as he turned toward the two oarsmen facing them as they rowed in silence. "These classics. Do they talk about fighting and bloodshed and strife? Or are they books of poetry whispering about silly love and other such nonsense?"

Decimus Julius Virilis lifted his head slightly and chuckled. The tribune actually was amused. Amused how, in Greek, the two of them were having ostensibly a casual conversation about literature, something over the last few years he had sorely missed in his last two legion posts. But equally amused on how easily the young man beside him caught his true intent in starting the conversation.

"Ah, centurion. Grand adventure! Gods conspiring to destroy we mortals ... mortals turning upon their friends and strangers and striking them down. The stuff that makes for an evening's worth of reading pleasure. You will thoroughly enjoy reading them, my boy!"

Quintus Flavius nodded absently, his eyes assessing the men in front of him for a second before he turned to examine the contents of the boat. It did not take him long to see both the dark stain on the curved wood of the bulwark beside him nor the three tiny threads of cloth caught in a sliver of wood and moving gently in the breeze.

Silently, he kept his eyes on the stain and pieces of thread. A young centurion he was in the Urban Cohort. But experienced. He already had had his share of murder investigations under his belt. He was experienced at seeing the obvious signs of a possible murder scene. A blood splatter only a few hours old on the bulwark of a fishing boat and three tiny threads of cloth hanging from a sliver of wood spoke volumes to him. Slowly his eyes moved back toward the nearest oarsmen.

"Be prepared for an afternoon's entertainment, centurion. It may be coming faster than you anticipate," Decimus stated jovially, a thin, curious smile on his thin lips as he too eyed the oarsmen in front of him.

"Oh, I am looking forward to it," Quintus answered, spreading the thin snarl of a wolf across his lips.

Decimus relaxed and stared out at the countryside sliding past them as the boat continued up river. But he wondered to himself: did the three men disguised as fisherman speak Greek? It was possible but not probable. If they did, were they aware of the sophistry he had used to warn his young comrade of a possible trap? Again, possible. But turning to eye the two oarsmen in front of him, he nodded in a friendly fashion before turning his attention back to the riverbank.

Possible. But highly doubtful.

In silence, the two sat in the boat as the oarsmen moved them up stream. Five miles past the outer wall of Ostia the steersmen moved the tiller and the boat cut across the gentle stream of the Tiber and headed for the riverbank on the far side. Beyond the bank was the aromatic, grim looking salt marshes. As the boat plowed into the soft mud of the riverbank both oarsmen jumped out and pulled the craft higher up onto the bank. One of them motioned for Decimus and Quintus to disembark before disappearing up a narrow trail that faded into a set of low hanging brush.

The two who had rowed took the lead in front of Decimus and Quintus. The older man followed. For a half hour they twisted and wound their way deeper into the marshes on a narrow trail sometimes so narrow they had only room enough to put one foot directly in front of the other.

Decimus noticed it first. The deeper they traversed into the marshes the natural sounds of animals that inhabited the marshes seem to lessen ominously. Ahead of them he noticed the two men's gait increasing. Noticed how both of them seemed to be tensing. Their heads dropped lower into their shoulders. Their hands clenched into fists.

He recognized the signs. A fight was near at hand. As he

walked, a hand slid down to rest on the pommel of his sword. He knew from long experience that he who could draw first and strike the most savagely stood a better chance of surviving.

A few moments later they moved around a white brined pool and stepped into a small clearing. Stunted trees, dark and twisted, walled in the clearing creating dark shadows that crawled across the open space suspiciously. As they came to a halt in the middle of the clearing, from out of the darkness, two more roughhewn, bearded men stepped into view with swords in their hands.

"We have our orders, tribune," the leader of the men grunted, the one who had worked the tiller of the boat. "Our master knew of your presence in Ostia and suspected you would make inquiries. So he devised this trap to ensnarl you. We have orders to kill you and dump your bodies into the marshes. If you pray to a god or gods, I will give a moment or two for you to prepare yourselves."

Decimus slid the forged steel blade of his old legionnaire's gladius from its sheath and faced the two oarsmen who had led the way into the marshes and grinned savagely.

"Five to two the odds are, fisherman. Surely you jest?"

"Not fisherman, Roman," the man said, revealing his sword and smiling grimly. "Slaves ... gladiators from one of my master's establishments. Told to kill you and hide the bodies. I salute you on your bravery, tribune. But you will die, and I will be the one to run you through."

And with that, the man took a running leap toward Decimus screaming a defiant war cry and swept the blade of his sword high into the air to strike a downward blow toward the tribune's head.

CHAPTER ELEVEN

The clash of steel rang out with a vicious, ringing, clash of murderous intent. Decimus found himself facing two foes who pressed heavily upon him looking for a weakness in his defenses. The tribune's blade wove and dipped as he parried and countered every killing blow. Much to the surprise of the gladiators facing him—much to their chagrin—they realized they faced a foe who was well versed in the use of a sword. For indeed, twenty-five odd years soldiering across the known world had taught the old tribune well. Decimus Virilis moved in unpredictable patterns and did not only use his sword to fight. Occasionally a fist or a foot would come out and deliver a powerful blow on one foe or another. A blow strong enough to make the man grunt in pain and step back from the melee to regain his strength.

Behind him he heard Quintus Flavius laugh. An arrogant, confident laugh of someone who trusted himself in his use of the weapon in his hand. The power of the centurion's blows was physical as his steel drove past one gladiator's guard and bit deep into the man's flesh. Screaming, the wounded man staggered back into one of his comrades. The momentary entanglement of combatants was a deadly mistake. The centurion's blade came slashing horizontally across, severing the second man's sword hand from his wrist.

Both wounded gladiators, blood flowing from their wounds and wheezing in pain, backed away from the young centurion, and ran for their lives. The moment they retreated, the remaining gladiator facing him ran as well. The moment they disappeared the young officer turned to assist the tribune.

It was unneeded.

On the ground in front of the handsome, older legionnaire was one dead gladiator while the older one who had brought them here was backing away, a grim smile on his lips. He lifted his sword in salute toward Decimus.

"My compliments, tribune. Our employer forgot to tell us you were skilled in the use of the blade. Because of this lack of information, I underestimated my opponent. The next time we meet, the outcome will be different."

Into the stunted darkness of the trees surrounding the brine pool, the gladiator dissolved. Standing victorious in the middle of the clearing, Decimus and Quintus Flavius eyed the field of battle in silence for some moments.

"You are wounded?" the tribune asked, half turning to look at the younger man.

"Untouched, sir. And you?"

"My age is catching up with me, centurion. Ten years ago I could have fought all day without losing my breath. But today?" A brief smile flashed across the tribune's lips as he looked at Quintus Flavius and shrugged. "Old age is something I am not looking forward to."

Quintus Flavius grinned boyishly and nodded. Old or not the tribune in front of him had fought like a tiger. Facing two skilled gladiators and killing one spoke volumes to him about the man's skills. Which, frankly, he found unsurprising. The moment he laid eyes on the tribune he knew he was in the presence of an accomplished killer.

"For a young man your skills with the sword are remarkable. You were trained well."

Quintus Flavius shrugged as he followed the tribune over to the dead gladiator.

"Our family owns a gladiator school. One of the best around. The family made sure the master of arms tutored me. The training, I might add, was grueling. The old man who was the master of arms would club me severely with a wooden gladius whenever I made a mistake. I still have bruises from his reprimands even though it has been years since our last lesson."

"His training came in handy today," Decimus said, frowning, as he bent down and examined the body of the gladiator. "Ah. What do we have here?"

Between his finger and thumb, the tribune pulled up a portion of the dead man's tunic and inspected it closely. The centurion bent down and watched carefully. With the precision of a surgeon, the tribune used his sword and cut a rectangular piece of cloth from the dead man's tunic. Standing up, Decimus examined the cloth intently before lifting the cloth to his nose and sniffing it gently.

"Here, what do you make of this?" he said, handing the piece of cloth to the younger man.

Quintus Flavius took the cloth from the tribune and looked upon it with disgust. Prompted by the impatient tribune, he reluctantly lifted the cloth to his nose and inhaled. "Wine," He said, lowering the cloth from his face. "Relatively fresh."

"Indeed so, centurion. Now can you tell what kind of wine did this man recently spill upon himself?"

"What kind of wine?" the centurion repeated, looking down

at the piece of cloth in his hand for a moment before lifting it to his nose again.

He took a long, deep sniff of the wine's scent and held it in his lungs for some seconds before exhaling. Closing his eyes, he tried to remember the various wines he had tasted. Tried to remembered their aromas. And found himself exhaling and being decidedly confused.

"Greek," Decimus said, smiling into the face of the centurion's confusion. "A strong wine Greek sailors from the Isles of Samos prefer. I know this because for some time I was stationed in Greece. Developed a taste for this particular wine myself. So ... what does all of this tell us, Quintus Flavius?"

"What does it tell us? Well..." the centurion hesitated, looking down at the dead man and then at the marsh clearing with a thoughtful mask on his handsome face. "They told us we were expected. Their master expected someone to come snooping and made arrangements to greet us. The old gladiator who complimented you said something to the effect his master owned a gladiator school. Perhaps with that bit of news we might find the current owner of your mysterious scroll. Hmm ... from the wine's aroma we know the gladiator recently had a round or two of a wine vented in Greece. It might, or might not, suggest our gladiator friends are recent arrivals to our shores. Possibly from Greece. So maybe ... maybe ... we make a few inquiries. We hunt for any connections which link a school of gladiators, Greece, possibly Atia Graccia, and our dead Servius Lavinus together. If all the threads can be woven into one cloth, perhaps we have found or killer."

"Excellent, my boy. Excellent. A wonderful exercise of the intellect!" Decimus exclaimed as he rose to his feet and smiled in pleasure. "I compliment you on your piecing together strands of the puzzle and weaving it into a possible supposition."

It was the way the older man said it which made Quintus

Flavius smile roguishly. There was a certain timber in the older man's voice which warned him the compliment was not the full complement it appeared to be. Coming to a standing position he waited for, euphemistically, the other shoe to fall.

"An astute observation on the possible connection between a Greek gladiator school and his owner. But you may not have carried the supposition further along. Perhaps there is a more sinister explanation here we should consider? One that throws an entirely different light on the subject?"

"A more sinister explanation? How so?"

Decimus looked thoughtfully at the man in front of him and nodded. For a few seconds he remained quiet as he studied the dead man at their feet and allowed his thoughts to gather into a coherent pattern. When, at last, he had completed his silent analysis he turned and started striding down the path toward the Tiber, motioning a hand toward the young man to follow.

"Consider the possibility that our friends lying in wait for us happened to be a serendipitous gift handed to their master. Our sudden appearance so soon in Ostia could not have been foreseen. But when we did arrive, their master had the tools on hand to hastily devise a means to remove us permanently from the scene. Consider, Quintus, the possibility those who are behind all of this and possess these damming scrolls may be gathering tools and personnel for something far more serious."

The two men moved briskly down the path toward the river. The centurion, following the tribune, kept quiet but allowed his mind to race across the hundreds of possibilities the older man suggested. When they reached the river, they found the boat they had arrived in gone. Cursing underneath his breath Decimus stared at the wide river thoughtfully with hands on his hips.

"We must hurry. Help me build a fire so we might attract a fisherman or a bargeman to come to our rescue."

The younger man did not hesitate. Using his sword, he began chopping away at the tall grass and stunted trees lining the riverbank and throwing them into a large pile. Decimus assisted in gathering the fuel for the fire and when satisfied at their efforts, stepped back and pulled from a leather pouch a flint and a piece of iron. It took only three strikes onto the flint to spark roaring flames and billowing smoke. It took another half hour before a wide barge coming down river pulled over to the bank and retrieved tribune and centurion from their exile.

A half hour Decimus hoped he could afford to waste.

CHAPTER TWELVE

The eloquent Gnaeus greeted them at the door to the apartments in the military barracks. Even before Decimus and Quintus Flavius could enter the room the mute's hands were flying furiously before him as he gave his report to the tribune.

Walking across the wide room, the tribune poured wine for he and his young centurion but kept close attention on the small servant's hands. Frowning, he handed Quintus his wine and then drank from his own.

Quintus, for his part, watched Gnaeus closely. Amazed at the animation in the man's hands and the expressiveness of the man's face, he waited to hear what had been revealed.

"Apparently Felix Graccus has returned to Rome only minutes after our departure. Gnaeus says the senator left in a rush. Tertius Julius remained in the villa for some time. But when he left, he left with a scowl on his face and apparently in a very foul mood. He journeyed back to Ostia. But the interesting item is this. Soon after Tertius Julius' departure, a servant on horseback galloped away from the villa heading in the direction of the river. Not toward Rome. Not toward Ostia. But toward the Tiber. In the general direction of the salt marshes we so recently visited."

The centurion sipped his wine quietly and mulled over the news. A reasonable man might suspect the three had sent word to the gladiators to expect a visit soon and to kill whomever showed up. But would that be true? Were all three involved? Were all three equal conspirators?

Another thought crossed the centurion's mind. Was Atia Graccia involved in the murder of her husband? What motives would there be if she was? She certainly seemed genuine in visibly expressing the loss of her husband. But a consummate actress could do the same.

"We shall set Atia Graccia aside for the moment and concentrate our efforts on finding the ship captain, Caius Septimus." The tribune lowered his wine and looked at Quintus Flavius. "It is crucial we find this man and his ship as soon as possible. If I am correct, the safety of the Imperator and the peace of the land rests upon it."

"I know his regular haunts, tribune. I will find him. If you want, I will assign a detachment of the Urban Cohort to scour the city."

"Do more than that, my son. Alert the garrison commander and tell him the Imperator has requested a full century of his best men to be placed on standby. You will then present yourself to the legion commander here and make the very same request."

The centurion sat the goblet of wine down, saluted the tribune and left immediately. Decimus watched the young officer leave and seemed unsurprised the young man had not asked questions concerning his very real sense of dread hanging over them. There was no need for surprise. His assessment of men and their timber had so far favored him well. He saw in

Quintus Flavius the makings of a very good officer. A young man with a keen mind. One who already suspected what he so feared was near at hand.

The silent Gnaeus watched the centurion leave. Standing behind the short form of Gnaeus was the leaner, taller frame of a rested Hassad. He too kept his eyes on the tribune with a frown on his face.

"Prepare yourselves," Decimus said softly, smiling at the two. "Armor and weapons. Pull out my armor as well. We may see some stiff action in the next few hours, and it will not be pleasant. Have we heard anything for Rufus yet?"

Both men shook their heads before moving to large packing chests and opening them. Rufus was in Rome. By himself. In a city filled with jackals and wolves.

Surrounded by enemies on all sides.

CHAPTER THIRTEEN

All through the day and late into the night two centuries of soldiers searched the city looking for gladiators and the elusive sea captain. Inns, whore houses, empty buildings, warehouse ... ships. Every ship moored or anchored either in the river or in the artificial harbor was thoroughly searched.

They found nothing. No hidden hive of gladiators. No Caius Septimus.

The longer the search continued without results, the black mood settling onto the tribune's shoulders grew darker with each passing hour. In the end, in the early hours of a new morn, Decimus gave the order to the two centurions in command of the legionnaires to return to their barracks. Everyone was exhausted and in a foul mood. In grim silence, with Quintus Flavius, Gnaeus, and Hassad, Decimus watched the men form up and march off down the cobblestone streets in good order. When the last column of men disappeared around a building, he turned to the three standing behind him. They too were exhausted. Exhausted but waiting for him to give the orders to continue searching. Shaking his head gently he carved out a thin smile of gratitude and told them all to return to the barracks and get some sleep.

Gnaeus silently gestured, asking, what was the tribune going to do? Decimus said he would return to the barracks shortly but first he had some thinking to do. He would stroll down to the river underneath the moonlight and observe the harbor for a while before finding his bed. All three men in front of him folded arms across their chests and frowned in disapproval at his answer. If he was not returning to the barracks with them neither would they. It was far too dangerous to be wandering about the streets of Ostia at two in the morning alone and unprotected.

Decimus started to protest but paused. And then laughed softly in the darkness. Of course they were right. Without saying a word, he clasped his hands behind his back, and began walking down the middle of a narrow street toward the Tiber. With, dutifully, his three companions following a short distance behind.

Reaching the river, the tribune strolled back and fourth down a long stone pier which jutted out into the glittering moonlit waters of the Tiber, head down, arms still clasped behind his back. Deep in thought. Seeing the tribune was going to confine himself to musing on an isolated pier, Gnaeus and Hassad found large coils of rope to bed down onto and soon were fast asleep. Quintus Flavius found a mooring post to sit down. Removing his helm, he sat it down by his feet and then rubbed a hand through his sweat-stained hair. He heaved a sigh of relief. But made no effort to lie down. As Gnaeus and Hassad's soft snores filled the hot night air, he watched the tribune strolling up and down the pier in an aura of deep thought. In the darkness a soft breeze strong with the smell of the sea wafted through his curly hair as he watched the tribune with quiet admiration. Even a measure of fondness.

There was something about the man which reminded him of his father. His real father. Not the one who was currently married to his mother. Not the soft, egotistical, vain fool of a wine merchant wallowing in his gold. No. This tribune ... reminded him of his father seventeen years past. Of the time he last saw his father alive. Standing, oddly enough, on a pier not too far from this one in his military uniform kissing his mother goodbye as he was about to board a troopship and head for the wilds of Spain. Looking splendidly like the hero he was.

Father never returned home. Spain, and those who warred against Caesar Augustus, had consumed him. He was seven when he last saw his father. Seventeen years had come and gone. And for each day of those seventeen years he remembered the image of his father standing on that stone peer. Now, so many years later, he sat in the darkness on a mooring post beside a pier and watched a soldier moving slowly through the night. The moonlight painted a surreal portrait of slivery white across the tribune's face and silhouette. A portrait that could almost be his father's.

Clearing his throat and running a hand down his face, Quintus Flavius looked down at the stones of the peer and tried to push the thoughts of his father out of his conscious. His father had perished doing his duty. As any true Roman would do. If there were gods, if there was an afterlife, he hoped his father was looking down upon him from above and observing that he too was doing his duty.

As any true Roman would do.

In the distance the tribune heard the young centurion clear his throat. A lone dark figure sitting hunched over, legs apart to brace himself, elbows braced against his thighs— exhausted after the day's arduous searching. Yet dutifully awake and attentive.

He found himself looking upon the young man fondly as he

walked on the return leg toward the city down the long pier. The lad had potential. There was a native intelligence there that needed sharpening. Needed to be focused and fused into clarity. There was no question the lad was a natural leader. There was no question the young officer was fearlessly brave and skilled in the use of the sword. Both Hassad and Gnaeus had in their own ways informed him of their acceptance of the lad. Two critical judgments which impressed the old tribune tremendously.

He found himself pleased at the thought he may have discovered a protégé. Found someone with the required intelligence to do what he did so well. To observe. To deduce. To see through the veils of men's lies. To seek the truth.

He paused to look out toward the mouth of the river. He counted more than a dozen heavy ships anchored just a dozen yards away. Bathed in silvery moonlight, the ripples of the river water glistened like brilliant jewels. The panorama was a picture a muralist would desire to paint on a rich man's villa. As he stood and observed the scene, he felt the warm breeze of the night blowing in gently from the sea. Above, the heavens were ablaze with bright stars. There was no denying the obvious. It was a beautiful night.

He smiled in the darkness with a dry, grim sneer.

The face of beauty hiding somewhere in the darkness a genuine threat of violence about to erupt in bloody conflict. Beauty and death ... two opposites that could not be separated.

Somewhere out there, in the deep cloak of darkness, a ship filled with death rode calm waters and patiently waited for word to come. A ship of hardened assassins lie waiting for the order to come which would shred the empire into another bloody civil war. He was convinced of it. He felt it in his bones. It had to be discovered and destroyed as soon as possible. Destroyed even before he tracked down those who had ordered it to sail from Greece to Ostia. For, if the order was given and *death*, in this case from the hands of gladiators trained for the arena and savage to their very souls, raised its ugly head in the streets of Rome, the blood would flow for years to come. Maybe for decades to come from its grisly aftermath.

Decimus doubted not the ship was real. It was out there. Somewhere. Somewhere near and in position for a quick strike. A ship filled with trained, experienced, gladiators meant someone with immense wealth was at the heart of this conspiracy. Someone with immense power. Someone with a thirst for revenge which had no bounds. Unrestrained vengeance suggested something old and nurtured from out of the past. Whoever was behind this conspiracy needed the sharp edge of a sword to begin the process. Not just one sword. But dozens. Perhaps hundreds. Hundreds of swords purchased to exact a secret insult long concealed from the world meant one patrician family was exacting payment from another patrician family. He knew of only one family large enough, powerful enough, to generate such hatred. The Julii. His adopted family. Gaius Octavius Caesar, in rising to supreme power, had been ruthless in his rise to fame and glory. People, by the thousands, died in the struggle. Patrician families who defied the Julii suffered immensely. *Which* family conceived this form of revenge could be any of a dozen or more.

A diabolical plan. A deadly dance of power which, at its conclusion, either guaranteed the grisly deaths of those who had hatched this maniacal exercise… or would offer up to them the power and wealth of the Roman Empire itself.

There were three questions gnawing at him as he stared out across the calm waters of river and sea. Where was this ship of death hiding? Who was the mastermind behind this evil entity? And lastly, why was the order given to murder Spurius Lavinus? Of the three in the puzzle, the murder of Atia Graccia's husband vexed him the most. What factors forced the conspirators to remove one powerful voice from the den of vipers? A viper himself who was no friend nor ally to Caesar. It did not make sense. No matter how he examined the problem nothing seemed logical about the death of Spurius Lavinus. If anything, it would make sense for the mastermind of this insidious cabal to keep such a man alive. If, as he suspected, the *real* threat of this cabal wished to keep his presence hidden from view, using a man like Lavinus as a shield, a puppet, would guarantee his presence to be unknown. If the plan succeeded, the power behind the cabal would rule *through* the arrogant but incipient creature effortlessly. He would wield power and be kept out of the limelight which always shown on an Imperator's presence. If the carefully laid plans of the cabal began to unravel it would be Lavinus who would be the one to suffer the humility of being nailed to the cross or fed to the lions. Or worse.

Either way, keeping Spurius Lavinus alive for as long as possible seemed to be the obvious course to take. So ... again ... he found himself asking the question over and over. *Who killed Spurius Lavinus?*

Irritably, he pushed that question out of his consciousness and deposited it in a cubicle within his memory. It was a question he would return to later. More critical questions demanded his immediate attention. With the most critical one being the need to find a ship full of gladiators.

They had to be close by.

Close to Ostia. Close to Rome. The death of Caesar Augustus would not be the end of the deadly plan but the very *beginning* of the terrible struggle. A group of skilled men would be needed to cut their way through the Imperator's Praetorian Guards and plunge their bloody knives and swords into the beating heart of Caesar. To do this the ship had to be very near. Close to Ostia. The port was less than twenty miles from

Rome. Less than an hour's hard riding to the city. So—one question kept running through his mind like some persistent itch which would not go away. Where was the ship hiding? More importantly, how were the gladiators going to approach Caesar Augustus before being recognized for what they were?

Information.

He needed information!

Shaking his head in disgust, Decimus unclasped his hands from behind him and walked down the pier with long, purposeful strides. Quintus Flavius, lifting his head to glance at the tribune, saw in the moonlight a change in the older man's gait and came to his feet immediately. Slipping helm over his curly hair, he went over to the sleeping men and kicked them awake gently. By the time the tribune joined them the three were waiting for him.

"We need to arouse the city engineer and demand to see a certain selection of maps. Somewhere in the salt marches we'll find our quarry. But before we find them, I need to know how a ship can hide so cleverly from prying eyes. Come! We have doors to pound on and must endure the sleepy grumblings of lazy bureaucrats roused from their warm beds!"

CHAPTER FOURTEEN

Their searching of the maps outlining the coastline to the north of Ostia revealed nothing. There were no hidden coves, no narrow channels with water deep enough for a ship to work their way into the salt marshes. There was nothing to indicate a ship whose cargo hold was filled with trained gladiators had ever anchored in the harbor.

Nothing.

As the first rays of a new dawn began to illuminate the windows of the city's main administrative building, Decimus found himself looking into the exhausted faces of three loyal followers. In their eyes, he saw exhaustion and frustration. Frustration not for doubting his convictions. But frustration in not finding what their leader believed was there. Even the young Quintus Flavius seemed irritated at not finding what he personally believed had to be there. Eyeing his three comrades, he knew he had pushed them to their limits. He knew it was time to step back. To give them a needed rest. And while they rested, to reconsider his assumptions and see where he might have erred.

Quietly, he gave the order to roll the maps up and slip them into their cases. In silence they left the administrative building and returned to their assigned apartment in the city's fort. Informing each to get some rest, he saw the three silent figures nod their heads and trudge off to find beds to flop onto. In moments the sound of heavy snoring filled the large room. Smiling to himself Decimus walked to the table in the middle of the room, poured himself a large goblet of wine, and moved out onto the veranda and into the growing warmth of an early morning.

Where was the ship filled with wolves ready to strike the Imperator?

Who was the master mind behind this diabolical conspiracy? Could it be Atia Graccia? Beautiful and intelligent. The wife of the oldest male member of the Livinii. Indeed, capable of being devious and understandably holding a grudge against Caesar. During the time of the Second Triumvirate when Octavius Caesar, Crassus, and Mark Antonius agreed to share power, the bloodletting in the political purges which swept through Rome and Italy devastated the Graccii. Family members were ruthlessly hunted down and slaughtered because they chose the wrong side to swear allegiance to. Her father, Felix Graccius, barely escaped with his life. So ... yes. There was motive for the Graccii to plot the downfall of Caesar. And between Atia and her father, Atia was the one far more cunning and dangerous when it came to plotting for revenge.

But was she the one?

Or perhaps it was more a family affair ... meaning the arrogant Tertius Julius Romanus was the one. The Julii were also savaged by the purges even though they were directly related to Caesar. But the Julii were openly arrogant. Tertius Julius represented them well. Arrogant, haughty, quick to be offended and harsh in the treatment toward their enemies. Too obvious in their motives. Their intent.

No.

Shaking his head, he stared out over the training field, now empty, and over the walls of the fort and at the city. He lifted the wine to his lips.

None of the three. Soldiers, yes, in this dark deed. But none were willing to risk their lives, their fortunes, their power on some half-brained plan they might have concocted on their own. Someone else ... someone more sinister ... someone more skilled in the art of concealing themselves from this intrigue had to be the kingpin. But who? Who?

A wave of aching exhausting swept across his nerve endings. Lifting a hand to rub burning eyes gently, Decimus walked back into the main apartment and found a chair. Sitting beside the table, he sat the goblet down, sighed deeply, folded hands across his stomach. And ...

Someone gripped his shoulder and shook him violently. With an involuntary flinch, Decimus realized he had been sleeping and jerked up in the chair to the excited face of the centurion bending over him.

"Sir, sir! We must hurry. We think we may have found Caius Septimus and his ship."

Coming to his feet, Decimus noted the presence of several Urban Cohort officers in the room. Gnaeus was at his side immediately, breast plate in hand, and signaled to the tribune they would have to ride hard on their horses north of the city and he had to don armor.

"What has been found, Quintus?" he said, turning his attention to the centurion.

"Two fisherman returning from a night's catch saw flames in the night and caught a whiff of something burning. A ship, tribune. Burning like a funeral pyre not more than five miles north of the city. And bodies. Dozens of bodies floating in the surf and lying on the beaches. They said they died of sword wounds, tribune. Slaughtered was more the term they used. The news has just arrived. Our horses are ready, and we depart upon your command."

For an answer the tribune waited until Gnaeus strapped the greaves over his shins and then strode out of the apartment rapidly. Mounting up, they rode through the busy streets of the city at a fast but controlled gait. Pedestrians and street vendors hurriedly moved out of the way, and they let loose the reins the moment they passed through the gate.

The ride along the hot beach underneath a clear sky and glaring sun would have been exhilarating in any other circumstance. Horses pounding through the surf, sea spray flying in the air; the screams of angry sea gulls exploding into the air as the horsemen sped past ... exhilarating indeed if it were not for what grisly scene awaited them at the end of their journey.

But grisly was the scene which greeted Decimus' eyes the moment they rode over a sandy hill jutting across the beach and descended to the far side. Splayed across the shore, smoke still rising into the clear afternoon air with flames hungrily licking across its bare, blackened hull, a large merchantmen tilted dangerously on its port side. The ship's rigging, masts, and upper works had been gutted by a raging fire. Here and there lying grotesquely along the hull were the charred, blackened forms of men who, trapped inside the vessel, tried to escape.

In the surf and dotting the narrow beach were the bodies of men, at least three dozen, lying motionless in the sand or floating face down in the water. They had indeed been slaughtered. Each individual had several wounds on their bodies and a half dozen ... oddly ... lie scattered about as headless torsos.

Gnaeus, walking beside Decimus, with the others leading their horses as well, had a puzzled look clearly written on his deeply suntanned face."You wonder why only a few have no heads while the others remain intact?" the tribune rumbled softly, glancing at his friend. "Surely it will be obvious to you once you put your mind to it, Gnaeus."

The silent Gnaeus looked at the nearest headless corpse and frowned. Twisting around to look at another, the mute legionnaire noted the strange tattoo of an eagle's claw tattooed on the back of the neck of a few of the dead men. The tattoo had been severely damaged from the edge of a sword slicing through the neck to remove the head. But on others who retained their heads the tattoo was very clear.

Still, he could not make the connection and, confused, turned to glance at the tribune and then at Quintus Flavius.

"Tell him, Quintus, while I hunt for the body of Caius Septimus," Decimus said, releasing the reins of his horse and sloshing through the surf toward the burning ship.

The young, curly haired centurion nodded and then shrugged at the mute. "My guess is whoever killed these men took the heads so they would not be recognized. What you see surrounding us are dead gladiators, silent one. From a certain school, we think, of gladiators originating in Greece. I suspect the tribune believes those without their heads must have fought at one time or another here in Italy and were popular among the masses. They would be instantly recognized. Once recognized we would know the name of the school, and thus, the name of its owner. Apparently, those who killed them all wished not to disclose that knowledge just yet."

For the next two hours the search through the wreckage was shrouded in remarkable silence. It was a grim task no one wished to do. Keeping a ready eye on the tribune, Quintus Flavius and Gnaeus searched for the body of the ship's captain as well. But the body of Caius Septimus was missing. Meaning ...

"Either he was killed at sea and his body thrown overboard ..." Decimus growled at the end of the search, standing with his comrades in front of their horses. "Or he was the one who commanded the butchering to take place. I believe the latter is more accurate. Either way we know this for certain. The surviving gladiators trekked down the coastline a mile or two and then apparently boarded wheeled transportation and left the scene of the crime."

"For Rome?" Quintus Flavius inquired.

"Most likely. If there is to be an assassination attempt of Octavius they would have to be in the city and close at hand. Assuming, of course, *they* are the weapons to be used against the Imperator."

Gnaeus frowned while his hands quickly palmed a question. The tribune watched the flying hands and nodded grimly.

"At first glance it would make sense the gladiators are heading to Rome to be a weapon. Most probably a weapon to be used against the Praetorian Guards and Caesar. But consider these possibilities. What if they are nothing more than a dedicated force brought to Rome to *defend* the person who is behind this deadly game? What if they are nothing more than a decoy? A decoy designed to pull us away from the real threat?"

"But why all this sneaking about, tribune?" Quintus Flavius asked, lifting an eyebrow. "Why not, like any honest head of a gladiatorial school, just bring this force to Rome openly? We have gladiatorial contests on a weekly basis now. Large groups of slaves trained for the arena come to Rome on a daily basis. There would be no questions asked. There would be no need to find a way to enter through the city's gates surreptitiously. Gladiators come and go by the hundreds on a daily basis. If they come to Rome just to be close by as a bodyguard for whoever is behind this affair, it would make more sense to lessen the odds of suspicion and just bring them into the city openly."

Decimus Julius Virilis did not reply. Instead, dark eyes played across the centurion's face for a long time. A time and silence long enough to make the young centurion uncomfortable. In the end the tribune grunted curiously and turned to mount his horse.

"We should hurry. I must confront Atia Graccia again. Before we leave Ostia we need to find out what she wanted to tell us when we first spoke to her. Mount up! We may have long hours riding facing us before this day is complete."

CHAPTER FIFTEEN

In the midst of the villa's servants packing crates for what appeared to be a long and arduous journey, they again greeted the beautiful widow of Spurius Lavinus in the atrium of the spacious house. She stood beside the towering statue of Mars and his upraised gladius in one hand. She was dressed in soft yellow with blue thread. Around her throat were an impressive necklace of blue sapphires and a sprinkling of diamonds. They were hardly needed to accentuate the woman's natural beauty.

"You plan for a long trip, Madame?" he inquired softly, eyeing the many trunks and cases already packed and waiting for transportation.

"Africa." She clasped her hands in front of her. "I have a son in Carthage I have not seen in ages. It occurred to me a voyage to Carthage would be more suitable to my womanly frailties if I journeyed in the summer months."

"Under the circumstance I would advise not to be too hasty, Madame. There is an ongoing investigating in the murder of your husband. Your sudden departure before the investigation's completion might raise some questions."

"I have nothing to hide, tribune. I loved my husband. Why anyone would suspect me in his death is beyond me."

"There is also this question about the letters I mentioned earlier. Letters which may, or may not, suggest a possible conspiracy." Decimus watched the woman's facial expression closely. "The two seemed to be linked. Don't you agree?"

"I ... I know nothing about conspiracies. My husband was a loyal follower of the Imperator. He would do nothing to threaten Caesar Augustus."

He caught the hesitation, the slight pause, in the woman's answer. He smiled thinly seeing the young centurion's face become more attentive with Atia Graccia. He too caught the nuance.

"Lady Graccia, your husband was murdered because he had these letters in his possession. That he held these letters in his hands cannot be disputed. Documents, I might add, that if revealed to the public would be quite damaging to the Imperator. Furthermore, you are well aware of the long history of your illustrious husband's family. Allow me to be brutal for a moment, Atia Graccia. The Lavinii and the Julii have never been allies. Cobra to Mongoose would better describe their relationships with each other. So, with that in mind, would it not be prudent on your part to tell me all you know concerning your husband's intrigues?"

Her hands moved spasmodically. Rotating over each other rapidly. She glanced to her left and right and there was a look in her eyes that was ... what? Genuine fear? Keeping silent, Decimus watched her as she half turned as if she was going to end the conversation. But she paused, dropping her hands to her side, and stared down at her feet with the look of a wounded animal caught in a trap.

She lifted a hand up and rubbed across a troubled brow. Turning, eyes still downcast, she faced the tribune and slowly lowered herself on the stone bench beneath the statue of Mars.

"A fortnight ago, in the midst of a terrible thunderstorm, my husband received a guest in his library late at night. Two men, dripping wet and mud splattered from a long ride, followed Spurius into the library. One man was Tertius Julius. The other I ... I don't know. He was wearing a long cape with a hood thrown over his head. Spurius saw me standing in front of our bedroom door. I started to ask him who were our guests. But he cut me off and told me curtly to retire for the night.

They stayed for two hours. Several times I heard them arguing loudly in the study. I never could make out what they were saying. When they finished, they came out of the study and left immediately, regardless of the storm's fury. It did not seem to matter to them. They left and my husband refused to tell me what they had discussed. Actually became quite angry at me for even mentioning it."

"Did either man bring with them a leather case which might have been large enough to contain a number of scrolls?" the tribune asked softly.

Atia Graccia, one hand still to a throbbing forehead, shook her head before answering. "Nothing. They brought nothing with them. I quietly asked the servants on the following morning if they had arrived empty handed. All assured me that was the case."

Decimus frowned, eyes narrowing. Was she telling the truth? Was she lying? did she know more than she was willing to reveal? Questions. More questions needing answers.

"Tell me about Tertius Julius. What was his composition? Was he excited? Angry? Dark in mood?"

"Wet. Very wet," the woman whispered, her eyes remaining downcast. "Like a dog who swam for miles in a raging flood. But

... but I would say his facial expression might be described as grim. Very grim. Tertius and I are old childhood friends. When he arrived that night he would not speak to me, nor even look in my direction when he entered the house. I thought that very unusual."

So Tertius Julius had ridden a very long way. A longer journey than the fifteen miles between Rome and Ostia? If longer, from where did his journey commence?

"Lady Atia," Quintus Flavius' voice broke the momentary silence gently, a furtive glance thrown toward the tribune in the process. "The following day, what were the actions of your husband? Did he seem upset? Nervous? Or was he in a jovial mood? Did he remain in the villa, or did he perhaps leave your presence for a while?"

"He ... he went to Ostia for a few hours, centurion. Left just after lunch. He didn't return until well past the evening meal."

Decimus Julius Virilis nodded in approval. The young man was taking initiative in the investigation. And one astute question had subtly nuanced the line of inquiry. Spurius Lavinus had traveled to Ostia. To see whom? To discuss what?

Yes. Yes! The young centurion was most promising!

"Returning to the night of the storm and the hooded man. Are you sure you have no idea the identity of this man?" the tribune asked, turning his attention back to Atia Graccia.

She hesitated a moment before shaking her head. She remained silent. Remained staring down at the atrium's pathway. Refusing to look up and into the eyes of either questioner.

"Very well. Upon his return from Ostia, what was the emotional make up of your husband?" he asked.

"He was ... well, somewhat excited. Yes. I would say excited. He would say nothing to me about what was going on. But he seemed well pleased. Even jovial. He ... he told me perhaps my desire to see my son in Carthage was a good idea. A month earlier I had broached the idea to him and seemed quite adamant about me not leaving him. But ... but now he was very agreeable on the idea."

Decimus eyes remained on the woman sitting on the bench for some moments in deep thought. Glancing toward his young protégé, he saw the man was about to burst with a desire to ask another question. Silently, a fatherly smile on his lips, he tilted his head to one side in acquiescence.

Quintus Flavius grinned, then just as quickly wiped the grin off his face and turned solemnly toward the grieving widow. Gnaeus, eyeing the centurion with a half smirk on his lips, glanced at the tribune and nodded. A nod that told the tribune his silent friend also approved of the young man's initiative.

"Lady Atia, forgive me for this question. But I have to ask. On the day your husband was murdered, where was he and his entourage traveling to?"

"To Brundisium, centurion. Why?"

"Brundisium. In the south of Italy on the Adriatic side of the peninsula. A major port. And, interestingly, a city where many gladiators from Greece and the eastern empire would sail to as they journeyed to Rome."

"Do you know why he traveled to Brundisium, Madame?" Quintus asked. "Your husband had business or holdings there perhaps?"

"He did," Atia Graccia said, and ... for the first time ... looked up and into the face of Quintus Flavius. "My husband owns several shipping firms in there, as well as a school for gladiators. He mentioned to me just before he left a number of gladiators had been contracted for an exhibition in Rome. He and the school's master were going to escort them to the city very soon and he wanted to see them before they left."

"Do you know the name of the school master?" Decimus asked quickly.

"No. I'm afraid not. All I can say is that it's a Greek name. One that starts with an A or possibly a T. I really don't remember."

Decimus nodded at his protégé and nodded again. They had two more possible leads to investigate. Brundisium and a Greek who happened to be the master of a gladiator school.

"Decimus," the woman began, rising to her feet and stepping close to the tribune. "Whatever nefarious affair my husband might have been involved in, neither I nor my family participated in any way. My family is innocent. You must believe me. I am innocent. All I wish to do is travel to Carthage and be with my son. I wish to leave Italy and not return for a long, long duration. Please ... please allow me to leave. Please!"

Decimus heard the pleading note in the woman's voice. Saw the fear clearly burning in her eyes. Knew there were pieces of information she had adroitly refrained from revealing to him. But information he could surmise perhaps.

What she hid from him gripped her in fear. Real fear. A fear that impressed Decimus. Atia Graccia was a very intelligent, very ruthless, woman when she had to be. She rarely felt unnerved. Yet was capable of feeling fear. But it would have to be a threat that would be, by its very nature, enough to undo even the most resolute of hearts.

What, he asked himself, could be the source of that dark emotion?

Nevertheless, he reached out with both hands and gently enveloped hers.

"Go to your son, Atia Graccia. Remain for at least a year in Africa. A long vacation would be the perfect medicine to restore beauty and equilibrium into your life. Go in peace, Madame."

A flood of tears filled her eyes as she lifted a hand to partially mask the emotion draining from her eyes. She turned and quickly slipped out of the atrium. When she disappeared from view the tribune and his comrades retraced their steps through the villa and out to their waiting mounts.

CHAPTER SIXTEEN

"Sir," Quintus Flavius began reluctantly, eyeing the tribune and Gnaeus cautiously, "Don't you think it might be wise to send word to Caesar that a number of gladiators may be in Rome and waiting for a time to possibly assassinate him?"

Gnaeus and the centurion flanked Decimus as they rode casually back to Ostia underneath a warm summer's sun. The paved road was dotted with a number of carts and horsemen, along with those who traveled by foot, either moving toward the port or moving in the opposite direction and heading toward Rome. Both Gnaeus and the centurion carefully observed those they passed on the road.

"I plan to the moment we arrive back in the city," the tribune answered absently. "But first we must hurry and find Tertius Julius Romanus. I wish to dig deeper into his participation in this affair."

They rode on in a cloud of troubled silence. Glancing at the young centurion, and then at Gnaeus, the older man could see each were in deep and troubling thought. Undoubtedly the gruesome discovery of dead gladiators floating face down in the surf and the burning hulk of a beached slave ship were being relived in their memories. Dire times laid ahead if this affair wasn't quickly resolved.

His eyes returned to the face of the youthful centurion. As they moved along in an easy gallop he knew the young man well enough to see he was working himself up to ask another question. He suspected he knew what the subject might be.

"Sir, about these letters. I take it you already knew of its existence?"

"For a number of years, Quintus. A thorn in Octavius' side since he rose to power."

"How has it been that no one has revealed it until now?"

"A few years ago, while I was First Spear in a legion serving in the Balkans, Octavius detached me from duty and asked me to find and personally place them into his hands. It took some effort on my part. But in the end, I did as the Imperator ordered. I retrieved them and gave them to him personally. But last year they disappeared from his personal belongings. For a year Octavius used his spies to quietly search the empire for those who took it. Matters came to a head two weeks ago when he heard Caius Septimus had the letters and was sailing from Greece to Italy with it. That is when Octavius asked me to step in and retrieve the vile slurs for him again."

"Ah," the centurion grunted unconvincingly as he rode his horse with a troubled face.

The tribune smiled inwardly. And waited patiently.

"Sir, if you don't mind me inquiring, the first time you found these documents, who claimed possession then?"

"A very wealthy Roman by the name of Sextus Domitius. A distant relative, by the way, of Spurius Lavinus."

"Hmmm... " the centurion rumbled carefully. "And uh, who removed these documents from the Imperator's personal files this time?"

"That, Quintus Flavius, is the central question we must find out. Caesar assured me the identification of the thief is a complete mystery to him. I believe him. Obviously it had to be someone who had access to Caesar's household. Someone whom Caesar and his staff considered loyal. But there is another question that has to be answered. One even more compelling to conjecture over. Care to guess what that might be?"

In the distance the walls of Ostia came into view and the horses automatically picked up their step. The road was now becoming heavy with pedestrian and wagon traffic. As they galloped past those on foot, eyes shot up to watch them past. Many with ill temperament and some with open hostility.

The centurion pondered the tribune's last question. The scrolls had been missing for a little over a year. Taken by someone close to Caesar. Obviously someone Caesar trusted. A year had elapsed. And only recently revealed to be returning to Italy.

"I believe you have it, my boy. Spit it out," Decimus said, smiling patiently as he sat on his horse and waited for the centurion's answer.

"I can only conjecture, sir. But a year has gone by, and the incriminating document only now surfaces. Why wait an entire year?"

"Indeed," the tribune answered, beaming. "Indeed. This collection of wicked lies has become just in the last few weeks a damning accusation hurled toward Caesar. One that would rip again the empire to pieces if it fell into the right hands. So a number of questions arise that require answers. Who stole the scroll? For what purpose was it going to be used? And why the elapsed time of an entire year before journeying back to Rome? Why now do they return to Rome? If, mind you, its destination was indeed for Rome."

"Not for Rome?" Quintus repeated, surprise on his face. "What other destination would these documents travel to?"

"Perhaps to Brundisium?" Decimus shouted over the growing chatter and clatter lining up to enter through the gates and into the city. "Into the hands of those who are secretly building an army of insurrection? Come. We must hurry and find Tertius Julius and converse with him. After that we will decide whether it is for Rome we ride to, or south to Brundisium."

CHAPTER SEVENTEEN

The house of Tertius Julius was a small summer home tucked away just two miles outside the city high on a hill which overlooked the sea. Surrounded on three sides by tall, imperial looking Cyprus trees, while running down the back slope of the villa were rows upon rows of stunted, twisted olive trees.

The villa itself looked old and slightly derelict. A low wall surrounded the house. One could see stones were missing and, like the house, in need of repair.

Gnaeus, leaning forward on his horse, grunted and eyed Decimus as he signed with his hands. Decimus nodded and gazed at the house again.

"Yes, a beautiful setting anyone should be proud to own. But our friend Tertius is too rich and too important to be concerned with trivial worries such as maintaining a house. But did you notice, my friend, the lack of anyone moving about? No servants. No dogs. The place appears to be abandoned."

The silent Gnaeus eyed the house again and frowned. Signing again to Decimus he waited until the tribune tilted his head slightly to one side before heeling the horse underneath him and galloping away.

"Where is he going?" Quintus asked.

"Reconnoiter the premise and the surrounding area. If this is some form of trap our sharp eyed Gnaeus will discover it quickly enough."

Quintus moved his eyes to the back slope of olive trees looking for any suspicious movement. Turning, he stared at the countryside behind him. For several minutes the two of them sat on their horses and waited for some sign from Gnaeus. It eventually came when the little man rode his horse in front of the gate of the villa and lifted an arm up to wave.

Indeed the villa was empty. Almost empty. Dismounting, the three of them eyed the villa's lawn and white rock roadway which paralleled the house. From the bits and pieces of cloth, broken and smashed wooden crates and gutted trunks it was obvious Tertius Julius and his slaves had vacated the home in rapid haste.

The heavy double doors to the villa were partially open. Pushing one further open, they entered the gutted remains of the interior and made their way cautiously over and around the broken furniture, the shards of shattered vases, the ripped and shredded curtains and drapes left behind. From one end of the villa to the other the three explored the eerie quiet of the abandoned home. But what they discovered in the very last room of the house stopped all three in their tracks.

A headless body sat upright on his knees, his torso and arms thrown across a low wooden table. He was dressed in a rough-hewn Greek chiton of dark blue with a long chalmys of the same color edged in red wrapped around his shoulders. Heavy, powerful legs propped the dead body up and over the table. Thick sandals on his feet, well-worn and old, made it obvious the man was not very wealthy.

Decimus, a frown on his lips, was the first to move. Walking into the room, he observed the body critically and reached down two fingers to touch his bare arm. Grunting in surprise he pulled his hand away and then reached over and gripped one of the man's hands. It moved freely and without resistance. Turning the hand over, the tribune eyed the dead man's palm closely.

"Quintus, your opinion, please."

The centurion came to a halt beside the smaller, finer boned tribune and looked at the hand the older man was gripping firmly. It was the hand of a man who knew hard labor in his life. A calloused hand and one broken finger which had badly healed sometime past.

"Could this be our Caius Septimus? Or sea captain?" the tribune asked softly, letting loose the dead man's hand. He reached out and ran a hand down one long scar on the dead man's bicep.

"I can tell you it is not Caius Septimus. Like I said earlier, the man and I are acquainted with each other. Septimus would be taller. And on his left hand his little finger is missing. This is not our man."

Decimus grunted as if in agreement with the centurion's conclusion. Stepping around the oddly positioned corpse, his dark brown eyes continued to examine the headless body closely. But something caught his eyes and stopping, he bent down to take a closer look. Gnaeus, accustomed to such odd requests, produced the bared blade of a dagger at the same time.

"Gnaeus, if you please. Use your dagger and cut off the upper portion of the man's chiton. I want to see his chest and ribs more closely."

In no time the dead man's torso was revealed. Quintus Flavius sucked in his breath in surprise. Across the man's back were the scars of dozens of whip lashes the man had suffered through his life. They crisscrossed the man's back like someone badly stitching a broken doll. But there was more. On his chest were the distinctive scars of someone who had been wounded. Wounded often.

"Another gladiator," Quintus said, looking at the tribune. "One who was either very bad in the arena and barely lived. Or ..."

Decimus lifted his chin in anticipation.

"One who sulked and resented being both gladiator and slave. One who would not allow his streak of individuality to be beaten out of him. A warrior captured and thrown into the slave pits perhaps. A man of honor."

"But why was he beheaded? And here, inside the villa?" Quintus asked.

"I would suggest he rebelled against those who were his masters. Perhaps a sudden, and violent, rebellion before he was subdued and beheaded. As to why he was beheaded, I suspect, again, he must be a well-known figure in the gladiatorial rings of Italy. His killers could not take a chance. Hmmm ... "

Tapping a finger on his lips thoughtfully, the tribune turned and examined the room carefully. Several times as he moved around he bent down and examined something closely either on the floor or on a wall. Once he bent down and touched some stain on the tiled floor. For several seconds both Gnaeus and Quintus watched the tribune before eventually Quintus broke the silence.

"What do you look for, sir? Perhaps we can assist you."

"Signs of a struggle, my boy. I am thinking our dead hero here opposed his master and his minion's plans and put up a fight to stop ... or escape ... before he was killed. So I am looking for anything that might prove his sudden attack might have wounded or killed those who eventually killed him. If you wish, the two of you can examine the other rooms while I go over this one carefully."

All three resumed their search. Again they traversed the villa slowly, carefully, examining each room in fine detail. When completed, the three exited the house and began looking at the manicured grounds surrounding the house. It was Gnaeus, in the end, who made the discovery.

Behind the stables a small door through the wall surrounding the house led out onto a twisting path which meandered off through jagged foliage of the olive grove. Just a few steps away from the wall Gnaeus discovered a piece of a cloth which had been cut from an expensive cloak and used as a bandage. The bandage was blood soaked and relatively fresh.

"Our party is not too far in front of us," Decimus grunted, rubbing his jaw thoughtfully and peering off into the grove. "With luck we might be able to track them down."

"But there are only three of us sir," the centurion pointed out. "If your suppositions are correct, Tertius Julius had a rather large party with him. Perhaps one with more gladiators attached to it. We would be facing a decided disadvantage."

"Yes. Yes. I realize that." Decimus smiled knowingly, glancing at the centurion and then back into the olive grove. "Nevertheless, let us take up the chase and see where it takes us. The game is afoot, Quintus. Can you not hear the song in your blood lusting for the chase? We are close, very close, to unraveling this affair. I am eager to see what awaits us!"

Gathering their horses, they led them by their reins down the path smothered by the twisting, contorted arms of the ever present olive trees. Leading the horses made for an agonizing slow trek. But the tribune insisted they bring them. Not knowing what they might face at the other end of this adventure convinced him a sudden and rapid retreat might be to their advantage.

The trail branched off several times in other directions. But a quick search of the path revealed that no one in the party they followed had decided to split off and separate. Returning to the main trail, they continued their slow trek. The olive trees gave way to a narrow gully filled with grass and Cypress trees and then plunged suddenly down the side of a cliff that overlooked the sea. Below, in the late afternoon sun, the three stood on the wind-swept edge of the cliff and looked down at the little cove.

There was no ship beached on the sands. But there had been one recently. A deep gouge in the wet sand indicated where the large boat had run itself aground. Around the water filled trough where the heel of the boat had come to rest, the sand was severely mauled from the tracks of several people climbing aboard.

"Gnaeus, stay with the horses while Quintus and I investigate. Keep your eyes open. This may be a trap. If so, mount and ride toward Rome. Warn the Imperator a threat is near and approaches him."

The silent one made a sour face, spat angrily to one side, but nodded and took the reins from their hands. In silence he watched tribune and centurion make the arduous and steep trek downward toward the beach. When they reached the beach itself he let out his breath, his face still curled in distaste and the thought of being left on the heights of the cliff, but turned his attention to his immediate environs and eyed them closely.

Below, both tribune and centurion examined the evidence of where the long boat had run aground and at the tracks which surrounded it. Decimus, kneeling, gently touched and outlined several tracks with his fingertips before grunting and coming to his feet.

"They were loaded down with something heavy. Very heavy. Several of the men lifted it up into the waiting hands of those inside the boat. See how deep the tracks are? See that odd triangular shaped hole in the sand by one of the tracks?"

"Very heavy indeed sir," Quintus grunted and kneeled to examine the evidence in the sand. "Several heavy weights boxed in wooden crates. What does that suggest?'"

Decimus turned toward the young officer coming to his feet and dusting sand off his hands. The young centurion with his dark curly hair being ruffled by the sea breeze, the deep dimples carving troughs out of his suntanned cheeks, the strong jaw, made for an imposing image. Chuckling quietly to himself, the older man turned and began walking up the beach, searching the sands for more evidence as he answered over his shoulder.

"Money, dear Quintus. A treasure in heavy coin. Payment of some kind for some service to people we have yet to discover. To pay the one who supplied the gladiators perhaps? Maybe. Or maybe a bribe to be paid to a cohort commander or two of the Urban Cohorts which might assure their participation in what is to come? Perhaps. Whatever the reason, the cost was not a trifling matter. Meaning the service to be rendered is to be significant."

"Tribune," said Quintus Flavius, with such a dark note in his voice it stopped Decimus in his tracks. The older man turned to the centurion. "Here, in the rocks. I found our wounded man."

Decimus stepped to the side of the centurion and gazed into a cut in the wall of the cliff. A deep fold in the soft rock which no one from the cliffs above would know existed. In this fold sat upright a dead body. Dressed in the simple rags of a peasant, the balding man looked to have been in his late forties before meeting his sudden and violent demise. Which, the edge of a sword drawn viciously across the soft part of a man's stomach, usually created.

Those who carried him this far had tightly bandaged his abdomen as best as they could. But it was obvious from the massive loss of blood there was no hope for the man. It would have been a grueling, horrible, death. Made even more so by being carried over rugged terrain in some kind of makeshift stretcher.

"Our gladiator was good with the blade, Quintus. His selection for the death blow indicates he wanted the man to suffer."

"Know this man, sir?" Quintus asked.

"I do," said Decimus, quickly jogging toward the steep trail that would lead them to the cliffs above.

Surprised by the agility of the tribune's moves, it took a moment for Quintus to catch up. He remained silent as they worked their way to the top of the cliff. But arriving by a waiting Gnaeus and the horses, almost breathless, he eyed the tribune and waited for an answer.

"His name is Caspian. He is one of the spies employed by Caesar's private secretary. Mount up. We must hurry to Rome. We have no time to waste!"

CHAPTER EIGHTEEN

Rome.

The largest city in the empire. Almost a million strong with a population increasing dramatically.

Spread out and rolling across the seven hills bracing the southeastern banks of the Tiber, the city was becoming a magnificent vision of imperial power. Of the seven sacred hills, Caesar Augustus, like so many others of the nobility, lived on the Palatine. In the early morning light just after dawn, standing at the railing of one of the several courtyards which surrounded the house, his eyes took in the thousands of cooking fires originating from the various apartment dwellings, street vendors, and villas lifting columns of smoke into the hot, humid air. Even here, standing in one of the many gardens of the magnificent residence, the aromas of the city assaulted his nostrils. Rome smelled like no other city in the world.

Rome *vibrated* with a personality all its own.

A sense of wealth, a sense of *power*, like the assault of an electric eel softly touching him, made the hairs on the back of his neck tingle every time he entered the city. A city of intrigue and danger. A city filled with secrets and cabals. A city definitely not for the faint of heart. This was Rome. The heart of the empire.

Below him, as he stood alone in the gardens of Octavius' home, he viewed the marbled magnificence of the Temple of Apollo and its surrounding buildings. To one side was the elegantly designed Grecian Library and further down the slope of the Palatine was the long, newly rebuilt Circus Maximus.

Fluttering from the tops of stadium seats surrounding the track of the Circus were hundreds of pennants indicating today would be a race day. Faintly, Decimus thought he heard the neighing of horses. Through the graceful Cypress trees and garden flora that littered the hill slope the house and temples resided on, he caught glimpses of clusters of people already making their way to the stadium. To his surprise, scholars were already moving back and forth along the paved squares of the temples and library.

His cousin had been a busy man since his purchase of the original small but elegant home of Quintus Hortensius. Soon after the Senate gave him the title of *Imperator,* Octavius began purchasing properties on the Palatine and expanding his household. He commissioned the building of the Apollo temple that his gardens and court yards abutted, along with several other smaller temples. The all-powerful Octavius, the most powerful man in the empire, continued to graciously decline the proposition of residing in the city's massive governmental palace. He accepted the honorarium of being called *Imperator*. But he exhibited great pains in paying due respect to the Roman Senate. He demurred from the offerings of others wanting to officially call him Emperor. Even as old as he was he still preferred to live in his private home and maintain an outward semblance of an ordinary Roman nobleman.

Under Octavius' rein the empire basically remained at

peace. The empire thrived and grew. Commerce exploded across the Mediterranean basin. New provinces were added. Rome's skyline changed tremendously through the efforts by the Caesars. Starting first with Julius and continuing with Octavius. The city was being reshaped into the most dazzling monument of power money could buy. Everywhere across the sprawling hills and valleys the city's walls encompassed, architects and master craftsmen were erecting marvelous designs built in marble and granite.

Caesar, the honorable old man who lived the sedentary life of a Roman nobleman in his own house on the Palatine, was the richest man in the world. One of the most generous men in the world. Without question the most powerful man in the empire. And ... without a doubt ... the most dangerous man in the empire.

This thought filled Decimus' mind as he stood by the railing and gazed out across the city. This dangerous, sometimes vindictive, streak that curled and wove through the soul of Octavius Caesar. He was all too familiar with it. Had seen it suddenly erupt like Vesuvius to the south— its wrath so intense its conflagration consumed all who stood too close to it. He had himself been the tool used by Octavius to exact revenge on those who had plotted against him. In the past justly so, Decimus believed. The empire was threatened. Octavius was being threatened. Someone had to be the weapon ... the *means* ... to remove the threat for the greater good. He had not hesitated. He acted with swiftness and due diligence. Had no regrets.

Now, again, he was the tool ... the weapon ... Caesar gripped to remove another threat from the empire. A sinister intrigue lurking in the shadows and being manipulated by a personality so far unknown. One which, without question, both threatened the peace of the empire and the life of Caesar Augustus. But ...

Behind him he heard the distinctive shuffle of his older cousin. Alone, this time, unaccompanied by guards. Yet not alone. For as he stood at the railing and waited for Caesar to join him, below, in the gardens and trees of the villa's grounds, dark forms of armed Praetorian Guards silently moved out in a protective envelope around the house.

"Decimus, you arrived late last night yet did not wish to disturb me. I take it the empire is still safe enough to allow an old man like me to enjoy one more night's deep sleep?"

The old man, dressed in a purple toga with silver threading reflecting morning sunlight, approached Decimus with outstretched hands and a smile on his craggy, drawn face. Over the Imperator's head was a purple shawl. Decimus gripped the hands of his cousin and smiled into the man's face with a look of concern. The elderly *Imperator* did not look well. The shawl over Caesar's head, even though the early morning air was now quite warm and comfortable, confirmed his suspicions. Age was devastating the old man hourly.

"Cousin, the empire is threatened, it is true. But you are too cunning and ill-tempered to allow just another of many inconsequential threats to worry you."

"Ha! There you have me, Decimus. Old and ill-tempered I freely confess. My bones ache. My feet ache. My soul aches. Sometimes at night when I try to sleep I wonder what will happen to all this when I die."

Caesar turned his head and gazed out over the eternal city. It gleamed beneath the morning light. It pulsed with life both men could physically sense. But Decimus knew his cousin wasn't viewing just the city. Caesar's eyes took in all. He was seeing the hills of far off Cappadocia. He was seeing the blue waters of the Egypt Nile. The rolling plains of Spain. He was seeing the world. The world as only a Roman *Imperator* would see it. A sense of melancholia filled Decimus as he looked into the old man's eyes.

"You know, Decimus, for all of his bad habits, my adoptive father, Julius, really did not wish to be remembered as the greatest of Romans. He had a far more encompassing vision. A vision for the empire. He didn't want to be remembered necessarily. He wanted the Roman Empire to live. To live eternally. He wanted to create a stable, vibrant, and just empire. One ruled by law. One that would surpass Alexander's vision of a Greek cosmos.

In the end, if his vision of that empire was completed, all who lived within the confines of its borders would have been Roman citizens. The rule of law would have become the guiding light. Not an emperor's decree. Not a tyrant's whim. Laws, justly executed, would end the corruption which plagues us all. From the most noble to the most base of men, each would know where they stood before the law.

But that's the ultimate irony is not, cousin? The true irony? For a vision to take place, for a world as new as Julius envisioned, he had to become what he wanted to destroy. He had to become a tyrant. He had to become corrupt. He had to gather the reins of power and grasp them so firmly no one would dare to challenge him. Not surprisingly, in the end he paid for that tyrant's grasp."

Decimus' dark eyes played across the old man's face. The old man gripped one of Decimus' arms gently. Caesar Augustus was a frail old man. But an old man with clear eyes and an ever sharp mind. His body was failing him. But not his intellect. It was the intellect which had always impressed him the most about Caesar.

"And you, Octavius? You succumbed to Julius Caesar's vision as well?"

"Succumbed?" the old man echoed, smiling weakly in amusement before turning to look up into Decimus's face. "Yes. Yes, I succumbed to it as well. I understood Julius Caesar, cousin. Underneath that Roman veneer of mocking superiority. I saw the true man. He loved Rome. He loved the empire. He loved the power! Yes, yes, there is no denying it. Power is an intoxicating bitch that folds you into her arms and seduces you unhesitatingly. It takes a strong man to push the seducer away. Julius could do it. Push her away and manipulate her to his will at the same time."

"As, it seems, you have as well, cousin. All these years leading the empire and people still admire you. Even worship you as a god. You appear to be exactly the same man as you were thirty years ago when I first entered your service."

From underneath the shawl that covered Caesar's balding head, Decimus heard an old man's amused chuckle. Caesar tugged on Decimus' arm, indicating silently he wished to move somewhere else. Hand still on Decimus' arm the old man turned and began moving slowly, painfully, toward a series of large carved stone chairs with bright purple silk pillows softening the harshness of the cold stone.

As Caesar lowered himself into the chair, servants magically appeared gripping serving trays filled with freshly baked pastries and flasks of chilled wine. In silence Caesar watched the young boys pour wine and fill a plate of fine silver full of pastries before bowing and withdrawing quickly. The tribune, seeing the old man reach for a pastry and finding it difficult to stretch a hand out to it, bent over and lifted the pastry dish and held it for Caesar to choose.

"You are a trusting man, Caesar. Still insist no one is going to poison your food? No slave to taste the delicacies you eat? Or has the latest one recently passed away?"

"There you have me, cousin. At my age I sometimes believe

it would be a blessing if someone put a pillow over my face and ended it quietly for me. Age and the accompanying pain that comes with it is a curse. I wake up in pain. I go to bed in pain. In between I try not to think about the pain. Fortunately the empire and its wants and demands distract me from my woes. But forgive me, Decimus. I ramble on like the old man I am."

The warrior watched the ruler pinch off a piece of pastry and lift it to his lips. In the old man's face was a myriad of emotions that complimented and yet opposed each other. Pain. Pride. Ambition. Regrets. Determination. Resignation. All there. And one other emotion. The waiting. Waiting for Death to slip into his bedchamber and take him on Charon's boat for the trip across the River Styx to Hades. Caesar felt its present close by. Knew it was coming. Yet resisted its calling knowing there was so much yet to be accomplished. So much that could possibly unravel like a badly woven tapestry after his death.

"You eye me, cousin, with concern. Fear not. I plan to remain in this world for a few years more. I will not retire into the afterlife until my replacement is ready to take the reins of power from my dead hands."

"So it is true? Tiberius will be your heir?"

"There is no other," the imperator sighed with a voice filled with resignation and regret. "Tiberius' son is too young and all the others are dead."

Tiberius Julius Caesar was Octavius' adopted son. The son of his second wife, Livia Drusilla. Tiberius' true father was a Claudian. Tiberius Claudius Nero. Octavius ordered the older Tiberius to divorce his wife, Livia Drusilla, in order that she would be free to marry the Imperator. It was a messy, sordid affair how Tiberius became a Julii. An even worse and more sordid affair happened. A few years later when Octavius, eager to marry his daughter to the heir of the empire, commanded

Tiberius to divorce his first wife and marry Caesar's oldest daughter, Julia the Elder.

For the glory of the empire men's lives are ruined. Decimus knew this dictate of Roman power applied to Tiberius Julius Caesar like no other. A brilliant general. A reluctant politician. An appreciative adopted son. Nevertheless, Tiberius seemingly had a curse about him. Groomed from birth to be a possible successor to the Imperator, Tiberius Caesar seemed to be the perfect candidate. Unquestionably brave. Unquestionably capable. Still, it was obvious the man did not want to become the supreme leader of the empire. Tiberius wanted to be a general. But more than anything he wanted to live a long and happy life with his first wife, Vipsanius Agrippa.

It was not to be.

Commanded to divorce Vipsanius and marry Octavius' daughter, what he received from his forced marriage to Julia was ridicule, shame, and debauchery. Debauchery on her part. So incensed at losing the love of his life and equally incensed at watching Octavius' daughter making him look like a cuckold fool, Tiberius astounded the Roman world with one bold act. He renounced his political ambitions, told Octavius he no longer desired the throne, and left Rome altogether.

Retiring to Rhodes, the famous general became a rural hermit among the island's inhabitants. And a source of deep political intrigues in Rome itself. Over the years as Tiberius lived on Rhodes much speculation was mulled over as to whom would the Imperator select for his heir. Even more speculation as to what Tiberius had said to his father which compelled the Imperator to allow Tiberius to leave.

Decimus knew Tiberius. In many respects liked the man. But, like many others, he too sensed a dark moodiness about him. A moodiness that, if ever coupled to unlimited power, and after all the hardships the man had to endure, offered the possibility that dark days might lay ahead for Rome.

But Tiberius was not the Imperator yet. Octavius was. Old as he was nevertheless the old man had bright, clear eyes. And an inquisitive mind. Decimus saw his cousin eyeing him silently, a half-smile on his old lips, quietly waiting for him to inform him of what he had found so far in the death of Spurius Lavinus.

"Who killed Lavinus, cousin?"

"How should I know?" Caesar answered, shrugging ancient shoulders. "That's why I sent you to ascertain."

Decimus smiled, stood up from the couch, and walked over to fill his cup of wine. "Can you tell me how Lavinus acquired knowledge of the Antonian letters?"

"Hmmm ... yes. That would be something you should know. A little over a year ago I received word some agent, a Roman citizen, freshly arrived from Greece was making discreet inquiries about the scroll. He was trying to bribe a few junior clerks on my personal staff to find out where the scrolls were stored and whether they could be obtained for a price. Large sums of gold exchanged hands. With more to come if he acquired the scroll."

"This agent," Decimus began, "You arrested him and had him interrogated. Yes? What did he have to say?"

"We did not, cousin. We decided to devise a scheme which, we thought, would both capture those here in Rome who still harbor ill will against my rule, and at the same time, eventually track down this mysterious Grecian employer. We made arrangements for the scrolls to be, shall we say, acquired in a believable way. From there it was our intent to string out enough rope which would eventually ensnarl the lot of them. But, unforeseen accidents foiled our plans."

"Lavinus' murder," Decimus said, nodding, "The freshly

arrived Roman citizen from Greece. Hmmm ... Have you any idea where they are now?"

"None," Caesar said, shaking his head and looking worried. "And now you tell me gladiators are being hidden somewhere in Brundisium to do what? Assassinate me?"

"That would be the most logical assumption, Caesar. Hidden openly in view in a gladiator school, who would suspect anything? But on the day when the assassination is to take place, they are moved and put into position. Are you to attend a public spectacle either here in Rome or in Brundisium soon?"

Caesar extended a hand toward Decimus for assistance to rise. Decimus gripped the old man's arm and gently lifted him off the couch. Wobbly on his feet, the Imperator of Rome gripped the younger man's powerful arm for support.

"I am not aware of any public appearances. But I will check my itinerary. If there are I will cancel them immediately."

"There is another possibility, Caesar. One even more evil to contemplate."

Caesar's old eyes turned and looked into Decimus' face.

"You suspect these killers are not hunting for me but are lying in wait for Tiberius?"

"He is your heir, cousin. If the viper strikes twice, cutting down the head of state and his immediate heir, who is left to claim the Imperator's laurels?"

"No one," the old man sighed, shaking his head sadly. "Chaos would rein. The empire would shred itself into a thousand pieces. Civil war would return."

Decimus nodded as he stood beside the tottering old man and kept him standing upright. In the distance, down at the base of the Palatine, toward the Circus Maximus, the peel of a dozen brass trumpets cut through the air. Too early to be announcing the first race of the day he assumed the trumpeters were practicing. The martial sound of the trumpets filling the clear early morning air filled the tribune's mind with distance lands and half-forgotten wars.

"So what do you propose we do, my young Decimus? Shall we round everyone up and throw them into prison? A hot iron pressed into yielding flesh has a way to loosening many a tongue."

"Why was Spurius Lavinus killed, Caesar? With his death already finalized, how do we apprehend his Grecian employer? I'm sure only Lavinus knew the name of the Greek. The others are nothing more than fellow conspirators only partially included in the overall plan. They would not have been informed of who was this conspiracy's mastermind. No. I propose we take a dangerous course, Caesar. We allow the rope to continue to unwind. We will continue with the waiting game. We wait for someone to make the first move. Sooner or later someone will make a mistake."

A rumble of soft laughter rolled out of the old man's weary chest. A laughter Decimus was familiar with. If there was anything his cousin loved, it was involving himself in devious and complex schemes. His rise to power relied more on his amazing cognitive abilities and his abilities of persuasion than they ever did in relying on raw military power. In the laughter Decimus knew his old cousin was agreeing with his plan.

"Go to Tiberius. Talk with him. See if he might not be the target you suspect he may be. Your assumptions could very well be right. Tiberius may be the sacrificial goat waiting to be led to slaughter. For the sake of the empire we must save my adopted son. At all costs."

Caesar made a gesture with his hand and several young servants hurried to his side quickly. Decimus, seeing he was being dismissed, separated from Caesar and bowed respectfully at the old man. Caesar, for his part, chuckled in amusement again.

"Good hunting, Decimus. For all of our sakes let us hope your intuition proves to be correct."

Silently Decimus stood and thoughtfully watched the old man shuffle off toward his mansion and disappear within. A Praetorian officer appeared, bowed, and stretched out a hand indicating the direction Decimus would use to exit the premises.

Unlimited, unquestioned power. How could power such as this not warp and twist even the best of minds?

CHAPTER NINETEEN

"What is our next move, sir?"

The boyish looking centurion lifted an apple to his lips and bit deep into the red fruit and waited for the older man to reply. Dressed in the common attire of a Greek peasant, the large-framed Quintus Flavius stood beside an open window of the small villa the older tribune owned on the Palatine. Big. Strong as a bull. Unassuming and likable. And intelligent. The key ingredient needed, the tribune believed firmly, to handle the delicate affair before them.

"We wait for Gnaeus' return," Decimus Julius Virilis answered, setting forward in the chair he occupied and reaching for an apple as well. "When our silent friend returns with news we will decide our next move. But very soon, my young friend, you and I must visit Tiberius and ascertain if he is cognizant of this conundrum facing us."

"Hmmm ..." Quintus growled, using the back of his hand to wipe the apple juice rudely sliding down his chin.

Decimus sat back, apple in hand, and lifted a brow. He

heard the young man's grunt. Heard the tone of concern in it. And knew what the centurion was worried about.

"Quintus, I have not forgotten about the shipload of gladiators. We will search for them shortly. But instead of rushing off to Brundisium and rattling all the slave cages in each of the gladiator schools, perhaps we could clarify their next move by identifying the target they are preparing to attack."

"But I thought you were sure their target is Caesar."

"Perhaps one of their targets may be Caesar. But is my old cousin the main target? Ask yourself this, Quintus. What happens to the empire when Augustus dies? Who assumes the mantel of Imperator after his death?"

"That would be Tiberius. Obviously."

"And what if there is no Tiberius? What if the famous general and adopted son of Augustus dies *before* the Imperator's expected death? Who then assumes the mantle of power?"

Quintus Flavius, chewing on a mouthful of apple, started to answer but paused and knitted eyebrows together thoughtfully. Another possible answer formed and, using the apple in his hand to gesture a confirmation, started to answer. But again he paused. Confusion overwhelmed his handsome face.

"You see the problem now." Decimus polished the red apple absently on his toga. "There is no one directly related to Caesar who is old enough to assume power. Caesar's natural children are dead. His grandsons are but babes in the arms of their mothers and will not become of age for years to come. So, with one stroke of an assassin's blade, killing Tiberius would sweep the empire into a maelstrom of fighting among the royal families. We know what such a maelstrom can, and will, do to the empire."

Quintus nodded in agreement, still chewing on the apple, his eyebrows again knitted in deep thought. Decimus, eyeing the young man fondly, lifted the apple to his mouth and bit deep into the fruit. Lowering the fruit from his lips, he shrugged and came to his feet all in one motion.

"Besides, I doubt we need to search for our shipload of assassins. I informed Caesar of everything. Including the discovery of a burning ship full of dead gladiators. If I know Caesar and his master spy for a secretary, Brundisium is already filled with imperial spies. If they are in Brundisium they will be found."

"And if they are not?" Quintus Flavius voiced quizzically.

"It will provide us with the only logical conclusion. If they are not in Brundisium, nor in Rome, it means they are not on the mainland. The only alternative left is they are again on board a ship sailing off the coast of Italy. Out of sight. But close enough to be summoned at a moment's notice."

Quintus Flavius tossed the core of the apple out of the open window and then turning back to the table hosting the large bowl of fresh fruit, reached for a second apple.

"Tribune, something else puzzles me. And has for a few days now."

"Oh? Speak up, lad. Never hesitate to voice your concerns when we are in the privacy of our own quarters. Among those whom I trust I insist on an openness between us. We must understand each other completely, Quintus Flavius. I must trust you. You must trust me. There will be times when that trust will be sorely tested. Therefore, we must each of us be sure nothing is kept in reclusion."

The centurion grinned sheepishly, reddening a bit. To be told he was a trusted member to the small entourage attached to the tribune was an acknowledgment and compliment which caught him by surprise.

"I worry about Atia Graccia, sir. You said earlier that of all the ones involved with Spurius Lavinus, she was by far the one most capable of creating a plot against Caesar. Perhaps even more diabolical that her husband. Yet when she asked for permission to leave Italy and journey to the African coast you agreed to it without hesitation. Why?"

A soft rumble of laughter escaped from Decimus' lips. A laugh of genuine amusement. The older man turned his back to the open window.

"Ah, so the young man begins to observe as well as see with his eyes. Very good, Quintus. Very good. Indeed, my assessment of Atia Graccia's capabilities are quite accurate. I know she is far more capable than her husband could ever hope to have been. There are people who have the *intelligence* to conceive a complex conspiracy against Caesar. Her father, Felix Graccius, is one. Tertius Julius Romanus is another. He is nothing more than a viper waiting to strike at the right moment. But to *plan* and *implement* a vast conspiracy, Quintus? To have the *steel* in one's spine strong enough to throw the dice and *act*? No. Only one person in those whom we know of so far is capable of that."

"Atia Graccia," Quintus Flavius echoed.

"Atia Graccia," nodded Decimus in confirmation. "If anyone has the nerve, the imagination, the gall to take on Caesar and convince others to follow her lead, it is this woman."

"So why give her permission to leave the country?"

"Can you not deduce my reasoning, Quintus? Does it not seem obvious to you why I would allow such an apparently insane move on my part to happen?"

"My only thought is you wished to see what she would do next. Does she flee to Carthage? Or does she alter her travel plans and attempts to disguise her moves. Her movements might give us evidence she is indeed the mastermind we seek."

"Exactly," said the tribune, beaming in delight at his protégé. "I suspect she was as surprised as you were in my readily agreeing to retire from the inquiry. I am quite sure she suspects a trap. I am also quite sure she has the capabilities of eluding the spies I sent along to watch her every movement."

"But once she boards ship and leaves, what then?" the centurion asked before biting into the second apple. "A ship at sea can change course. Or another ship can rendezvous with it and passengers can disembark. There are a number of possibilities which would allow her to disappear."

"Arrangements have been made," Decimus answered, half turning to glance out the window and painting a wide grin on his lips. "A naval vessel will follow along at a discreet distance to make sure her ship reaches Carthage. But Quintus, the point is this. If she makes any attempt to elude our spies, we confirm our suspicions she is deeply involved in the conspiracy. If she travels all the way to Carthage and disembarks we can safely conclude she is an unfortunate spectator and is indeed innocent. But for now, let us allow this discussion to wither away. Gnaeus has returned and I am most curious to hear what he has to say."

Quintus Flavius grinned. He too would be quite interested to *hear* the silent Gnaeus' report since the man had no tongue. Yet for a man with no tongue, the rough looking bandit that was Gnaeus could speak eloquently.

CHAPTER TWENTY

Gnaeus had much to say. The enigma that was the sea captain, Caius Septimus, now was a frequent visitor to the home of Felix Graccius. Tertius Julius frequented the Gracci home as well. All seemed to be on edge. Nervous. At all hours of the day and night servants carrying sealed scrolls came and went at a frenzied pace. The whole household seemed to be agitated. But most interestingly the staff of Felix Graccius seemed to be preparing to shut the house down permanently. Laborers, lumbering through the night with large wagons, hefted up heavy looking wooden crates and disappeared into the darkness.

So too the household of Tertius Julius. In fact his small home was almost barren of both artifacts and servants.

"The rats preparing their escape?" Quintus Flavius suggested after Gnaeus fell silent.

"Hmmm," the tribune mused as he rubbed a forefinger across his temple. "On face value it would suggest the strike against Caesar or perhaps Tiberius is close at hand. But both leaving at the same time? What of our sea captain? Are we to believe Caius Septimus will be the one who leads our unfound gladiators onto their victims? I am inclined to frown upon that idea. In the chaos to come, when the murders have taken place and the Senate is thrown into chaos, only a nobleman of strong will have to step in and calm the nerves of the panicked. Caius Septimus is not of patrician rank. He is not even Roman. No. He cannot be the one who commands the strike."

Quintus Flavius glanced at Gnaeus. Gnaeus shrugged and turned his attention to Decimus. For his part the tribune stood, hands behind his back, and stared out the balcony doors leading onto the second-floor veranda. Etched on the older man's face was a look of deep contemplation. Gnaeus, the centurion, Hassad, nor Rufus had the inclination to disturb the tribune's thoughts. Silently gesturing to the three to follow him, the centurion led the three into another room and began cutting bread and cheese for each. And being old legionnaires who had soldiered with the tribune for years, the three knew when food was offered it was time to eat for no one knew when the next opportunity might rise.

A half hour later Decimus entered the room, walked to the table with the remnants of cheese and bread setting on it, and filled a plate as well.

"Of the conspirators we have so far met, whom do you believe might be the weakest of the lot? Anyone?"

Gnaeus made a gesture with his hand.

"I have one vote for Felix Graccius," said the tribune. "Do we have someone else to consider?"

"I agree with Gnaeus," the centurion said as he crossed arms across his wide chest. "Graccus seems hesitant. Reluctant. Certainly more nervous than the others."

Hassad and Rufus remained silent. But with the nod of their heads they voiced their agreement.

"Ah. Very good. I concur. Felix Graccus has never been a

strong man. In the senate he has always been a follower. Never a leader. So, perhaps if we put pressure on our senator we might extract some information heretofore unknown to us. Offering him an avenue to extricate himself and perhaps his lovely daughter from this cabal, he might readily agree. We will talk to the senator tonight. Hassad, find our senator and discretely follow him. Do not let him out of your sight. Inform us an hour before supper time where we might find the good man.

But we must all keep eyes on another conspirator. One who might lead us directly to our gladiatorial assassins. Rufus, go with Hassad. Stay watching the senator's house until you spy our ship captain's arrival. Follow Caius Septimus. And Rufus, be very wary. The man is quite dangerous and knows spies might be watching him. He will not hesitate to kill if he thinks he's being compromised."

Hassad and Rufus came to their feet, hurried across the floor to reach for loaves of bread, in case their assignments proved to be long and arduous, and quickly left. Decimus, concerned, glanced at the two remaining. Both the big framed, handsome centurion, and the much smaller and wiry silent Gnaeus watched him expectantly.

"It is time we talk to either or second intended victim, or perhaps, the mastermind of this whole affair. Either way we must tread gently. Tiberius Julius Caesar's intellect is first rate. None of us should underestimate the man's capabilities."

CHAPTER TWENTY-ONE

Through the busy streets the three walked. It was, without question, a beautiful day without a cloud in the sky, with the sky an amazing color of translucent blue. Past vendors selling all kinds of delicacies, past magnificent pieces of sculpture rising into the heavens in front of the temples which dotted the city. If anything, Rome was known as a city of temples. Every god imaginable had at least one temple dedicated to them. There was even a temple for the unknown god. A temple which seemed to attract a goodly sized following.

Across the street from the Temple of Ceres, not too far from the main entrance to the Circus Maximus, the three paused to lean against the bar of a small wine shop. It was race day as they watched the festive masses gathering for the event. Thousands of Romans, dressed in their team's primary colors, milled about between the Circus Maximus, the Temple of Ceres and the Temple of Hercules. Today were chariot races. A sport enthusiastically followed by most Romans from the full strata of Roman society. Haughty patrician and the much more enthusiastic and raucous masses of plebian followers mingled in the crowd exchanging good natured banter and placing bets on one charioteer or another.

They walked up the southern slope of the Aventine and down the northern slope before imbibing in a shop between the Aventine and the Palatine. Tiberius' home was one of the several homes which resided in the Augustan compound at the top of the Palatine. The Palatine would be a steep climb. They would have to trod past the Grotto of the Lupercal, the supposed sight where the legendary she-wolf had suckled Romulus and Remus, the founders of Rome, in a cave on the southern slope of Palatine not more than fifty yards away from the grounds of Caesar Augustus' home. The Imperator spent a large amount of his own private wealth to build a small temple above the cavern. A sight Decimus had not yet taken in. He would not explore the temple and grotto today. Too bad. He had heard the temple was a remarkable piece of architecture.

Leaning against the bar facing the milling crowd, wine cup in hand, bracketed on one side by the taller centurion and on the other by the rough looking Gnaeus, his dark eyes took in the masses idly. Beside him he felt the stillness of Quintus Flavius and almost smiled. Since leaving the small home opposite the Aventine he had noticed the young man's thoughtful pose. He knew what the lad was mulling over. And waited for the centurion to break the silence. He did not have to wait long.

"Sir, about what was said earlier. Concerning the Imperator's successor ..."

"Quintus, before the Imperator adopted Tiberius, what was his full name?"

The brows on the young centurion folded together thoughtfully before he shrugged at his mentor.

"To be honest, sir, I haven't a clue. Imperial intrigues and politics have been the least of my worries. Until now, that is."

Both Decimus and Gnaeus smiled. The rough looking

Gnaeus took the wine bottle sitting on the bar and poured a second round for each of them. As he poured into Quintus Flavius' glass he made a set of quick hand gestures toward the older man. The tribune's smile widened as he silently saluted his servant and lifted the glass to his lips.

"Gnaeus said imperial politics in this city is a Roman's very soul, Quintus. More so if you are an officer in the Urban Cohort. Sooner or later we are all drawn into their spider's web of intrigues. Let me enlighten you. Before Tiberius became a Julii he was Tiberius Claudius. The son of Tiberius Claudius Nero. A Claudian. Does that name mean anything to you?"

"I am aware of the reputation of the Claudian family, sir. I understand they are closely associated with imperial power. I seem to recall that, years ago, Tiberius's father and the Imperator had been enemies. If I recall my tutors' lessons, Tiberius Claudius Nero threw his lot in with Marcus Antonius. Fought in several engagements against the Imperator's forces. But those animosities were set aside when Caesar declared a general amnesty."

"An amnesty was declared, young man. Enemies were pardoned. But old hatreds never die. Revenge still burns in the heart of many. There are insults far more grievous than merely being defeated in battle, Quintus Flavius. For Tiberius Claudius Nero, insult was added to the stinging blow of defeat when Octavius insisted Tiberius divorce his wife. Octavius had fallen in love with the Claudian's wife, Livia Drusilla. Madly in love. Both wife and child left the Claudian clan and became Julii. Livia Drusilla became more than just a wife to Caesar. She became his closet advisor. Some say she is, today, as powerful as Caesar himself. I would not dispute the claim."

Something tan, fast, running on sandaled feet, ran past the opening entrance of the wine ship and disappeared in the growing crowd. Decimus narrowed his eyes and frowned. He had not seen a face. Had not even seen the structure of the body the small person had. But for some reason he was sure it was not a child running gaily through the crowd. He had that uneasy feeling building in his gut. They were being followed. Not followed ... more like scouted. Reconnoitered. Reconnoitered as if a trap was being set in place somewhere for them to fall into. Saying nothing to his companions, Decimus sipped wine and waited for the inevitable next question to come from his young protégée.

The centurion, scratching his head and looking genuinely puzzled, glanced at the milling crowd outside the wine shop and mulled over the tribune's words.

"So, perhaps, Tiberius holds resentments toward Caesar for forcing his real father to renounce him in order to be adopted? Yet why now? Why plot such a devious, and I might add quite dangerous, conspiracy knowing that Caesar is close to dying anyway? A year ... two at the most ... and Tiberius will inherit the Imperator's office. He will become the new Caesar."

Decimus sat his empty wine glass on the bar. Glancing at the taller centurion he slapped the younger man fondly on the shoulder and exited the wine shop heading toward the Palatine.

"Good. You have seen the obvious. Tiberius is not a reckless man. He is not foolish. There is a love hate relationship between him and Caesar. Always has been. At one point in the relationship Caesar banned Tiberius from Rome. But in the end Livia Drusilla has always stepped in and convinced Caesar to forgive her son. And now, with Caesar so close to his death, he has no choice but to declare Tiberius his heir. You are therefore correct, Quintus Flavius. Tiberius in all likelihood is not the mastermind of this cabal of conspirators. Yet that possibility exists, and we should be aware of it. Still, my instincts tell me he is more the potential victim than the perpetrator. We shall soon find out."

Entering the milling throng of waiting racing fans they began their brisk walk toward the tall slope of the Palatine and the wide marble steps leading toward the top. Above them, glimmering in the sunlight, were a number of small Grecian styled temples or the rough, plain looking outer walls of a nobleman's residence overlooking the Circus Maximus. As they moved again the tribune became aware of the unsettling feeling he was being watched by someone in the crowd. Even the centurion, striding beside the small tribune, brow furrowed in thought, felt it. Turning his head left and right his eyes penetrated through the crowd looking for whoever it was who might be watching them. Hundreds were laughing and talking and gesturing in animated conversations. But no one seemed particularly interested in their passing by.

As they began their ascent up the steps toward the Imperator's compound the handsome young centurion decided to trail the tribune while the silent Gnaeus set the pace in front of them. Rising above the grounds below them, Quintus Flavius glanced behind him and spoke.

"So I take it, sir, you now add the Claudian family to the list of suspects?"

"Quintus—" The tribune glanced at the centurion behind him before returning his attention to their ascent. "When investigating the murder of a patrician and the possible assassination of Caesar, there is no choice but to suspect everyone."

CHAPTER TWENTY-TWO

They were ushered into a large room with walls filled with scrolls. Rare pieces of Greek statuary of the Greek God Pan playing his flute or Bacchus, the god of wine, lifting a large leather bag of wine over his head and tilting his head with mouth open to partake. Heavy curtains of purple lined with gold thread had been pulled back and tied with golden ropes to reveal the well-manicured inner gardens of the house. Roses and chrysanthemums filled the garden boxes dotting the bright green grass and exploded in bright colors underneath neatly cropped Poplar trees. It was a beautiful home. A home that bespoke the power and wealth of a very powerful man. A man who loved art, beauty and knowledge in equal proportions. A man of taste and distinction.

A man, the tribune thought privately to himself, who could be both gracious and ruthless at the same time.

Behind them a set of doors were opened by a servant who hurriedly stepped aside and bowed his head. Almost immediately the Roman general and heir to the throne came striding into the room, both hands outstretched, a genuine smile of pleasure on his handsome face as he approached the tribune.

"Decimus Julius Virilis! My old friend. I heard you had retired finally from the army. How long has it been since we last served together? Two? Three years?"

Gripping Decimus Julius Virilis' hands firmly Tiberius shook them with a fond exuberance. The last time he had served in a legion commanded by Tiberius it was by a cruel twist of fate. *Legio IX Brundisi*, ill prepared and freshly arrived into the wild, mountainous country of Dalmatia, was struck with a horrendous calamity. Every commanding officer in the legion, except for Decimus, was killed instantly in a shattering explosion which rocked the legion encampment. The few remaining soldiers, surrounded by a determined enemy intent on slaughtering them, somehow survived. But only by fighting savagery with savagery.

"In the Dalmatian uprisings three years ago, sir."

"That's right. In Dalmatia. What a sordid affair that was, Decimus. It was you who saved the Brindisi legion, old friend. Perhaps even saved us from losing the war. I'll never forget the image of your grim, blood-soaked figure standing on that hilltop commanding the few surviving legionnaires when we came upon you. But your brilliance in tracking down the conspirators who murdered Senator Sulla and his staff was a display of genius, old friend. Genius! Come, let me pour you a glass of wine. I am very pleased to see you again, old friend. Very pleased."

Tiberius did not wait for servants to scurry forward and pour wine. He filled glasses for everyone. To the silent Gnaeus, the general gripped the man's arm and shoulder firmly and greeted him almost as heartily as he had greeted the tribune. When Decimus introduced Quintus Flavius to Tiberius, the heir to the throne mentioned that he had heard the tribune had absorbed an Urban Cohort officer into his retinue, and also mentioned his respect and admiration for the branch of the Flavian family Quintus hailed from. Honored, Quintus Flavius remained silent and bowed his head politely.

The general lifted his glass toward Decimus in salute. "To Decimus Julius Virilis. The finest soldier I ever shared many a cold meal with deep within enemy territory. Always victorious. Always lucky."

After the salute the heir to the throne fondly slapped the tribune on the shoulders again and laughed. Lifting a hand up, he gestured to all they should move out into the gardens for their discussion. Stepping into the sunlight, all three noticed how expertly the man they came to interview directed them to the middle of the gardens. Out of earshot from any within the house who might be willing to secretly eavesdrop on their conversation.

"Caesar tells me you are quietly working for him on some hush hush investigation. Should I be worried?"

"Perhaps, sir. Perhaps. Indirectly it does involve you. I do not wish to be blunt or too direct, general. But there is a strong chance you may be the target of an assassination attempt in the near future."

Quintus Flavius and Gnaeus drifted to one side of the expanse of green grass and turned their backs toward Tiberius and Decimus. Discreetly removing themselves from hearing the conversation behind them, they began inspecting the villa's many doors and windows. The tribune warned them that what was said today had to stay between him and Tiberius alone. Neither the centurion nor the silent Gnaeus protested.

"I face often one rumor or another about a possible assassination attempt, Decimus. What makes you and my father think this one is more dangerous than the others?"

"There have already been several deaths in this affair,

general. Including the murder of a senator by the name Spurius Lavinus. There is also the troubling revelation that a ship load of gladiators has arrived and are now tucked away from view waiting to be summoned by their masters. For what purpose one can only surmise. And then there is the resurfacing of an old set of letters. Letters filled with scurrilous lies."

The last remark made Tiberius narrow his eyes and glance at the tribune quickly. The smile on the general's lips evaporated to be replaced by a mask of indecipherability.

"I heard about the Lavinus murder. But I had no idea it was related to that other matter. Do we know who currently possess them?"

"No. I am making inquiries now. Caesar has impressed upon me the importance of having them either returned to him as soon as possible. Or destroyed beyond any possible recognition. But they are not why I am here, general. I worry for your health. There appears to be a good chance that both you and Caesar might be the targets for this viper's pit of assassins. Tell me, do you plan to make any long journeys soon? For instance, do you plan to journey south toward Brundisium within the month? Or perhaps north toward the Alps?"

Tiberius turned and faced Decimus, a scowl twisted his handsome face. "To Germania within the fortnight. Caesar has asked me to return to that old command and take up the reins again. My plans were to ride to Ostia, board ship, and sail to Gaul. From there I was going to tour a few of the garrisons and then ride on to Germania."

"It is in Ostia that the majority of our murders were committed, general. I suspect the gladiators in question are aboard ship waiting for your arrival. It would not be out of the realm of impossibility for them to stage an attack on your ship and make it look like a pirate raid. Your escort would be overwhelmed, and you would be lost at sea."

"And the empire, if Caesar is cut down, would be thrown into chaos," Tiberius growled, nodding grimly. "Decimus, wise you are in these matters. I know Caesar would not have asked you to take the lead in this affair if he did not have complete confidence in your abilities. As I have as well. I must return to Germania. My departure cannot be extended much longer. So tell me. What should be my next move?"

Decimus eyed the general, tapping his lips with a finger thoughtfully with hands clasped, and mulled over possible alternatives for a moment before answering.

"This could be an opportunity for us, general. But it will be a dangerous plan. One that would still place your life in jeopardy. One Caesar may not be willing to take."

"I will handle Caesar, my friend. What have you in mind?"

Quickly Decimus outlined the plan to Tiberius. As he spoke, the more the plan was verbalized, the wider the grin spread on Tiberius' lips. Finally, at the end, Tiberius lifted his head and laughed out loud and slammed Decimus on the shoulders fondly.

"Decimus, you old fox. I love it. I will begin making arrangements immediately. And I know just the event to make the announcement publicly to Caesar. I can see the surprise on their faces even now."

The tribune, almost smiling, remained standing solidly in front of Tiberius. There was another matter to be discussed. One that he knew he had to tread carefully over.

"General, there is something else. Something I wish not to discuss but something of such importance it has to be discussed. The death of Spurius Lavinus."

Tiberius glanced to his right toward the backs of Quintus Flavius and silent Gnaeus some distance away before turning his head in the opposite direction and glancing toward the nearest window facing the inner gardens. Gently gripping

Decimus' arm, he steered the tribune several feet away from the open window.

"Caesar warned me of the Lavinii's interest in the Antonian letters some weeks ago. Told me he was beginning to hear reports that several interested parties were eager to get their hands on it. One of the parties being Spurius Lavinus. I knew Caesar had them safely tucked away in one of his many private vaults and thought nothing else about it. But then I heard they were stolen. Caesar was beside himself with anger. His secretary, Caius Lucius, ripped the city to pieces hunting for it. A couple of spies working for Lucius were arrested and tortured under the suspicion they lifted them from its well-guarded vault. But it appears they were innocent. And then, a few days ago, I heard about the murder of Spurius Lavinus. I found that piece of news to be very odd, Decimus. Very odd indeed."

The balding tribune kept his dark clear eyes glued to Tiberius' handsome face and listened in silence. Every gesture, every facial nuance the general telegraphed to Decimus told him Tiberius was telling him the truth. He wanted to believe Tiberius. Yet he knew the man all too well.

"Did Caesar ever indicate he actually knew Spurius Lavinus received the letters?"

"No," Tiberius answered, shaking his head and smiling ruefully. "You know the old man as well as I do, Decimus. He will tell you what he wants you to know and not one iota more. The only name he mentioned concerning those who were interested in acquiring them was that one name. No one else."

"Have you heard any rumors as to who might have killed Lavinus?"

Again, the general shook his head *no*.

"Not a word. Caius Lucius' spies were just as rattled by Lavinus' death as I was. I got the distinct impression Caesar was taken by surprise as well. Everybody within Caesar's private entourage has been wondering about it. Do you suspect someone?"

"Not yet" the tribune replied slowly, shaking his head. "His death creates the impression that someone higher up, the real mastermind of this affair, was concerned over Lavinus' loyalty. There are hundreds of candidates who might have been in league with the dead man."

"So what is your next move, old fox?"

Decimus shrugged.

"Continue my investigation, sir. Keep searching. My primary goal is to find the letters. The secondary goal is to thwart the conspirators. Since they appear to be both one and the same you can see how difficult the assignment is. But let me ask you one final question, sir. Have you ever heard of a man by the name of Caius Septimus?"

"Septimus ... Septimus? Hmmm," Tiberius said, rubbing a finger across his left temple thoughtfully. "I seem to recall a naval commander by that name. Served Caesar's father faithfully. But may have gone over and sided with Marcus Antonius after Julius Caesar's death. But to be honest, I haven't heard that name mentioned in years. Why? Is he one of the cogs in this vast machine of intrigue?"

"Apparently so, general. But we should find out shortly."

"Ah, well!" Tiberius exploded, grinning widely and throwing hands onto his narrow hips. "Splendid! If you will excuse me, Decimus, I will hurry off and quietly talk to Caesar and make arrangements for our little moment of fun later in the week. Good hunting, old friend. May the gods smile upon you always."

Decimus bowed as Tiberius turned and disappeared into the villa. Servants led them out of the house. In silence the three trekked their way back to the Aventine, each vaguely aware that they were being followed.

CHAPTER TWENTY-THREE

In the darkness Hassad raised a hand and pointed to the modest walled home of a patrician setting underneath the plumage of large poplar trees. The house sat between two narrow streets. Ominous looking streets, currently barren of traffic, filled with shadows and dark places where spies could hide in secrecy. On either side of the home, larger walled estates sat in the darkness. Both were brightly lit and gaily raucous in the amount noise drifting over their walls. They heard musicians, laughter, and a number of different voices in avid conversations drifting down the dark streets. But the house of Felix Graccius was as dark as an Egyptian tomb and just as silent.

"You are sure our quarry is within?" Decimus whispered softly, leaning closer to the thin figure of Hassad.

"I found him here the moment I arrived this afternoon. There was a torch burning brightly in his bedroom chambers in that second-floor window to the right. I thought I saw movement through one or two of the windows. About an hour ago several men showed up, one of them being, we believe Caius

Septimus, and entered. They were there for about an hour before Septimus alone exited the house. Rufus, following your instructions, followed. Since then the house has gone absolutely silent."

"Could he have left by a different exit?" Quintus Flavius whispered, peering down one narrow street suspiciously.

"No sir," the dark figure replied, shaking his head. "Earlier I searched the house looking for secret exits. I am positive the only exits available are ones that open out into the street to my right. I would have seen our man's departure no matter which exit he would have used from this position."

In the distance, not too far away, a couple of dogs began barking angrily. Loud, insistent barking. The kind of insistent chatter from dogs who have stumbled upon intruders invading their domains. For several seconds Decimus and the others stood in the deepest part of the shadows and listened intently. Several seconds went by and then there was the distinct howl of a dog being smitten viciously. The barking ceased from both animals as swiftly as it had started only moments before.

Quintus Flavius, eyes turning to stare at the tribune, saw the older man holding his military cloak around his shoulders with one hand while lifting a finger to his lips in the universal gesture of silence with the other. Almost instantly Hassad made a motion with his hand and pointed toward one of the narrow streets which bordered the Gracci residence.

At first nothing was to be seen. Only a dark street partially lit by a few burning torches on the upper walled estate bordering the street. But then, in the darkness, the suggestion of movement. Hugging the shadows as best as they could, two cloaked figures, hunched over and barely visible, sprinted from out of the darkness,

and slipped through the main gate of the Gracci house, disappearing from view.

"Come!" Decimus spoke firmly in a low voice, "Swords!"

Each drew the ugly steel of a gladius and gripped it firmly in their hands as they followed the tribune across the street and into the outer gardens of the dark and silent house. Finding the front door gaping half open, they entered the home and into a dark well of blackness. Almost at once, from upstairs, they heard the clanging racket of steel ringing off a hard tile floor followed by the muffled scream of a woman. Hassad led the way swiftly up a wide stair to the second floor. Past the open door of the bedroom, the three entered and came to a swift halt. Before them was a particularly gruesome sight.

In the middle of a bedroom barren of any furniture was the body of Felix Graccus lying in a massive pool of blood. His clothing had been partially stripped from his body and strewn across the tile floor. Even in the darkness it was apparent he had been stabbed multiple times. Beside the ghostly pale white body knelt Felix Graccus' daughter, Atia Graccia. Hands covered half of her face as her entire body shook in silent anguish. Staring at the body of her father the woman rocked forward and backward in anguish as heart wrenching little sounds of misery escaped from her throat. Behind her stood the massive figure of a bare-chested Nubian. He too stared down at the body in abject horror.

"Light! Give me light!" shouted the tribune as he took a step deeper into the bedroom, sheathing his blade in the process.

Around him Gnaeus, Hassad and Quintus Flavius scurried to find an oil lamp or torch which might be quickly lit. Almost instantly flames erupted in the darkness from torches held high by Hassad and Gnaeus. Bright flickering torch light threw the darkness to one side and illuminated the bedroom brightly. Decimus, glancing swiftly to his left and right, brows furrowed in deep thought, scanned the room intensely.

One glance at the body told the tribune the man had been

tortured before being murdered. Expertly tortured from the look of the man's missing fingernails. It was also obvious that whoever had tortured the senator was looking for something. The bedroom walls had been partially dismantled by something blunt and heavy. Gaping holes in the walls and the plaster littering the tile floor suggested the search had been both vicious and rapidly done. Several sections of the tile floor had been pried away as well.

"Search the house," he said, half turning toward Quintus Flavius. "All of you. See if the fiends left any evidence behind. Quintus, after you have finished your search, go next door and introduce yourself to the patrician living there. Make inquiries as to whether they heard a man's screams coming from the house. Ask them, servants and all, if they saw anyone entering or leaving the house today."

Quintus Flavius nodded when the tribune finished giving his directions and handed the older man a burning torch before exiting the bedroom with the others. Decimus, for his part, held the torch over his head and watched the weeping woman for a second before turning his attention to the black skinned Nubian.

"You understand my words, slave?"

The Nubian stared at Decimus, fear visibly in his wide eyes, and remained silent giving only a nod of the head. Atia wept desperately, still on her knees beside her father. Glancing down at the woman and then back up at the slave, he remained silent for a moment before speaking. Holding the torch above his head, the flickering light of his torch plus the one the Nubian held hissed and flickered creating a room full of dancing shadows and ominous forms slinking across the plastered walls.

"Why did your mistress not board passage in Brundisium for Carthage?"

"Her father not come as promised," the giant answered in broken Latin. "Fear gripped my lady. We hurry to Rome to find father. Too late. Too late we find him."

Decimus watched as the pale Atia lifted herself off her knees and stood up. What once had been a ravishingly beautiful face was now that of a haggard, grieving old woman. In the flickering torch light, the transformation from beauty to that of a fabled witch's visage was startling as she faced him, eyes looking down at the floor in front of her.

"You killed my father," her voice whispered with an eerie hiss. Her tear stained face and hair wildly disheveled from the hysterical mourning added to the fantastical image of a witch rising up from the bloody floor. "You and the man you work for murdered my husband as well. Searching for phantoms that don't exist. Searching for safety. Searching for something you will never have! All of you kill the innocent. The pure of heart. The weak. I curse you! I curse all of you!"

Suddenly her head came up. Her eyes filled with red rage and bored into the tribune's. A hand came up and slammed him viciously across the face. Decimus made no move to stop the blow from falling across his cheeks. The slap echoed across the barren walls of the bedroom. The blow so fierce, the tribune unintentionally stepped back. He held onto the torch firmly and gazed into the woman's eyes.

"Atia Gracci I did not kill your husband. In fact, I was given the task by the Imperator to find those who did."

"Lies! Lies!" she hissed, a note of madness beginning to creep into her voice. "My husband had no intention of pursuing that cursed set of letters of Antonius until Caius Septimus came to our house and insisted on him accepting them! The moment Spurius took possession of it our lives were no longer our own. Misfortune and death have stalked us ever since!"

"Atia, I swear to you on anything you consider holy, I had

no hand in killing your father or your husband. All I can tell you is that I will find those who killed both and bring them to justice. This I promise."

"Ha!" she shrieked shrilly, breaking out into harsh laughter. "A promise you cannot possibly keep, you fool! Can you not see? Are you blind, Decimus Julius Virilis? You, like the rest of us, are being manipulated by forces far stronger than any of us! They do not blink an eye when they commit acts of monstrous atrocities! Their souls are nothing more than empty pits! You are nothing but a straw man soon to be blown away by a fierce wind. Hahahaha! A straw man! Hahahaha!"

The madness set in swiftly. Insane laughter gripped her and would not let go. The timbre of the woman's voice began rising as she staggered back throwing hands up to her face and looking more like a wild animal than the woman she had been. The laughter grew more insane as it increased in volume. So loud that both Gnaeus and Hassad came running into the room with looks of concern on their faces.

Quietly, he told both servants to suspend their searching of the house and escort the woman and her servant to the Vigiles station and acquire an armed escort. From there they were to take them to his small home on the Aventine and stay with her. They were to make sure no harm came to her nor allow her to harm herself.

In silence, he watched the woman and her servant, escorted by his two men, exit the bedroom. As she began walking to the bedroom's door, clasping hands in front of her with white knuckles, she lifted her head and gazed into the tribune's face with eyes of haunting fear. Eyes which told him she knew she was condemned to death and only waited for the final blow to fall.

CHAPTER TWENTY-FOUR

"We must find Caius Septimus, and find him immediately," the tribune said upon the return of Quintus Flavius. "He is a person who comes and goes at will. Every time he appears he brings death with him. He must know who is the one who orchestrates this grim comedy unseen."

"Sir, the neighbors. All I talked to swear no one came or left the Gracci household until Caius Septimus arrived sometime this afternoon. Yet a servant in charge of supplying the house next door with firewood swears there is a secret passage leading into the Gracci home through an outcropping just north of the house. Twice in the last two weeks he says he has seen figures late at night coming and going. Two, three at a time."

"Let us find this passage, Quintus. Perhaps we might find something of interest."

Gripping burning torches in their hands the two exited the Gracci house and entered the narrow streets. North of the walled house a short stone bridge swept across a rugged creek bed with steep, treacherous walls. In the darkness with only torch light to illuminate the way it was difficult to descend the almost vertical cliff. But a path just wide enough for one to traverse carefully, one step at a time, was discovered after leaving the street above and moving down the wall three or four meters.

Pressing their backs firmly against the sharp stones of the rocky wall, the two moved cautiously along the paths with only the hissing, spitting torches in their hands breaking the silence of the night. As they moved down, they noticed the path sweeping around an outcropping of rock and disappearing around it.

"Careful here, Quintus. By my reckoning we should be almost directly beneath the Gracci's northern wall. If there is a secret passage, we should be almost upon it now."

They were.

Inching their way around the outcropping, they discovered the opening to a cavern when a cold shaft of wind blew across their sweating backs unexpectedly. Turning, lifting torches high over their heads, the blackness of the cavern opening was just wide enough for one man to squeeze through with difficulty. The tribune did not hesitate. Leading with the torch held directly in front of him, he slipped into the darkness and disappeared immediately around a rocky wall. Only a small bubble of light told Quintus the tribune was close at hand. Following the tribune, the centurion found himself soon standing beside the older man's shoulder and staring in amazement at the sight of a wide set of marble steps which swept up into the blackness and disappeared into the nothingness.

Ascending the steps cautiously, torches held high over their heads and slightly in front of them, they found themselves staring at the incredible. The cavern opened into a wide, vaulted cathedral of natural stone. Six steps above them the steps ended. There stood a wide, marbled dais with a slab of uncut marble in the middle. Even in the faint glow of flickering torch light the sight was terrible to behold.

"Look, Quintus. There is where they tortured our victim before killing him in his bedroom," the tribune said, pointing to the slab of raw marble covered in blood in the middle of the cave.

"A ritual killing?" Quintus Flavius whispered in puzzlement. "Are we dealing with some strange religious cult?"

The tribune did not answer. Gripping the hissing torch, he moved slowly around the raw marble slab and noted how the blackness of dried, coagulated blood contrasted with the white purity of the marble. He grunted with interest when he discovered lying on the slab the small row of brass instruments of torture, covered in blood, and obviously recently used.

Holding the torch high again, his gaze fell upon the marble steps disappearing into the darkness above behind the bloody dais. He noted the thick coating of dust which covered each step of the staircase except where, over the last few days, a number of people had disturbed the blanket with their rapid coming and going. Moving close to the step he knelt to one knee and began examining the dust intently. Twice Quintus Flavius saw the tribune's hand reach out and almost touch something in the dust hesitantly. Curious, he decided to move closer to the steps and observe the tribune's investigation more intently.

As he did the tribune spoke.

"Quintus Flavius, you say you are familiar with this Caius Septimus. Yes?"

"Yes sir, we have had our run-ins before."

"Does this man have a damaged right foot?"

"The last I saw of him he did not. He was hale and hearty and fully intact except for that one missing finger."

"Look here," the tribune said, pointing to several footprints in the dust covering the steps. "A man with a damaged right foot comes and goes several times from this house. A man always followed by two others directly behind him. See?"

Once pointed out to him the centurion saw it quickly enough. There was something odd in the way the man sat his right foot down at an unnatural angle when compared to his left foot. Yet from the appearance of it, the damaged foot did not seem to inhibit the man's ability to move.

"An old wound perhaps," Decimus said. "Improperly set and long healed. Still, this man is in the prime of his life and quite capable."

"A gladiator perhaps?" Quintus Flavius muttered out loud, frowning as he turned and stared at the bloody slab of marble. "Someone not afraid of blood and expert in the use of torture would fit the description of a gladiator."

The tribune faced the young centurion and nodded in approval.

"Quintus, you beginning to read my thoughts? Yes, my thought exactly. A gladiator, perhaps. The one in charge of those brought over from Greece. Who knows? Come. Let us follow the steps up and see where they lead us."

The tribune led the way ascending the steps, holding his torch in front of him as he carefully observed what the dust told him on the cold marble steps. Twice he paused, knelt, and examined a step more closely before rising and continuing the ascent. At the top of the stairs they found a partially open stone door. The aromas coming in from the darkness on the other side of the door suggested the storage room of the Gracci residence. With torches flickering from the stiff breeze blowing through the door, both tribune and centurion left the grotto behind and entered the dark cellar.

For the next three hours tribune and centurion rummaged

through the home looking for more evidence. In the end, as the sun was beginning to color the tiled roof tops of the city and completely exhausted, the two decided to quit the search. The journey back to the Aventine and to the tribune's small house was a silent test of endurance.

CHAPTER TWENTY-FIVE

Atia Gracci moved as silently as a ghost as she stepped out of the door of the house and walked bare footed in the grass toward the edge of the hill. Surrounding the tribune's home was a grove of apple trees. Apple trees heavy with fruit. The woman reached up and plucked a dark red orb and bit into it as she turned away from the trees and faced the Greek styled architecture of the Virilis residence.

On the far side of the yard Decimus stood watching her. His sharp eyes took in the jarring change in the woman. There was no color in her complexion. In stark contrast to the white of her skin was the black attire of a grieving matron in mourning. A contrast that enhanced the suggestion the woman had aged a decade or more in a matter of hours since discovering her father's brutal death the night before. He watched her for a few moments, noted her vacant stare as she munched on the apple, holding it with both hands like a newborn infant, before turning and reaching for a tall bottle of wine setting on the stone table beside him. Pouring two goblets of wine, he sat the bottle down and, taking both goblets in hand, strolled silently across the thick grass toward the woman.

"Here, my lady. Drink this. It will help immensely in reviving your desire to live again."

The woman jumped, startled when the tribune spoke softly yet in a deep voice. Turning, she tried to smile but could not. Nevertheless, a hand came out and took the glass of wine from his hand.

"You startled me, Decimus. I was told you and your able assistant had returned home only hours earlier from searching my father's house. I ... I thought you would still be resting."

"Sleep is a mistress that eludes me often, Atia. Years campaigning in one foreign land or another fighting Caesar's wars has taught me sleep is a commodity only the innocent can enjoy."

"Then I must be very guilty, tribune. Very, very guilty. I have been unable to sleep since ... since ..."

"Not guilty, Atia. More like terrified," he added, lifting the wine to his lips.

"Terrified?" Atia echoed, eyes filling with tears as she looked into the tribune's sun tanned, craggy face. "Once, yes. Terrified more than you could possibly imagine. I knew the moment when the man who accompanied that strange sea captain arrived at our home all of our lives were in jeopardy. I thought I had convinced my husband to disavow any interest in those cursed letters the captain offered him a week earlier. I knew the moment I heard from Spurius' lips what this Caius Septimus offered we would be nothing but pawns in a far larger, far more dangerous game of intrigue. A game of power so devious and sinister none of us would possibly be able to control. Or survive. The gods must have touched my soul with the gift of prophecy, tribune. I hear them laughing even as we speak."

Decimus eyed the woman in front of him with interest. Of

all the conspirators involved in whatever grand scheme they conspired against the Imperator and his family, she was the one whom he suspected might have been the queen of the coven. Yet, seeing the genuine grief racking her soul, noting how the last few nights of horror had taken its toll on her, it was apparent she was but another pawn in this dark chess game. This pawn had been intuitively against the thought of either husband or father entering the game. She instinctively knew a trap somewhere lay waiting for them all if they succumbed to the intoxicating perfume of conspiracies.

"Why did you expect your father to join you, Atia? Did Felix Graccius agree with you? Agreed that this was some act of suicide if he participated?"

With eyes full of tears, Atia Gracci held the wine cup with both hands close to her bosom, then stared off at the house.

"Father did not trust this sea captain. He heard this man commanded a large pirate fleet somewhere off the coast of Greece. There were rumors the man's father had been a loyal follower of Tiberius Claudius Nero. The Imperator's natural father. Heard many rumors that made the man quite unsavory. The moment I saw Caius Septimus I knew we would not deal with them. Both Spurius and father made it quite clear to the man we would not participate in any political intrigues. But, a few hours later, Septimus returns with this stranger. The stranger insisted he converse with Spurius and father privately. There was shouting. Lots of shouting. When father and my husband emerged from the meeting father looked very worried. Frightened even. Spurius looked ... looked ... very excited."

"What was said in this meeting?"

"They would not tell me," she whispered, using the back of a hand to wipe tears from her cheek. "Neither one would say a word. The only thing said came from father just before he returned to the city. He gripped my arm as I went to bid him farewell and whispered into my ear that we had to leave. Leave Rome and Ostia and flee to some place where we would be safe."

"Describe this stranger, Atia. Did he by chance have an odd-looking tattoo on the back of his neck? And, perhaps, a leg that did not work properly which gave him a noticeable limp?"

"Yes," she answered, eyes opening in surprise. "How did you know? Do you know this man's name? Where he comes from? What he said that captured my husband's fantasies? Please! If you do, tell me. I must know!"

"This man killed your father, Atia. We found evidence of his presence below in a grotto tucked underneath your father's house. A secret passageway led from the house down into the grotto. As to his name, I know not. I was hoping you would tell me."

Atia Gracci stumbled once but regained her stance. She moved to a marble bench and slumped to a sitting position before burying her face in her hands. For some seconds she sat like this before lifting her red rimmed eyes up toward the tribune.

"I have no name to give you. It was never mentioned in my presence. All I can tell you is that he is Greek. Perhaps once a gladiator. Others have said they knew him to be a pirate as well. His presence with this Septimus fellow seemed to confirm that. Apparently my husband knew him quite well. That is all I can tell you."

"It may be enough," he said quietly. "If I can identify the gladiator's tattoo perhaps I can identify the man. But I must ask you another set of questions, my lady. Specifically, the involvement of Tertius Julius Romanus in his cabal."

"Ah Decimus," the woman sighed, wiping away tears and shaking her head on the verge of breaking down emotionally again. "The night this limping man arrived with Septimus, soon afterwards came Tertius Julius. He seemed greatly excited at meeting this stranger. To what extent he is involved with this man, or with any conspiracy, I know not. You will undoubtedly ask him. If he is still alive."

Indeed, thought the tribune. *Was Tertius Julius still among the living? And if so, where had he hidden himself? Was he still in Rome? Or was he, like rats scuttling a sinking ship, fleeing for his life as well?*

CHAPTER TWENTY-SIX

Rufus returned forty-eight hours later with news he had found the viper's nest which hid Caius Septimus from the world. Just outside Rome, a mile off the road leading to Ostia, the sea captain and three other men found a large farmhouse to spend the night in. The farm had an extensive set of buildings, all made of stone and large enough to house a dozen people or more. Surrounding the farmyard was a low stone wall of unusual thickness. The house and its surrounding buildings sat on a hill overlooking the road, with the ground between the road and the farmhouse cleared for tilling and thus offering very little cover for anyone who wished to approach without being seen.

"We take a century of the Urban Cohort with us and surround the farm, tribune. That way we capture all within," Quintus Flavius said, clenching a fist in front of him and grinning with anticipation. "If the gods are smiling on us tonight perhaps we capture this gladiator pirate and his band of brothers as well."

Decimus, frowning, shook his head.

"Or we have a long and arduous fight with trained gladiators who do not fear death knowing what is in store for them if captured alive. No, Quintus. You and I will travel to this farmhouse and observe. Observe first before we make any move. If we see movement indicating a number of potential hostiles are within we send for a detachment of Praetorian Guards. Hassad, Gnaeus, and Rufus will stay here and protect Atia Graccia. They will also devise a plan which will allow them to scour the city and find Tertius Julius for us. Come. Let us be on our way."

Night had fallen over Rome again. And with the darkness, that queasy feeling of danger settled in as well. Rome, at night, was a city of imminent danger and sudden death. No one moved late in the city unless well-armed and under escort. Even though there were laws forbidding citizens from carrying concealed weapons within the city's walls, no one in their right mind paid heed to such laws. Dark streets, roving gangs of miscreants, and madmen looking for the next victim, filled the Roman nights. The city's *Vigiles* and *Urban Cohorts* were, by law, created to clean the streets from crime and corruption. But in reality neither para-military organization came close to being strong enough to make any headway.

As darkness settled over the city, the tribune and the centurion began their journey. The night was without moonlight. Thus the journey even more treacherous. Armed with sword and daggers, the two moved rapidly through the semi-deserted streets of the city. Almost immediately they caught the faint sounds of footsteps following them. Neither made any attempt to look back. They did not want to inform their trackers they knew they were being followed. But tribune and centurion, each in their own way, moved their heads slightly to the left and to the right as they tried to ascertain the number of those following them.

At the large three gated *Fornix Augusti,* a marbled arch built by Augustus to dedicate his victory over Marcus Antonius and Cleopatra in the naval Battle at Atium, the two stepped close to one of the marbled columns and compared notes.

"Six," Quintus Flavius said, nodding his head. "I count six different men. Their foot patterns, once you get used to listening for them, are quite distinct."

"Yes, I tend to agree with you," said the tribune as he stared across the wide street leading to the Forum. "They will not attack us until our return. Right now they have orders to follow us and see what business we are up to. Over there is the Pons Aemilius. One of Rome's heaviest trafficked bridges day or night. We'll cross the Tiber there, hire out our mounts, and journey the rest of the way on horseback. But I assure you, my boy, our return home will be most interesting tonight. Most interesting indeed."

"Hmmm, a most joyous thought," the centurion returned, shaking his head. "A fight on a dark Roman street facing three-to-one odds. Something a young Roman officer dreams of, tribune."

In the darkness Quintus heard the tribune chuckle softly just as he stepped away from the arch and began walking. To their right the towering buildings and temples of the Forum were well lit with burning torches scattered about in strategic spots. But the Forum looked deserted. Immediately west of their position the low rumble of wagon and oxen traffic rumbling across the stone Pons Aemilius was easily heard. As they made their way closer to the bridge they began passing ox carts and wagons heavily laden with various materials. Dour looking laborers sat in the wagons, heads down, completely uninterested in the two strangers who moved past them.

It took some effort to cross the wide bridge. Making their way past the long line of oncoming traffic was difficult. Yet eventually they made it over the Tiber, found a merchant willing to rent horses, and rode away from the city at a fast gallop on the road leading to Ostia.

CHAPTER TWENTY-SEVEN

It was a relatively short journey on horseback. The farmhouse Rufus described was easily found in the night. Hiding the horses in a thick copse of elms, the two made their way through the trees swiftly, but silently, toward the low walled farm stead.

Discovering a small hill that overlooked the farmyard and all its buildings, the two squatted down on their haunches and took up the lonesome vigil of observation. Pulling cloaks over their shoulders, neither man said anything for several minutes as each surveyed the farm below. A half hour slipped as the night began to cool rapidly. At the end of the silence both watched a large red moon rise up over a set of small hills, and at the same time, heard the distinct sounds of a horse's rapid approach.

A rider slid off his horse and made a mad dash to the main entrance of the farmhouse. Throwing open the farmhouse door, a bright shaft of light shot out into the darkness for a moment before the door closed with a bang. Neither Decimus nor

Quintus Flavius uttered a sound nor moved a muscle. Ten minutes later the door to the farmhouse banged open again and the rider who appeared only minutes earlier ran back to his horse, leapt onto its back, and galloped away at high speed.

"A courier bringing news?" Quintus whispered softly in the darkness.

"Or a rider bringing a word of warning to his master," came the reply.

Both men lapsed into silence again and kept their eyes on the farmhouse below. Another half hour rolled by. The night became cooler. The red moon rose higher into a star filled night, weaving strange moving shadows in the woods. But the night was disturbed again, this time with the door opening softly below and the farmhouse illumination within flooding onto the moonlit ground of the farmyard below. Motionless, the two watched as a lone figure, powerfully built, stepped out into the night and faced the wooded hill.

"Caius Septimus," whispered Quintus Flavius, leaning closer to the older tribune.

Decimus said nothing but viewed the figure below with narrowed eyes as Caius lifted a hand to his face and bellowed out into the night a loud voice.

"Decimus Julius Virilis! I know you are up there. You and your lap dog, Quintus Flavius. I am alone and unarmed. There is nothing to fear from me. But we do have urgent business to speak of. Come down, the two of you, and let us cease playing these silly games of hide and seek!"

"Come," the tribune grunted, rising to his feet quickly and moving through the undergrowth.

Startled, Quintus Flavius eyed the older man for a second and then came to his feet swiftly. Throwing away caution and stealth, the two made their way down the tree lined hill and thick undergrowth noisily before stepping onto the dirt road leading from the highway behind them to the farm house. Striding down the middle of the road, shoulder to shoulder, the two entered the farmyard and came to a halt in front of the smaller, but heavier muscled seaman.

"So you are this legend called Decimus Julius Virilis. I pictured you as bigger. More evil looking," the seaman grunted, shaking his head and smiling wickedly. "And you, Quintus. I see you've put on a little muscle. Filled out some. Almost a man you are, eh?"

"Man enough to throw you into a Roman dungeon, you pirate. Why did you kill the father of Atia Gracci so cruelly?"

"I did not kill the old fool, centurion. At first I thought it was you and your master here who killed the patrician. But upon reflection I thought otherwise. Are the two of you saying you had no hand in this man's death?"

"We found Felix Gracchus in his home with his daughter kneeling beside him covered in his blood," Decimus grunted quietly, observing the man's face in the bright moonlight. "What is this important information we must discuss?"

"I found him earlier in the afternoon when I came to his home," the powerful little man said. "He had just been slaughtered. You know what this means, don't you? It means Felix Gracchus was silenced. He must have found the scrolls and knew who had them close to his person. The knowledge became his death sentence. As it will become to a number of others before this investigation is over."

"Investigation?" Decimus echoed. "Are you saying we work for the same employer?"

"Yes. We both work in the dark and pry into hidden secrets of powerful men. I have been employed by the Imperator's spy master for the last five years. I have been working on this case for over a year. Ever since the scrolls were stolen. Your insertion into this affair has seriously compromised my position. One wrong move by either of us and our quarry bolts like a jittery colt to some far off place where we will never find him."

"Why should we believe you, Septimus?"

"More importantly," the tribune growled suspiciously, "Who is our real quarry?"

Caius Septimus rubbed a calloused hand across the stubble of his chin thoughtfully, and then shrugged as if a decision had been made.

"The conspirator whom I am trying to weasel into his confidence calls him Caestus. He's an ex-slave who rose up through the gladiatorial ranks specializing in the art of pugilistic brutality. He says he is Greek. But my suspicions make me think Egyptian. He has ties to a number of gladiatorial schools up and down the peninsula. More importantly, he is held in high regards by one of the largest pirate brotherhoods who operate in the waters between Greece and Egypt.

A very dedicated and very ruthless man, tribune. He will go to great lengths to make sure this conspiracy plays out to its ultimate conclusion. But I believe he is not behind this cabal of vipers. Caestus takes his orders from someone else. Someone very powerful and very rich."

"Who?" Quintus shot back irritably, glancing into the darkness of the night suspiciously.

Caius Septimus shrugged ever so minutely and opened his palms in silent acknowledgement of not knowing. Decimus, eying the man in front of him, nodded as thoughts raced through his head. What the pirate in front of him revealed made sense. Whether it was the truth remained to be proven. But a ruthless, dedicated agent in service to the primary ringleader of the cabal whose primary mission was to implement plans into action was precisely what would be needed in an endeavor such as this.

"Where is this Caestus now?"

"I was to meet him here earlier this evening to go over the plans for your assassination, tribune. Apparently you and your lapdog's sniffing around has become a decided nuisance for him. The last I saw of him he seemed quite irritable. He mentioned your name several times. Plans are afoot to hunt you down and remove you from the game as quickly as possible. I would tread lightly, tribune. This man is not one to trifle with when he becomes irritable."

"You said you were to meet this Caestus here," Quintus Flavius echoed. "I take it he was not here when you arrived."

"He was not, centurion. A slave was here sent to inform me a change in plans. I am to catch up with him somewhere in Rome. Where I do not know. I was told he would send word to me on the moment of my arrival. But tribune, I must warn you ... apparently tonight is the night you are supposed to be dispatched to the Elysium Fields. Assassins loiter around all the gates encircling Rome waiting for your arrival. Most of the assassins are gladiators trained in the art of the silent kill. I believe you had a run in with them only a few days earlier. I hear the leader of this small group is eager to correct his earlier mistakes. If I were you, I would wait until sunrise and insert yourself in the middle of a large contingent of travelers entering the main gate. Daylight and a crowd of fools surrounding the two of you might save your life for one more day."

"A warning I will take seriously, Caius Septimus. But what else do you know of this cabal's plot? Whom do they plan to assassinate? The Imperator or his adopted son? Do they plan to kill both? When will they strike?"

"If I knew what you asked I would share with you, tribune. But Caestus is no fool. He keeps to himself the plans of his master and only feeds me tidbits here and there whenever it is necessary for me to know. I assume the master plan is to kill both Augustus and Tiberius Caesar. But there may be more to this plot. We both suspect the obvious. Yet this Caestus is a complex creature. As is his master. Whoever that may be. Sometimes I have this impression of looking down one dark alley expecting to find my quarry when in fact he is far, far away and involved in something altogether different. It is important for both of us not to assume the obvious."

Decimus' eyes played across Caius Septimus' weather beaten visage and remained silent for a moment. He found himself impressed with the pirate's caution and intellect. He could see why Augustus' private secretary recruited Caius Septimus as a spy. To be a spy meant one had to be daring and fearless. But daring and fearlessness without intellect were talents wasted. Obviously this man had all three. Making him either a formidable opponent, or a spy and assassin of the first rank.

"We must separate, tribune. I am expected in Rome, and you must find a way to return to the city without having your throat cut. I suspect your journey will be far more interesting than mine. Good luck to the both of you."

With this, the pirate turned and walked away. In a few moments a dark figure astride a powerful horse slipped around the simple peasant's farmhouse and galloped off into the night.

"Do we return to Rome tonight? Or do we take the rather surprising astute advice of this pirate and wait for the morrow?"

The tribune painted a hard, cruel little grin across his thin lips.

"Let us return to Rome, my boy. We should not be so rude as to give our waiting host a reason to suspect anything amiss."

Quintus Flavius watched the tribune walk back to the hill where their horses awaited them. At first a frown played across the young man's handsome face as he kept his eyes glued on the back of the tribune. But then the frown dissolved away, replaced by a grin which almost matched the cruelty which spread across the tribune's face just moments before.

He should have known. The old Roman had plans of his own.

CHAPTER TWENTY-EIGHT

The ride back to the Tiber was swift yet cautious. Even at this hour of the night the roads leading to Rome were filled with wheeled traffic and groups of artisans and laborers on foot. It was a simple matter of slipping out of a clump of trees and inserting themselves into the traffic flow. Hardly anyone noticed nor cared when two men in uniform slipped into the stream. Up and down the column were individual soldiers from a dozen different legions making their way back to the city. Walking, gripping the reins of their horses following behind them, tribune and centurion walked in silence for some distance before the tall centurion made a sour face in the darkness and cleared his throat softly.

"Something on your mind, Quintus Flavius?" the tribune asked casually, lifting his voice over the raucous laughter and bantering going on in front of them.

A group of brick layers, fresh from Syracuse, were making their way to the city in search of employment. Eight men, dressed in peasant's clothing, with several lugging long leather bags filled with wine strapped over their shoulders, were more inebriated than sober. Their entertainment of ribald poetry, scandalous singing, and off color humor was entertaining their fellow travelers immensely. No one, therefore, paid any attention to the two officers leading their horses along as they walked.

"This Caestus, sir. He knows we are aware of him. He must be assuming by now we have some inkling as to what his plans may be. I worry over the idea that perhaps his plans have altered. Whatever foul deed they are planning might, out of necessity, be let loose sooner than later."

The tribune nodded, smiling thinly as he glanced back at his horse. The young officer was coming along, he thought to himself, his smile widening. Sharp. Astute. An innate talent for observation and detail. Given a few more years of seasoning and he would become a valuable weapon in Caesar's almost unlimited arsenal.

"We have to assume he knows we are very close to unraveling this affair. That knowledge compels him to, at the very least, attempt a second assassination. The men we confronted in the swamps a few days ago were there on another mission and did not expect us. They said they were there to remove us permanently. But likely not. There was no sense of urgency to destroy us then as there appears to be awaiting us tonight. Thanks to our pirate friend warning us about tonight's festivities, it gives us a slight advantage. Caestus' employer knows, the longer we dog his trail, the odds increase someone in his organization will make a fatal error. An error that may very well reveal names. Names of powerful friends who wish to remain anonymous. I suspect we have taken both this Caestus and his master out of their comfort zones. We've forced them to act perhaps a bit rashly. An advantage to us if we can find a way to survive tonight."

"You expect our gladiator friends are truly waiting for us?"

"I do hope so," the tribune replied. "The race is coming down to the final stretch, centurion. There is no room for unexpected chances to thwart their intricate plans. If that is the case, hiring a number of simple cutthroats to lie in wait for us near the city gates will not suffice. Gladiators trained to kill swiftly and silently, and we assigned to be their main entertainment, will be the main menu tonight. With luck we might throw a net over our deceptive opponent."

"You've planned to trap those waiting to trap us?"

"Indeed so," the older man nodded. "Men stationed discretely at every gate to assist us in case there is an attack. My hopes are to capture a few of them alive and question them personally."

Quintus Flavius took in the older man's image enveloped in darkness for a few seconds in deep thought. Decimus Julius Virilis, with his high forehead and thinning hair, looked every bit like an heir to that famous name. Even in the cloying night one felt the man's complexity and deep intellect. Yet there was another aura quite visceral as well. The odd sensation being in the presence of someone who knew how to project power and authority, yet someone who had lurking in the deepest recesses of his soul, the knowledge and compunction to turn inward. To become a monster in the darkest of meaning.

Perhaps soldiering for two and a half decades in the legions of Octavius Caesar, seeing and participating in the various horrors a Roman legion inflicted upon its opponents, turned a man into a monster. He certainly could attest to that fact. As an officer in Ostia's Urban Cohort he had had his fair share of run ins with ex-legionnaires. Cruelty for the sake of cruelty and a willingness to shed blood was an all too common a factor he dealt with policing the city.

But the common legionnaire was petty in his cruelty. He lived for the present and never thought about the tomorrows.

Never had anyone accused the common legionnaire of being a man of intelligence. It occurred to him, narrowing his eyes thoughtfully, that a potential lurking monster, gifted with deep, cutting edge intellect, held the possibilities for something truly malevolent. Something truly horrifying in his potential for terror. As the tribune turned to stare at him questioningly, he wondered to himself what would he do when, at long last ... if it ever did ... this monster within the tribune revealed itself.

CHAPTER TWENTY-NINE

Nothing happened.

Returning to the city, they crossed the same bridge they had earlier traversed fully expecting to be attacked the moment they stepped into the wide expanse of the *Forum Bovarium*. But, making their way past the various temples and public buildings setting in cold splendor and towering over them in deserted silence, no one stirred or made themselves visible. Not even a dog or one of the many wild foxes known to live somewhere near the Tiber who explored the forum at night looking for a meal was seen.

But, approaching the first steep incline leading up to the Aventine and moving past the massive dark marbled outer facing of the *Circus Maximus,* the sound of laughter, high up in the arena's empty seating encircling the track, came to their ears. A man's amused, sardonic laughter. Decimus paused, turned to face the famous racing track, and lifted his head to peer into the night. For a long moment, both tribune and centurion stared at the track, neither offering any comment, yet both fully realizing what was taking place. And who it was that was so amused by their presence.

Caestus aimed his laughter toward them. The laughter taunting both the tribune and centurion. The sound informing the tribune he was aware of his plans to capture him and arrogantly defy the Julian family member in the process. Staring into the night Decimus stood impassively like a statue revealing not the slightest emotion for the younger centurion to observe. And then, quite suddenly, he turned and began walking briskly away from the Circus Maximus, his hands clamped behind his back, his head down as if deep in thought. Not one word was uttered until he stopped just before entering through the heavy, iron studded door which led into the outer gardens of the small villa within. Pausing, Decimus turned and gazed at Quintus Flavius.

"The game is afoot, my boy. The game is afoot! Like the pugilist he used to be, this madman punches and dances across the ring urging us on to strike back, knowing that if we do, his counter punch will surely be devastating. We need to know more about this Caestus. Who is he? Who was his family before he became a slave? Who owned him during his last years of servitude? From where does his obvious wealth come from? We find the answers to those questions, we surely will find the mastermind who is behind this cabal."

"He knew when and where we would be when we left the city, tribune. Why did he not strike us down then? Somehow he knew we had set a trap for his men on our return. How is that possible? Is he in league with sorcerers? Or, perhaps, with Caius Septimus' allegations, we live in a world where only spies and suspicions exist, and no one knows the truth."

A brief smile flashed across the older man's handsome face before evaporating completely. A hard, calloused hand came up and gripped the younger man on his shoulder in a fatherly gesture.

"In the service of Caesar, Quintus Flavius, one never knows exactly what troubled waters we must wade through before reaching the far shore. The best we can do is to keep our wits about us and our emotions in check. Observe everything, my boy. Question all that you hear. And the most important advice of all ... trust no one!"

"Not even you, tribune?" Quintus asked, a wicked smirk playing across his youthful image.

"Me most of all," the older tribune growled agreeably as he threw open the door and entered the villa's gardens.

CHAPTER THIRTY

Down the wide, polished marbled floors marched the tall figure of Decimus, dressed in toga of wine red stitched in fine gold thread. The soft whisper of sandaled feet was a gentle reminder to him that he was in the halls of the greatest power on earth and in a palace filled with powerful, and dangerous, men. The hunter and the hunted came in all sizes and shapes. But whether found in the thick forests of Germania, or the rolling deserts of the Carthaginian plains, or here in the civilized world of politics and imperial power, one had to remember that sometimes the hunter might soon discover he had actually become the prey and the prey was now the relentless hunter.

Keeping pace step by step by his side, dressed in the simple attire of a Grecian freeman, marched the silent, hardened old leather of his ever-faithful Gnaeus. He, like Decimus, knew the man they had come to see in the halls of the palace. Years of service in one legion or another, along with those times served on detached service for the Imperator, had forged a dark and secretive relationship with master of Caesar's spies. A relationship, nevertheless, fraught with potential danger and grudging respect.

The morning crowd of supplicants was sparse as the two men followed the minor bureaucrat past thick marbled columns down one hall and another. But as they marched deeper and deeper down dark halls the mass of strange faces of army officials and citizens thinned precipitously. That Caius Lucius had an office within the confines of the palace did not surprise either Decimus or Gnaeus in the least. Of course there would be no carved sign above Caius Lucius' office door saying, *Office of the Chief of Spies*. In fact, there would be no signs at all. At first glance one would think they were walking past the offices of some nameless bureaucrat who occupied just one of the hundreds of offices of bureaucrats an empire had to employ to run it efficiently.

That was the brilliance of Caius Lucius. He hid himself from prying eyes within the palace by making no effort to hide himself. Anyone familiar with Caesar and his rule knew, or at least had heard, the name of Caius Lucius. No one in their right mind wanted to meet Caius Lucius socially or professionally. No one.

"Ah, Decimus Julius Virilis. And Gnaeus, my old friend."

The chief of spies was a rather small man of stunning inconsequence, physically speaking, to behold. Nothing leapt out to one's eyes which would set Caius Lucius' looks apart from others. Yet that too was the brilliance of the man. The unremarkable appearance of the spy made him infinitely forgettable. He was a chameleon. He could disappear into a crowd and never be discovered again if he so desired. He came and went unseen and unheard as if he was a whiff of odd wind ruffling one's robes on a hot morning's excursion through a crowded forum.

It was these talents which made him the eyes and ears of

the Caesar Augustus. It was his ruthlessness, when called upon to be used, which guaranteed Caesar's reign to appear as if peace and tranquility had finally settled onto the empire.

"Hail, Caius Lucius. It has been a long time indeed," Decimus answered, offering a hand and gripping the forearm of the smaller man firmly as they exchanged greetings.

"The imperator has informed me I must assist you in your investigation in any way I can, Decimus. Of course I will comply with his wishes. But I confess it puts me and my organization in an uncomfortable position."

The taller tribune and the silent Gnaeus followed the chief of spies through two rooms filled with scribes busily at work on various scrolls before finally entering the inner sanctum reserved for the man himself. Motioning to chairs for the two of them he strolled around a large desk and sat himself down in a plain looking chair, resting elbows on an armrest and setting fingertips of both hands together in front of him.

"I'm sure you met my own agent late last night on a farm just outside the city. I cannot begin to tell you how long and arduous task it took for him to infiltrate the outer ring of conspirators in this cabal. I must confess, the Imperator's request of inserting you into this investigation has upset my plans immensely. But ... no matter. The Imperator is my employer. I live to serve him."

"A fact I am well aware of, Caius. I do hope your pirate captain survived the night and finds himself alive and useful to you. To alleviate any further complications, I propose that we separate our inquiries and proceed independently of each other. But in order to do this I would ask that you fill me in on the details your organization has already discovered. For instance, who is this figure who calls himself Caestus?"

Caesar's chief of spies sighed. He came out of his chair and walked across the room to a small table holding a decorative

Grecian bowl filled with ice and a small jar of chilled wine. Reaching for the jar, he quickly poured wine into three large stone goblets and handed a goblet to each guest before returning to his chair again.

"To be frank, Decimus Virilis, we are not exactly sure who this Caestus is. We know he comes from Greece. We know he owns several gladiator schools scattered across Greece and Thracia, as well as a few here in Italy. We also know he has extensive shipping operations which plow the waters from Greece to Egypt and Greece to the Parthian kingdoms to the East. He is very wealthy. Has extensive contacts and business relationships with a number of Roman senators and is highly regarded by many. Creating, as you no doubt can appreciate, a conundrum for us. So far we have no direct proof this man is actively involved in any hostile intentions aimed to harm Caesar. At the snap of his fingers he can bring forth dozens of highly placed Roman citizens who will gladly sing his praises to the heavens if asked. We tread cautiously in our investigations. My hopes are Caius Septimus will find a direct link proving his involvement in the murders of Spurius Lavinus and Felix Graccus."

"May I ask what are your thoughts on why these two senators were so brutally murdered?"

Caius Lucius shrugged eloquently and then sipped his wine in silence as he kept his eyes on both the tribune and his voiceless servant. Dark eyes played across the tribune's face as he sat his plain, unadorned stone goblet on the desktop in front of him.

"One can only assume both noblemen were somehow becoming a liability to Caestus and his master and had to be removed. What other explanation can there be?"

"You are sure Lavinus was a participant? As well as Gracchus?"

"Absolutely," the chief of spies said. "The Augustan Letters were delivered to the House of Lavinus by Caestus. He was escorted to the Lavinii home by Caius. My spies discovered the possibility that in turn, Lavinus was supposed to carry the letters to some fellow conspirator in Brundisium. A conspirator we have yet to identify. Lavinus' death had to be some act of desperation. We know when Lavinus left his villa just outside of Ostia he had them securely hidden in a small wooden chest. When his body was discovered, first by my spies, and then by your centurion of the Urban Cohort from Ostia just before your arrival on the scene, the letters were missing."

"So the question remains. Who killed Spurius Lavinus?"

"I haven't a clue." The small man shrugged before shaking his head in mystification. "It doesn't make sense believing Caestus is our killer. Only hours earlier he felt confident enough to hand the letters over to Lavinus for transportation. Lavinus was an eager participant in this affair. He often whispered to friends and allies his desire to find something which would make the few remaining years Caesar has left on this earth to become a living hell for him. When he heard the Augustan Letters might be available he, along with Felix Gracchus and Tertius Julius Romanus, each contributed three thousand talents in gold to purchase them."

"You have proof the three paid nine thousand talents for the letters?"

"Only the hearsay evidence of slaves speaking to my spies, Decimus. The three were adept in juggling their contributions around in such a way no money trail could be found."

Decimus sat in the plain chair facing the desk of Caius Lucius and remained silent for several seconds as he studied the face of the chief of spies. The nondescript odd man had a face that was completely unreadable. So bland, so common of features, he suspected the spy was capable of uttering a bald face lie with the same degree of sincerity as an ascetic would in uttering the unalterable truth. So one was left with a sinking realization. When Caius Lucius spoke how was one to know when Caius Lucius spoke truthfully or not?

Why, for instance, did he have this unsettling feeling running through his mind he was being lied to? Outwardly he and the chief of spies were allies. Both had been tasked by the Imperator to track down the mastermind of the cabal and bring him to justice. Yet there lingered this nagging thought that his old acquaintance was hiding something from him. But why? For what purpose?

He felt a tap on his shoulder and turned to look at Gnaeus. The tough old ex-legionnaire's hand moved rapidly and eloquently before falling silent. Decimus nodded, grunted his approval, and brought his attention back to fix onto Caius Lucius.

"Gnaeus asks me to inquire as to what was the source of Spurius Lavinus' hatred toward Caesar. A question I've been wondering about myself."

"Ah, Decimus. May I compliment you? You surround yourself with men who are keenly observant and stoutly self-confident. I have always been impressed with the grumpy old Gnaeus here. Adding this Quintus Flavius to your staff only solidifies my admiration. For such a young officer in the Urban Cohort he seems quite adept in handling himself in difficult situations. His reputation as a swordsman is well known to me. But his intellectual skills have come recently to my attention. Pleasantly surprising me, I might add."

"We will gladly relay to him your compliments, Caius Lucius," Decimus answered. "Now ... to the question at hand. What fueled Spurius Lavinus' hatred toward Caesar?"

"The second Proscription. Spurius Lavinus lost a grandfather and an uncle during the Second Triumvirate. In fact, I suspect that is the glue which brought Lavinus, Felix Graccius, and Tertius Julius Caesar together. All three lost loved ones. Loved ones ordered disposed of by Octavius while he served as the junior member during the Triumvirate."

A cruel snarl of an amused laugh escaped from the chief of spies' lips as he slipped out of his chair and walked over to refill his wine goblet.

"As you well know, Decimus. We Romans love our revenge. Fools say *Time heals all wounds.* Not for a Roman. A true Roman cherishes his slights. Dwells in the darkness of his revenge. He can wait an eternity, if he has to, before he strikes. The Lavinii, the Romani, and the Gracci have been waiting for a long, long time to repay the debts with the Imperator."

Fifty years earlier, in 43 BCE, soon after the murder of Julius Caesar from the hands of Brutus and a number of Roman Senators, the empire plunged into a set of civil wars which rocked the growing empire to its very core. Warring factions divided the empire up into zones of influence. At first the fighting erupted in an effort to track down and destroy the factions who allied themselves with those who murdered the first Caesar. That took about four years to complete, ravaging the empire in military conflicts from Aegypt to Hispania in the process. But after the battles, after the last foe was dispatched, three Roman leaders remained standing. The very young Octavius Caesar. The experienced, yet cunning opportunist Marcus Antonius. And a Caesar loyalist, yet a somewhat forgettable politician, by the name of Marcus Amellius Lepidus.

Three powerful, ambitious, experienced politicians who, each one of them, secretly plotted against the others to gather in the reins of power for themselves. But after four years of hard fighting, their coffers, and their armies, needed replenishing. Thus the creation of the Second Triumvirate. An unnatural cessation of hostilities settled across the Roman domains. A set of rules were rammed through the Roman Senate which allowed the three men to be co-equal in their rule of the empire. But everyone knew the hatred felt between Octavius Caesar and Marcus Antonius would eventually erupt and plunge the empire into another series of devastating wars.

But they would come later. During the strange, ill-fitting peace which settled across the empire during the Second Triumvirate, the method to exact both revenge on their enemies and to refill their respective coffers with gold was the creation of a Second Proscription.

Each triumvirate leader submitted a list of names of their alleged enemies. The lists named friends, loyal followers, brothers, sister, fathers, uncles, admirers of another faction leader's entourage. Thus becoming alleged enemies to one faction leader or the other. The names of the list were rounded up and either executed or sold into slavery. Their lands, their possessions, their wealth were confiscated as well and handed over to the faction leader claiming grievance.

During the time of the Second Triumvirate it was dangerous times to be a rich or politically ambitious Roman. Hundreds of innocent Roman citizens were rounded up and executed. Vast wealth exchanged hands in wholesale lots. Steadily, ruthlessly, the three factions leading the empire grew in power and wealth.

But during the Second Proscriptions loved ones suddenly disappeared and were never heard from again. The perfect source for creating pockets of simmering revenge in those who had lost loved ones because, rightly or wrongly, their names were found on a list. The tribune sat for a few moments in his chair and ruminated over the many facets that was the Second Proscription. It was very easy to conceive the possibility hundreds of aggrieved families would harbor ill will toward Caesar. But how many would be aggrieved enough to plot against the Imperator? Not that numbers alone were needed to be a telling factor for a cabal to be successful. Only a few of the truly powerful, and truly wealthy, families needed to participate.

"You have faith that this Caius Septimus is loyal to Caesar?" he asked, turning to watch the chief of spies return to his desk to sit.

"As much as I have faith in you, Decimus, " Caius Lucius answered, a weak sycophantic smile spreading across his bland features. "But I will confess, I fear for the man's life. He walks among vipers with essentially only his wits to assist him. This Caestus is no fool. How long Septimus can continue his charade remains to be seen."

The high browed, thinning haired tribune nodded and then came to his feet. Taking some time to adjust the brightly hued material of his tunic, he finally stepped forward and clasped the spy's forearm firmly.

"My thanks, Caius Lucius. You have been open and frank in your answers. For that, I thank you. Let us both fervently wish this affair soon comes to a violent yet fruitful conclusion. And let us hope this talented spy of yours finds a way to save himself from a terrible death."

"Agreed, my friend Decimus. May we both succeed in our collective endeavors. My prayers go with you in keeping your journeys safe from harm's way."

Twenty minutes later, sitting on a marbled bench in front a small Greek temple dedicated to *Pallas Athene,* the two sat for some seconds and silently watched Romans of all levels in society going about their business as flocks of pigeons fluttered about noisily across the open square. When, at least, each was convinced they were not being spied upon and none were close enough to overhear them, the tribune leaned toward his short, sun tanned, silent servant.

"We must find out more about this Caestus. You still have a number of old ex-army drinking buddies here in Rome, do you not? Old buddies who help in the training of gladiators?"

Gnaeus nodded and his hands moved to provide an answer.

"Good," Decimus said. "This Greek trainer you just mentioned. He still lives?"

Again, the silent Gnaeus answered in the affirmative.

"Very well. Find him. Get him drunk. Get him talking. Ask him about what he has heard about this Caestus. If this man is indeed Greek and an ex-gladiator, surely your friend has heard of him. Perhaps your friend knows others who can tell us about our man of mystery. Offer a few discreet rewards to those who may become recalcitrant in their answers if it is necessary. Find out as much as you can in the next two days and report back to me. But Gnaeus, be careful. We flirt with danger in this quest of ours. Those whom we hunt will not hesitate in removing you from this life if they grow suspicious."

The old, wrinkled ex-legionnaire grinned a rakish smirk of insolence and spoke rudely yet silently to his patron before coming off the marbled bench and disappearing into the heavy Roman crowd. For his part, Decimus watched his friend until he could no longer be seen before rising to his feet and turning to head back to his villa.

Danger lurked in every face. Every passerby. But then ... grinning mercilessly ... he remembered this was Rome. The greatest city in the empire! And a city always dangerous anytime night or day.

CHAPTER THIRTY-ONE

"I know he is old, but just how old is the Imperator?" Quintus Flavius asked as he sat on a wooden stool beside a table gripping the pommel of his sturdy, heavy bladed *gladius* with one hand and running a whetstone down one sharp edge of the steel blade.

He had listened silently as his mentor revealed all that Caius Lucius had told him just hours before. When the tribune mentioned Caesar's direct involvement in the Second Triumvirate the young man's eyes lit up.

"Somewhere in his eighties," the older man answered softly as he stood in the opening of the villa which led out into the gardens. He held a goblet of wine in hand. "An old, tired man, Quintus Flavius. A man who knows he has little time left in this world. That knowledge weighs upon him heavily."

The sound of the whetstone sliding down the cold steel of the blade was, for Decimus, an almost comforting sound. How many times had he done exactly the same with his weapon while he served in Caesar's legions? He smiled cynically. More times than he cared to remember. Idly he felt the weight of a gladius in one empty hand and the weight and firm grip of a legionaries' *scutum*, or shield, in the other. A legionnaire was a sword and shield man. The sharp blade was a vicious thrusting weapon designed to cut through armor and flesh in sharp, but short, stabbing motions. The scutum was the rectangular curved shield designed to protect a legionnaire's body in the thick of battle.

Serving in the legions of Caesar was bloody work. Not something the timid or frail could long endure. Serving more than twenty years in the service of Caesar forged a man's soul in the fires of battle and bloodletting. The hardships endured, the thirst, the hunger, the long marches, the sun beating down on one's armor and slowly roasting one into a sweating mass of aching flesh, all worked their magic and molded a man's resolve a certain way.

Of course, there was the fear one felt standing in the ranks of your maniple facing an enemy for the first time. The thrill... the terror ... the excitement all wrapped up in one confusing packet of raw emotions! Facing the possibility of certain death for the first time surrounded by men, both hardened veteran and raw recruit, who felt the very same emotions was an unforgettable experience. To march slowly into battle formation, to move across the front of an assembled enemy standing only a few hundred meters away screaming in rage at you and brandishing their arms, was an experience only a few could claim as their own.

How many times had he marched into battle? Nine times? A dozen? More? Who knew. A cynic's smile played across his thin lips again. Too many to count. But each time was unique. Each time was memorable. Each time was an intimate dance with Death.

But each time had taught him how true exhaustion ... true desperation ... felt. He had brushed against Death's cold hands too many times not to feel his waiting embrace. So, in a way, he knew how his old kinsmen felt. Knew the exhausted resignation, even the quiet willingness to fall into Death's embrace that Caesar must be feeling each time he awakes to a new morning. And ... surprisingly ... vaguely experienced a sense of envy knowing his cousin's departure from this plane of existence was close.

" ... Tribune!"

The sharpness in Quintus Flavius' voice was like a slap in the face. Decimus had not realized his rummaging into the past had taken him so completely. Forcing himself to return to the present, he noticed the stout looking junior officer of the Praetorian Guards standing in the room's interior doorway standing quietly at attention.

"Tribune, Cornelius Flavius has requested a private audience with you. He will not state the nature of his request. But, seeing he is a palace official requesting a formal audience, I suspect nothing unnaturally suspicious. For now."

There was a dry, sardonic tone in the centurion's voice. A sardonic lilt that, for a brief second, made the young centurion in the Praetorian Guards glance toward Quintus Flavius and flash an impish grin.

"Cousins?" Decimus asked, a fatherly look of amusement filling his face.

"My uncle's second youngest son. A thorough drunkard if I ever knew one. But then, nothing new there. We of the Flavian clan are noted for our love of the grape. Eh, Corny?"

The young face of Cornelius Flavius reddened for a moment from being called an old family name. But he recovered quickly, came to rigid attention, and formally saluted the tribune of the Urban Cohort that was Decimus Julius Virilis.

"Hail, tribune! My mistress wishes to convey her respects and felicitations to the honored Decimus Julius Virilis. She bids me to remind you of her long friendship and patronage over the years and continues to be both friend and patron for years to come. She requests the honor of a private meeting with you tonight, an hour after the evening Vespers, in *The Temple of Hesperus Minor* which is located behind *The Temple of Mars Ultor*. She asks that I return with a formal answer, sir."

He glanced at Quintus Flavius and then back toward Praetorian centurion, Cornelius Flavius. The family resemblance was striking. Their facial features were almost a mirror image. Young, curly haired, confident. From their eyes glowed that familial trait of sardonic wit and vast intelligence.

His smiled widened.

"I thought you said this was to be a private audience, centurion." Decimus commented, his eyes fixed on Cornelius Flavius. On the other side of the room his cousin's lop-sided grin widened in pleasure.

"With all due respect, tribune. We are alone. The ugly drunkard standing in the room with us is just a cousin of mine. Meaning, of course, his presence and opinions expressed are inconsequential to either of us."

A rude, yet pleasant, guffaw of humor escaped through Quintus Flavius' lips as he sat hands on his hips and smirked at his cousin playfully. For his part, Cornelius Flavius disregarded his cousin altogether.

"Tell Livia Drusilla the honor is mine, centurion. Inform her my continued devotion and gratitude toward her and her honored husband remains steadfast as always. I shall be eagerly awaiting her arrival."

The Praetorian nodded, came to attention and formally saluted the tribune, then half turned to leave. But he hesitated and glanced at his cousin.

"Not too far from Mars Ultor is a new wine shop specializing in Greek wines and cuisine. I hear it is excellent. Say we meet there, two hours before the meeting of my mistress and the tribune for a quick bite to eat and a glass or two of wine?"

The tribune nodded ever so slightly in agreement and turned his eyes back toward his smiling cousin.

"An excellent choice, young cousin. You will, of course, be picking up the tab for tonight's pleasantries."

"Why should I pick up the tab this time? Did I not pay the last time our paths crossed in Ostia?"

"You did. And it turned out to be a most pleasant experience."

"Bah! You whining tight wad," Cornelius Flavius grunted then grinned.

"Bah! You parsimonious welcher," Quintus Flavius instantly retorted, the exact same grin as his cousin's on his handsome face.

The two, arm in arm, and talking to each other at the same time as only family members can, left the tribune alone before Quintus returned. A wide, boyish grin was still on the centurion's face. Decimus, handing the young man a goblet of wine, chuckled in amusement.

"I take it your side of the Flavian clan is a large one?"

"Immense," Quintus Flavius answered, the grin on his face widening with pleasure. "Father had three brothers and two sisters. All of them married. All of them producing vast herds of children. I have cousins in the army. Cousins who are in politics. One is the vice-consul in Hispania. Two are architects. A couple, including that one you just met, serve in the Urban Cohort here in Rome. We are like locusts, tribune. You cannot be an official in the army or government and not be near a Flavian."

"Ah," Decimus said, a smile on his lips. "Most interesting."

"Which, a thought occurred to me as I escorted that clumsy oaf out just now. I told Cornelius to contact our other cousin,

Justinus, and invite him to join us tonight. He too is in the Urban Cohort here in Rome. They might have valuable information which might interest us in our investigation. For perhaps a bottle or two of fine wine, they might share."

"What kind of information could they have which would call for such drastic ransom?"

"Any information concerning Tertius Julius Romanus and his whereabouts. Or perhaps a rumor or two about this Caestus. I am assuming, of course, we are extremely interested in finding this Romanus before he too takes a sudden ride across the river Styx. If we can find him before this Caestus finds him perhaps we might extract from him much needed information."

Decimus stared down at the surface of the dark wine in his goblet he held in one hand before lifting it to his lips. Yes. Quintus Flavius would become a very skilled investigator. It would not take nearly as long as he first anticipated.

Lowering his goblet, he looked at his protégé again.

"You are assuming Caestus killed Spurius Lavinus and Felix Gracchus and now hunts Tertius Romanus? Why would Caestus want to kill his fellow conspirators now?"

"Two reasons come to mind, tribune. Either whatever this cabal is planning is soon to take place and this ex-gladiator has orders to remove fellow conspirators. In effect, to remove loose links in the chain who might, for one reason or another, wish to change sides and stop the madness before it happens. Or ... "

"Or?" Decimus repeated, waiting for the young man to utter the second part of his theory.

"Or perhaps there has already been a fatal leak in the plan and Caestus is seeking out the traitor to repair the damage before the cabal unravels entirely. It is the only working theory that makes sense to me, tribune. What other theory is there to consider?"

"One comes to mind," Decimus replied, looking at his wine again as he lifted the goblet to his lips once more.

Quintus Flavius blinked a few times, his face an open book of puzzlement, and stared at the older man. A half second or two ticked by and then the young centurion's face exploded in utter surprise.

"By the gods! You suspect Caesar is assassinating them. But that means he already knows who the cabal members are! No ... wait a minute. He ... he can't actually know. Otherwise why ask you to investigate the death of Spurius Lavinus in the first place? Or find these secretive Augustan Letters he claims to have been stolen from his possession? It makes no sense! Why have an assassin cutting the throats of traitors, while at the same time, forcing us to investigate their murders?"

From out of the tribune's chest came a rumble of soft laughter. Quintus, growing irritated, lifted his wine goblet and gulped his wine down in one swallow and slammed the goblet on the table beside him. Decimus' laughter died away as he walked close to the young man and put a fatherly hand on his stout shoulder.

"A lesson just learned, my young friend. Caesar does what Caesar thinks is necessary. I do not know if Caesar is behind all this. But I have my suspicions. I have known my kinsmen most of my life. I know how he thinks. This is exactly something he would do in order to eke out his revenge, and at the same time, disguise his murderous intent and make it appear as if he is the innocent victim. Never underestimate the cunning of we Julii, my son. Never."

"So, from here on, what are our intentions? Do we continue with the investigation? Or do we just confirm our suspicions and then retire from the field? I find this option completely unsatisfactory, by the way."

The tribune patted the centurion's shoulder fondly again

before stepping away toward the open entrance leading out into the gardens before answering.

"My suspicions do not equate proof, Quintus. We will comply with Caesar's wishes. He wants us to investigate the death of Servius Lavinus and he wants us to find the stolen letters. So be it. Caesar has commanded. We will obey."

CHAPTER THIRTY-TWO

In the twilight of soft burning candles which barely illuminated the small temple, he stood half hidden behind a marbled column and eyed the few souls who came to worship the goddess Dawn. The small *Temple of Hesperus Minor* was an old temple dating back to long before the birth of Julius Caesar. From its non-descript exterior of simple brick and tall, narrow Greek columns encircling the small round temple, one would have thought the architect who accepted the commission in designing the temple did so with little heart into the task.

But looks were deceiving. Stepping into the deep shadows and strategically placed flickering orbs of candlelight, the interior of the temple transformed the supplicant to the goddess into a whole new realm. Like the ring of the exterior's four tall white marbled Corinthian styled columns supporting the temple's domed roof, four columns supported the blue tiled ceiling of the interior. But the ceiling was breath taking to behold. Artisans of the first rank created the starry heavens of a summer's night in a number of different hues of blue. In the candlelight the stars glistened and winked in the temple's soft lighting. The blues were the darkest and the stars the brightest around the curved dome's outer edges. But as a worshipper's eyes followed toward the center of the room the blues began to lighten and the stars began to dim. Giving the impression as if dawn was approaching.

Dead center of the temple's polished slate gray stone floor stood the ivory and golden statue of the goddess Dawn. She stood on one foot, with one arm raised gracefully above her head, her delicate open hand supporting the small golden orb of a newborn sun. The overall impression was that of the goddess flying swiftly through the night sky, bringing with her the joy and warmth of the sun's radiating light.

Eyeing the exquisite detail of the ivory covered statue informed him that the unknown architect of this temple had worked with a limited budget. His decision to design the temple's exterior as plainly as possible, thus allowing his true artistry to shine within the temple's walls, had been a wise choice. *The Temple of Hesperus Minor* was a small architectural wonder hardly any Roman knew existed. Knowing this, a slight breath of regret swept through him curiously.

But he pushed it aside when, directly opposite from his half-hidden position, he saw a set of flickering shadows dance across the curved brick wall. Three shadows. Two rather large and massive. One so small and dainty it almost blended into the shadows of the two in front of her.

Livia Drusilla. The beloved consort to Caesar Augustus. The second most powerful Roman in the Empire.

No one doubted the small woman, so charming and so frail, yet so beloved by the masses, wielded immense power. Everyone knew she and Caesar conferred with each other as equals when it came to ruling the growing empire. In the public's eye she comported herself as the model Roman wife. Gracious, compassionate, a generous patron to the arts, even the enemies of her husband looked upon Livia Drusilla with admiration and affection.

But he knew better. He had known her for most of his adult life. He had heard the rumors. Talked to those who knew Livia Drusilla even longer than he. He knew about the heated, tempestuous love affair she and Octavius had flung themselves into the moment the two first laid eyes on each other. She was, at the time of the affair's beginning, the wife of the very powerful Tiberius Claudius Nero. She was already the mother of Tiberius and was pregnant with Tiberius Nero's second child as well. She was not even twenty yet. But, even deep in her pregnancy, elegant to behold. And extremely intelligent. Factors, everyone said, Octavius could not help but fall in love with.

At the time of their first meeting both were married. Augustus' wife, the shrewd Scribonia was, as some quietly suggested, a precursor to Livia Drusilla. But older. She was, at their marriage, years older than Octavius. But this marriage was not a marriage for love. This was a marriage of politics and political survival. For both her and for Caesar. Not nearly as attractive, perhaps not quite as graceful and natural around men who commanded vast power and wealth, nevertheless Scribonia was a shrewd judge of men and, more importantly, in command of vast wealth in her own right. Her previous husband prior to marrying the young Octavius Caesar had been Publius Cornelius Scipio, an heir to the famed wealth and Scipio name.

But when Octavius first looked upon the beauty of Livia one could say that, for the first time in Octavius' life, Roman politics slipped back a few notches as being the driving force in his life. Love ... Romantic Love ... gripped his soul in a kind of lustful madness upon seeing Drusilla. Octavius ordered Tiberius Nero to divorce Livia. He quickly divorced from Scribonia. The two married after a brief, extremely brief, courtship.

One would think a man like Tiberius Nero would have been insulted receiving a command to divorce his wife so that the most powerful man in Rome could marry her. Just the opposite. So pleased was Nero that he stood, in lieu of Livia Drusilla's deceased father, in the wedding ceremony to give her hand in marriage to Octavius.

Of course the rumor mongers were rampant of this sudden, and swift, turn of events. It was whispered in the softest of voices it was not so much that Octavius fell madly in love with his new wife as it was Livia Drusilla's wiles and charms which drove Caesar to near madness in his desire to possess her. Rumors also circulated for months on end that Tiberius Nero became very pleased and condescending in accepting the decree after a vast fortune mysteriously fell into the family coffers.

Decimus, still hidden in the shadows of the temple, allowed himself a moment's worth of a cynic's smile. Whether it was love, or money, or politics, or power, both Caesar and his wife knew what they wanted the most in their lives. Each other. Both had grown old together. Both still listened to and respected each other's cunning and advice. Both ruled the empire together as equals.

Both could be very devious, as well as very dangerous, when it came to playing in the arena of Roman politics. Factors he was all too aware of as he stepped out of the shadows and revealed himself, arms out and palms open, to Livia and her escorts.

CHAPTER THIRTY-THREE

"Hail, dear friend. I am so pleased you accepted my invitation." The woman, still standing straight and true, still with the light step in her gait, clasped both of his hands warmly.

"The pleasure is mine, my dear. It has been some time since we last spoke. But I see the years have been good to you. You still are the loveliest of all."

"Ha," the still sprightly Livia Drusilla laughed, the pleasure glowing in her smile as she slipped an arm around one of his. "You always were a gracious flatterer, Decimus. One of the few who had a talent in making me smile every time we met. A flatterer ... nay ... more of a consummate flirt, full of joy and mischievous delight in those dark eyes of yours. I cannot tell you the number of times your presence near us made both myself and Gaius smile in delight. Yet at the same time, instill in us a feeling all was well in the world."

"Well, well ... a fine compliment, my lady. But you must be mistaken. I am, and have always been, a simple soldier. Even in retirement it seems like I continue soldering for your wily husband and my elder cousin."

She turned and looked up at Decimus, her eyes lit with a mysterious fire, before she lifted a hand up and pointed into the darkness.

"Do you mind if we walk a little, cousin? I find that I think better, perhaps articulate my thoughts better, if I exercise my old legs some. Which is why I chose this temple for our meeting. A circular temple in the dead of night gives me my exercise in a secluded, and I might add safe, place away from the ever-present busybodies of the palace."

"Why Livia. If I did not know you better, I would think you have something devious and quite cunning to reveal to me. But I know you for what you are, cousin. A meek woman full of Roman virtue and matronly duty."

She heard the dry sarcasm and wit in his words as, arm in arm, they began walking slowly around the temple. Her Praetorian Guard escort stepped away, closer to the various entrances leading into the inner sanctum to keep anyone from entering. The tinkling voice of genuine amusement filled the semi-darkness as they floated in and out of the bubbles of torch light partially illuminating the temple.

"Decimus, you know me all too well. Perhaps as only my husband knows me. Yet you use that dry humor of yours like the thrust of a knife flashing in the night. Just like Gaius Octavius. I confess, I find the men of the Julii cunning rogues one and all. And a most attractive lot as well. So I'm sure it comes as no surprise to you I would be informed about the plans you and Tiberius have devised to discover and capture these mysterious gladiators recently arrived upon our shores."

"I was sure your son would not keep secrets from you, dear cousin. I suspect your concerns revolve around what possible dangers Tiberius might face if we are indeed lucky and come across the prey we seek."

The elderly woman sighed as her free hand came up and patted the muscular arm she held onto gently as they walked. In the torch light Decimus saw her head bend as she stared down at the dim marble floor they traversed over with a tired looking matronly smile on her lips.

"I know my son is a grown man, Decimus. He's led armies into the field and has become one of our finest generals. I cannot protect him from the dangers any mortal must face while being a soldier. But there are other dangers, far more insidious and cruel I can, with some discretion and sleight of hand, perhaps shield him from. Of course I would do this because he is my son. Any mother who is in the position I am in would. But there is another reason. One that supersedes that of being a mother."

They continued walking in and out of the bubbles of torch light which almost pushed the gloom of the temple's emptiness away. He turned his head and looked at the profile of the old woman's face. It was easy to see the flower of beauty she was in her youth forty years earlier. Time had treated her with kindness. Her mind was as sharp and as cunning as ever.

"Let us not quibble over sentiments, cousin. Octavius and I are old. Far too old to rule the empire much longer. Both of us will be gone soon and this heavy burden of keeping a tight rein on the many forces wishing to tear the empire apart will fall on someone else's shoulders. Those shoulders will be those of Tiberius. It is our mutual desire to make sure Tiberius survives and assumes the mantel of power without undue strife and turmoil impeding the transition."

"Cousin, I assure you your son will not be in any danger. Precautions have been put in place to satisfy the safety of his presence."

"I know, my old friend. It is not the little adventure the two of you are soon to partake in which I am talking about. It is the larger picture, the real dangers, which I wish to convey to you that worries me. This Spurius Lavinus investigation Gaius has asked you to look into is but one example I refer to. I feel it in my bones, Decimus. Forces are gathering. Dark forces determined to ruin Tiberius's ascension to power. I fear not only for my son's life, but for the life of the empire as well. Too much blood, too many fortunes, too many dreams have been ruined in bringing peace and stability back to Rome just to see it shatter like a piece of fine Greek pottery."

"Eloquent words, Livia. And genuine fears many of us who love this empire of ours have often considered. Is this not the reason why your husband sought me out personally to assign me this investigation? Knowing full well, mind you, of my desire to retire from active duty."

There was her soft tinkle of laughter as she squeezed his arm warmly.

"We Julii do not retire, cousin. You knew your services would be needed after you left the army long before you officially left your last position. I am sure Octavius made that clear to you on many occasions."

It was his turn to utter a soft chuckle. Yes, without question, he long suspected Caesar had plans after he left the army. Many times Caesar had mentioned this problem or another requiring a man with both discretion and tact, yet also possessing the willingness to act swiftly and efficiently when the moment required it. He often said finding men of such timber was an extremely rare accomplishment. Decimus remembered how the old man's eyes sparked whenever this subject came up.

Yes, Livia Drusilla was correct. The men of the Julii never retired. At least, not willingly. The turbulent times Romans currently found themselves living in kept a man active and alert. Or very dead and very forgotten. Years of civil unrest, grand uprisings, scheming politicians, and open warfare ... with seemingly the family Julii deeply involved in each ... kept the family constantly alert for the new threat to their very existence. Even more so now. Now that the family claimed the cloak of authority over the whole empire. For it was an empire now. The old Roman Republic long since dead the moment Julius Caesar and his famous *Legio XIII Gemini* crossed the Rubicon and marched on to Rome to take the city by force almost sixty years earlier.

Sixty years of bloodshed. Of schemes and cabals. Of madmen lusting for power. Of dreaming about ruling an empire. Sixty years.

"Livia, what is it that you are asking from me. My devotion? My loyalty? You and your husband have always had them."

"I know, old friend. I know," she said, still pulling him along in her slow gait around the temple's inner space. "You need to find the mastermind who is behind this cabal which apparently stimulated Spurius Lavinus' thirst for revenge. But more than that, Decimus. Far more. You need to promise me you will become something far more important in this old woman's heart. Something I cannot command you to do. But something I pray nightly will come voluntarily."

"And what would that be, dear lady," Decimus asked softly.

"Be the friend, the one true friend, Tiberius has never had when he assumes the role of Imperator."

CHAPTER THIRTY-FOUR

With a thoughtful expression, he watched the elegant curtained couch, deftly carried on the shoulders by four impressively tall blond bearded Franks, move across the small plaza in front of the temple and disappear into the darkness down a narrow street. Five purple clad, heavily armed Praetorian Guards marched in front of the couch, while ten more followed in the wake of Livia Drusilla in precise military formation. As he watched the entourage fade into the darkness his mind was like a chaotic nightmare of jumbled thoughts. A thunderous lightning storm of contentious contradictions rumbling among the mountain tops.

What were Livia Drusilla's true intentions? True, she had come to him pleading for her son. The city, the whole empire, knew that once Augustus died the old days might return again. The killing. The sudden disappearances of loved ones. The stark figure of civil wars again ravaging the countryside with rapacious armies. For young Tiberius to survive he would have to display a will, exhibit an iron hand, to those who wished to deny him his ascension. He would indeed need loyal friends once he assumed the cloak of Imperator. It would be dangerous times once Tiberius assumed the crown. He would find enemies everywhere he turned.

Yet.

He could not shake from his thoughts that Livia Drusilla had come to him with a subtle warning. Or, perhaps more accurately, with a subtle threat. A veiled threat that hinted she was active in her son's rise to political power. Tiberius Caesar was not to be harmed. She looked upon him to make sure no political threat emerged strong enough to threaten him. That had been obvious. Something he expected the powerful woman to convey to him. But was there more? Was this feeling of an implied warning real? Or was it something else? Something more sinister.

Folding arms across the front of his elegant white toga he nevertheless heard the distinctive footwork of Quintus Flavius rapidly ascending the temple steps to his left. In the darkness he felt the taller presence of the younger man come directly to stand behind his left arm. Yet he could feel the centurion's impatience. Smiling, wiping the thoughtful gaze from his lined face, he turned and looked up into the young man's face.

"Tribune, news. Both about our Tertius Julius Romanus and about the mysterious Caestus. My drunkard lot of a cousin heard from one of his informants that Tertius Romanus is still in the city. He is hiding in an apartment building down by the river not far from the Aventine. The apartment belongs to a junior officer in the Praetorian Guards. For reasons I cannot fathom, the man agreed to allow Romanus stay there temporarily. The news is Romanus is about to flee. He is packing a few essentials and is about to depart for Ostia and leave on a ship heading to Alexandria. If we hurry, we might catch him just as he steps out of the apartment building."

In the inkiness of the night, the hulking form of Quintus

Flavius towered over the smaller, more compact tribune. Yet even in the darkness sharp eyes would have known who the youth was and who the seasoned, hardened legionnaire was. One stood tall and eager. Incapable of standing absolutely still. The other was like a statue. Absolutely motionless. Calm. Calm and deceptive in appearance.

"Your cousin trusts this man's word?"

"He is an informant, tribune. One never trusts the news they bring entirely. Still, this is a piece of news we cannot disregard. We have to look."

"Agreed." The older man reached up with a calloused hand and squeezed the younger man's shoulder fondly. "We must check it out. Come. Let us hurry to this dangerous rendezvous and face full on whatever might confront us."

"And what of the news about Caestus?"

"Later," Decimus said, waving a hand dismissively. "We undoubtedly will learn more, with a little persuasion on our parts, from the lips of rich and soft Romanus than from the ex-gladiator. Therefore, we pursue Romanus first and then turn to Caestus later."

They descended the stairs of the temple and hurried away to the east. Into the night's shadows they sank as they hurried. Down incredibly narrow streets filled with silence and dread. Past crumbling buildings of wood and stucco, filled with the loud voices of those too drunk, or too angry, to care anymore whether they lived or died. Yet, as they hurried in silence and stealth, their eyes and heads swiveled constantly to the right and left and behind them. They skirted past small bands of roving thugs, an ever-constant threat in the Roman night. They stopped and sank into darker shadows as they waited for the few uniformed *Vigilis* or urban cohort night watch members patrolling the streets. Even for them, being caught this late by the night watch would be most inconvenient, and perhaps more injurious to their health, before being released from custody.

No honest Roman moved through the darkness like a common thief. No honest Roman would be found meandering through the streets without a proper escort and a mass of burning torches to light their way through the serpentine streets. This was Rome.

Yet both tribune and centurion seemed adept in eluding detection. An hour later they pushed their backs against the cool surface of a brick curtain wall which surrounded the gardens of an elegant apartment building.

"The apartment to the left of the entrance. I see one candle burning in a window. That is where Romanus hides."

Decimus nodded gently in the darkness. Eyes narrowed suspiciously, he took in the scene before him. The apartment building in the darkness was three stories tall and built of brick. It sat in the middle of a small park of trees and beds of well-manicured flowers. Two guards stood on either side of the entrance. They were armed with swords. Roman law forbade sharp edged weapons to any of the citizenry within the boundaries of the city proper. For the two guards to be armed and so brazenly open about it meant that someone of importance lived in the apartment building. Someone authorized to have an armed bodyguard.

"The entire upper floor belongs to Darius Milinius. He is the junior officer I mentioned earlier. He is an optio in the fifth cohort of the Praetorian Guards," Quintus Flavius whispered, anticipating the tribune's next question. "Most of the time he is not there. But two guards are always assigned to each entrance into the building. Apparently the man is a collector of fine art. Hence the need for security."

An optio in any Roman military organization was the second in command, usually a senior NCO, of a century. A century in a typical Roman legion consisted of eighty men. Six centuries, or roughly four hundred eighty men, made a Roman army cohort. Eight to ten cohorts made up an entire legion of roughly five thousand men. But in the Praetorian Guards the cohort was doubled. Each cohort was a thousand men strong. Five cohorts kept the Imperator safe from harm within the walls of Rome. The best of the best, some said, plucked from the legions served in the Praetorian Guards. Decimus wasn't sure that was exactly accurate. But there was no question the Praetorian Guards were trained superbly and staffed by dedicated men fiercely loyal to Augustus.

"Should we just present ourselves in front of them and inform them we are here to arrest Romanus?" Quintus Flavius whispered.

"We ... "

Decimus never finished the sentence. A sound like the soft whisper of cloth moving across brick, came to the ears of both centurion and tribune. A whisper of cloth moving across stone not more than a foot from where they knelt in the dark shadows clinging to the stone wall surrounding the apartment building. Almost immediately they were aware of bodies slipping over the walls and landing silently into the thick grass beside them. Four darker forms kneeling, like they were, in the grass and absolutely motionless. Both men thought they saw the gleam of steel partially lit by an errant moonbeam cutting through the canopy of trees towering over them. The four figures were armed with the long, curved blades so favored by gladiators to end the lives of their opponents in the ring after a hard contest fought. The four kneeling men were unaware of the presence of Decimus and Quintus. Their full attention was aimed at the apartment building and specifically at the two unsuspecting guardsmen standing on either side of the apartment's main entrance. As they watched, one of the men gave a short, sharp hand signal and the four dark figures submerged themselves into the deeper shadows of the gardens and faded away into blackness.

"We must warn them," Quintus hissed barely audibly. "They have no idea their deaths are imminent!"

"Too late," Decimus answered, shaking his head. "Look."

Across the short expanse from where they hid themselves, four more men appeared out of the darkness on the far side of the gardens and leapt onto the half asleep guard. As they attacked one, the four who had almost dropped into their laps just moments before, launched themselves onto the other guardsman. Both guards went down at the same time silently. Both men died before they hit the ground. As they watched, eight black demons rose up out off the ground and swiftly entered the building in complete silence.

"How many entrances to this building?"

"Three," the centurion whispered.

"Each entrance guarded by two men?"

"Yes," came the reply.

"Each sentry attacked by four gladiators. Twenty-four men assigned to kill six men. There can be only one outcome to this mission. If Romanus is indeed in that apartment, he is already dead. If he is not, then it is true. The gods do smile upon the insane and the foolish. In either case there is nothing we can do. With odds this large arraigned against us all we can do is remain here and observe."

Reluctantly, the centurion nodded in silence, his eyes blazing with anger, his right hand gripping the pommel of his still sheathed gladius. Eyes returning to the building not more than a heartbeat or two later both men saw a large swath of dark figures rush out of the building in two groups of twelve. Between the two groups was a black figure wrapped in heavy cloth being man handled by four men and displaying the twisting contortions of someone being bodily carried away swiftly. Yet as they watched, two of the gladiators stopped and turned to face the building. One of the dark figures handed something to the other and then knelt to one knee quickly. As their comrades slipped out of the gates leading through the outer wall of the complex both Decimus and Quintus saw the flash of sparks and then the swift flash of a small fire cut through the darkness. The figure kneeling rose to his feet and retrieved whatever it was he had handed his comrade seconds earlier.

What followed next was both sudden and terrifying. Tribune and centurion saw both figures step toward the building. Arms flew over their head. The two men raced out of the gardens just as the sound of cheap pottery shattering against stone came to their ears. There was a loud *whooosh!* and suddenly the night was ripped asunder with a gigantic ball of whitish-blue flame splashing into the open ground floor entrance of the apartment building. The searing flames expanded at an alarming rate, its hungry tongues of ghoulish delight reaching up and further into the building.

"*Fire!*" both Decimus and Quintus Flavius screamed at the top of their lungs as each came to their feet and began running toward the building. "Get out! Get out! Fire! Fire!"

Only two things a true son of Rome feared in life. They being the ever-constant threat of plague sweeping through the poorer sections of the city, killing hundreds, if not thousands, in a matter of weeks. And fire. Plagues and disease were a daily terror which stalked the rich and the poor on a daily basis. One could not walk the streets of Rome without eventually stepping around or over the body of someone who had died from one pestilence or another. For the most part the sudden and swift eruptions of contagion lasted only a few days in one section or another of the city. Leaving the rest of the city relatively safe and unharmed. But *fire* ... fire was a terror which haunted the dreams of every citizen. A fire left unattended even for a few brief moments meant it would soon engulf whole neighborhoods. Towering flames would leap high into the sky hungrily and consume anything and everything it touched in unyielding fury. Most, if not all, of the city was merely a gigantic tinderbox waiting for the right spark. The fear everyone felt was the horror of waiting for the moment when that inevitable conflagration happened, and the entire city was consumed on the altar of total destruction.

Both tribune and centurion entered the burning building and rousted its inhabitants out of their rooms forcefully. Half dragging, half carrying many of the older inhabitants out in their arms, they dumped them on the street and then raced back into the building again. The flames swept through the building with incredible speed. Each time they flung themselves through the flames they wondered if it would be their last moments of life. But each time they came out of the building with someone and deposited them into the waiting arms of people who had come to either help fight the fire or to observe the horror of the doomed trapped inside.

Fire fighters, both of the city's vigiles and of private fire departments, arrived on the scene with their pumping engines and buckets at almost the same time. Soon long lines of bucket brigades stretched out across the city's streets to the nearest public cisterns of water. Hundreds formed the lines, passing one bucket at a time back and forth to those who tried their most valiant to halt the ravaging hunger of the flames. In the end it became a battle which lasted the entire night and consumed not only the apartment building where Tertius Romanus had been abducted from, but one other elegant apartment building as well. When the first rays of sunlight lit the streets of Rome it found dozens of the city's citizens covered in singed hair and blackened robes lying exhausted in the city's streets. Many sat upright, hugging their knees, their faces covered in soot and ash and stared at the still smoking remnants in a sullen stupor. Others, too exhausted to drag themselves back to their apartments, dropped to the pavement and went immediately to sleep. A detachment of Praetorian Guards came marching down the street filled with gawking onlookers, parting the crowd like a warship parting the surf, then came to a halt, broke out of formation and then began moving everyone off the street.

For tribune and centurion, exhausted and covered with soot and ash, they sat leaning against the wall of a building saved and watched the guards do their work. As they watched, the commanding office pivoted on his heel and looked in the direction the man he was questioning pointed to. The burly looking officer then marched across the street straight toward them.

"Hail, tribune!" the officer growled, saluting the still sitting Decimus.

Decimus nodded, too tired to return the salute, and eyed the young man curiously. As he did, he heard Quintus Flavius grunt in amusement.

"Ah, the noble Darius Milinius has returned to his home and hearth. Our apologies, old man. The tribune and I tried to save as many of your neighbors as we could. But the treasure trove of Grecian statuary stuffed into your rooms was just too much for two mere mortals like us to lug out in time."

The scowling face of the junior centurion of the fifth cohort of the Praetorian Guard took in the smoking remnants of what once had been his apartment and grunted in disgust before turning back to the tribune and centurion.

"If I ever find out who committed this atrocity and tried to burn down the city, I and most of my men, will be very eager to nail their asses to the cross after we've worked them over with iron bars. Until then, allow me to convey to you my sincerest appreciation in your efforts. The two of you saved hundreds of lives in your timely intervention. Many of them I consider friends of mine. For that I owe you a debt of gratitude."

"Ah well, Milinius. We did a little more than that. We could not save all of your collection. But we did save one or two of your smaller treasures," the grinning Quintus answered. He pointed to the far end of the gardens. "The good tribune here apparently has an eye for beauty. I must say that Egyptian piece of a queen's bust and the Grecian statue of Venus are very pleasing to the eye."

A slave armed with a club stood in front of the bust of a very beautiful Egyptian woman and the other was a half sized marbled sculpture of what could only be the Goddess of Love rising out of the foam of ocean surf, her arms above her head, her long flowing hair seemingly blowing in the breeze. The centurion stared in amazement at the two pieces in total shock. The two pieces represented exactly half of his accumulated wealth. Whereas moments before he thought his fortunes had plummeted into the depths of agonizing poverty. But, with the casual shrug by the Urbani centurion, he saw he still was a man of means. His fortunes could be rebuilt.

"Tribune ... centurion. I am indebted to you both even more profoundly. If there is anything I can do for you do not hesitate in the asking."

The tribune broke into a crooked smile, the soot on his face combined with the smile creating a mask of malicious deviltry. Lifting a hand up toward the centurion, Darius Milinius grasped the tribune's forearm and pulled him up onto his feet before assisting Quintus Flavius up as well.

"Your payment for services rendered will come to you shortly, young man," Decimus said. "Day after tomorrow I and my friend here will be in the need of a full century of your

Fifth cohort. In the service of the Imperator and sanctioned by him, of course. It will be bloody work, Milinius. We hunt for renegade gladiators and intend on capturing as many of them alive as possible. Think you can provide for our needs?"

The Praetorian officer eyed the tribune intently and then nodded, a wiry smile creasing his lips. Glancing at the tall Quintus Flavius and then back at Decimus, the centurion folded arms across his chest and grinned even wider.

"Your name and the news of your new commission from the Imperator precedes you, Decimus Virilis. Our orders came down a week ago. The guard is to assist you at any time when called upon to do so. We of the Fifth are at your service wherever and whenever you need us."

"Very good, young man. Word will come to you shortly to inform you when and where your men will be expected. Until then, rejoice in the fact that the gods still smile upon you."

CHAPTER THIRTY-FIVE

Bathed in the deep golden rays of a late afternoon sun, she stood near a marble railing and stared at the back of the legendary tribune, holding a goblet of wine close to her bosom with both hands. She wore a gown of white Egyptian linen sewn with wine red and silver thread. The linen was thin and translucent, almost scandalous in its near transparence for a recently widowed Roman matron to wear. It fell across her long, lithe figure with a seductive beauty. The gown was comprised of several layers of the expensive and very thin cloth. But while it did not hide completely her statuesque frame from the eyes of any potential admirer, what was hidden by the gentle folds of cloth only accentuated her natural beauty. And the way she moved with such fluid grace across the gardens in the rear of the small Virilis compound could make any man stop and openly admire her sensual presence.

Her luxurious long hair was penned high atop her head with jewel encrusted pins, revealing a long, sensuous neck. The cleavage of her bosom, still firm and ripe, glowed in the late afternoon sun magically. More goddess than mortal, her beauty had become the toast of Rome the moment she matured into womanhood. Men lusted for her. Poor men. Rich men. Men from Rome. From Parthia. From Hispania. Men commanding immense power. Possessing immense wealth. She was aware of how her physical appearance affected the minds and souls of men. She had used that knowledge to make her way through the cruel world. A world dominated by strong men. Lustful men. Simple men.

But Atia Graccia preferred intelligent men. Devious men. Intelligently eccentric men. There was no one in all of Rome who was more intelligent and eccentric than the man standing with his back toward her. She knew men who feared Decimus Virilis. Powerful men who were, by anyone's reckoning, far more powerful, as well as far more wealthy, compared to the ex-legionnaire. Yet they trembled at the thought of meeting Decimus Julius Virilis in person. Among those who played the game, the reputation of the distant kinsman to Caesar Augustus was well known. The whispers of those who knew of soldiers and politicians disappearing mysteriously whenever Caesar sent this man off to investigate some malfeasance or another were rampant. So were the tales describing the barely audible mumblings of this man talking to ghosts in the dead of night. Even the incredible tales of the tribune's apparent capabilities of seeing into the future.

Yes, without doubt, this man intrigued her the most. Her husband, the late Spurius Lavinus, as incredibly wealthy as he was, nevertheless visibly paled when word came that Caesar had pulled the tribune out of retirement and had personally given him a secret assignment. Panicked so much he left the very next day after telling her a sudden disaster in Brundisium required his immediate attention. That very night, while enroute, bandits attacked his entourage and cut them down mercilessly.

Standing some feet behind him, watching him quietly talking to the gnarled little servant known as Gnaeus, she narrowed her eyes thoughtfully and wondered. What *actually* did the tribune know of her husband's murder? Did he know who the killers might be? Or even who might have given the order to slay her rich but spineless husband?

Just what was this man hiding from her?

She smiled to herself and relaxed. A puzzle. A conundrum. A man who harbored secrets and kept them to himself. This was what so intrigued her about him. Other men she could read openly and easily. No man kept secrets from her. Even poor Spurius Lavinus had been an open book to her. An open book to her even though he thought he had been the most secretive of men while in her presence. But this man ... this Decimus Virilis ... was like stone to her. Unreadable. Gracious and courteous. Even gallant in believing she was innocent of her husband and her father's horrible deaths. Thankfully, she admitted to herself. If her husband was truly conspiring against Caesar, as the tribune hinted, it was even more surprising this man's attentions toward her. When it came to political intrigues everyone knew Caesar Augustus was not a man to trifle with. Any other Roman official investigating her husband would have immediately assumed she too knew far more than she had so far revealed.

But, as she watched the tongue-less Gnaeus leave, she knew she could not remain in the presence of this man much longer. She had to travel to Carthage. Only there, surrounded by her son's servants and soldiers, would she feel more at ease. She would never be safe here in Rome as long as her husband's killers remained unchained. Nor could she continue to live in this vacuum of not knowing what secrets the tribune hid from her. She smiled with a coquettish delight when the tribune turned, and his eyes fell upon her seductive form.

"Ah, Atia Graccia. May I compliment you tonight? You are a perfect picture of Roman beauty. I stand before you bedazzled by your loveliness."

"You flatter me with your kind words. I admit of late, with all that has befallen me, along with the fears of what might lie ahead, I am afraid beauty alone will not protect me."

"While you remain here under my protection, no harm will come to you, my dear. Admittedly dark forces are at work. They may appear as if they surround us and threaten our very existence. But the morning will come, Atia. The darkness will be overcome."

A smile of apparent relief swept across her face as she reached out and took his right hand into hers and squeezed gently. Stepping close to him she allowed her bare shoulder to rub against his arm. Standing so close, and towering over her, she knew her charms would be quite enticing to behold. She felt the tribune relax and even lean slightly into her. The smile on her dark lips increased slightly.

"Decimus ... I ... I have a request to make of you. I know the Imperator must suspect me in whatever evil machinations my husband was involved in. But you must know I knew nothing. Whatever his sins were, I did not participate in. This you must believe."

"I understand your fears, lovely lady. A threat does hang over our heads. A threat that, if left unchecked, could plunge the empire back into the throes of civil war. Yet you must believe me. Neither the imperator nor I believe you are involved. You are nothing more than an unfortunate pawn in a grand game of chance that is being played. Now tell me, what is this favor you ask of me?"

"I must leave Rome, Decimus. I must hurry to Carthage

and be with my son. As you know, he is the appointed legate of the newly formed *XXIII Victrix*. With his new legion protecting me, and my presence far from Rome, I would feel both safe, and at the same time, relieve you of the necessity of housing me in your home for my protection. All of your efforts could then be channeled in finding those who killed my husband and possibly threaten the empire."

Her son, Claudius Lucius Lavinus, had been appointed legate, or an army commander, by Octavius only four months earlier. The *XXIII Victrix*, a brand-new legion, was being assembled from the sons of old army legions who had settled in Africa. Caesar, after defeating Anthony's forces years earlier, decided to whittle down the total number of legions either he, or his enemies, had assembled. All told, at the end of the civil wars, there were something like sixty legions to command. He retired and disbanded thirty-two legions from active duty. These veterans, whether they were loyal to Octavius or had fought against him, were fully paid off and land was found for them to settle on. Most of the veterans settled in Africa. Now, years later, these same veterans had fully grown sons ready to carve out their own fortunes in the world. From this plentiful crop of recruits, the XXIII was being built.

The new legion was going to be based in Carthage. Not the legendary Carthage of ancient Rome. But Roman Carthage. A bigger, more resplendent city set on the African coastline not too far from the ruins of Rome's ancient nemesis. Claudius Lucius Lavinus would have more than 20,000 men under his command. They would be composed of the 6000 in his legion, plus an equal amount of men in the auxiliaries every Roman legion were assigned, along with, since this was Africa, a size-able compliment of native cavalry at his disposal. In Carthage Atia Graccia would be safe. Safe from those of this still hidden cabal who may wish to dispose of her like they had her husband

and father. Safe, in relative terms, from the prying eyes of Caesar as well.

The problem was the long and arduous journey she would have to complete to join her son. Until those who lived hidden and secluded within this deadly pit of vipers were found and exposed, her life was in constant jeopardy. She would remain safe only if she continued to live under Decimus' protection.

"In a few days I suspect this evil we face will fade away and be properly forgotten by all parties involved. Once we've satisfied our concerns, I am sure arrangements can be made for your journey. But until then, Atia, I cannot allow you the freedom you request. You must stay here under my protection for the time being."

"But Decimus, why would I be targeted by these men? I knew nothing of either my husband's nor my father's desires. Surely these people know that. Do we even know who leads this conspiracy? Is this Caestus the leader? If so, why not find him and immediately arrest him. Once that is done surely all the dangers cease and I may, at last, hurry to my son's home in peace. Please, Decimus. Tell me you are about to apprehend this fiend and capture his band of murderous pirates. My heart aches. I wish to look upon my son's face as soon as I can."

The tribune smiled knowingly as he gently removed his hand from hers and then guided her hand underneath his arm for her to hold onto. As they walked across the white painted gravel pathway of the garden their sandals made a soft crunching noise with each step. For a second or two each remained silent and stared down at the pathway as the walked. But a movement from the side made Decimus turn his head. Quintus Flavius stepped into the garden. Tall. Handsome. With a bright look on his roguish features which instantly caught the tribune's interest. Stopping, he turned to Atia

Graccia and patted her hand still draped around his arm in a brotherly fashion.

"Atia, I promise. Give me only a week and all will be over. By the end of next week you will have the freedom you desire. One week. That's all I ask."

She glanced at the centurion with wiry concern and then turned her full attention back toward the tribune. She stepped in closer, lifting herself up with her sandaled feet and kissed him on his cheek.

"Very well, old friend. One week. I will hold you to your promise."

Stepping back, an alluring smile of seduction on her lips, she left him standing on the pathway watcher her retreat out of the garden and into his house with approving eyes. And then, sighing and shaking his head, he cleared his mind and turned to face Quintus Flavius.

"You bring good news this day, young centurion?"

"Aye, tribune. Remember my words from last night? That I had possibly good news about this gladiator we seek?"

He nodded.

"The news has been confirmed. Caestus' hideaway has been found. In Ostia. He was seen entering it late last night by one of my informants. A man with keen eyes and in desperate need for money. His services procured to scour Ostia and seek out either the gladiator himself, or find the lair his henchmen possibly hid themselves in. He has sent me word he has found both. If we hurry, we might bag them all in one swift thrust of the sword."

"Then by all means. We journey to Ostia to find this gladiator and his friends. Who knows? Perhaps we will find Tertius Julius Romanus as well. Alive and well and in the midst of his duplicitous friends."

Tribune and centurion hurried down the path toward the

other end of the house. As he moved, Decimus thought he saw the whisper of cloth partially visible just within the gloom of his house move deeper into the interior's darkness. Just the suggestion of something white. Something almost translucent. Something incredibly beautiful.

CHAPTER THIRTY-SIX

Bathed in brilliant moonlight were the white-washed walls and dark tiled roof of the hulking form of a large warehouse. A large warehouse setting on the banks of the Tiber about a mile inward from river's mouth and about two hundred yards away from the city's eastern gates. The warehouse sat alone on a sliver of firm land paralleling the river. Surrounding the warehouse was the river on the south, while the salt marshes so familiar to the tribune and centurion, surrounded the building's other three sides.

The only way to approach the building was to either traverse the narrow, twisting road which led from the city to the warehouse. Or to use the river and dock alongside the short but stoutly built wooden wharf jutting fifteen feet out into the river's dark waters. There was no other way to approach the building. The salt marches were impassable. The road so narrow it was barely wide enough for a two wheeled cart to traverse its narrow girth. Only the river and a frontal assault over the dock offered any course of action. There, tribune and centurion, along with a detachment of Praetorian guards, hid themselves underneath heavy canvas tarps in the middle of a long, wide river barge being manhandled down the middle of the Tiber by a few bargemen using long wooden poles. They navigated through the dark waters expertly. Understanding the limitations at hand, Decimus observed the dark forms of closely packed men in full armor. A full century of the Praetorian Guards ... one hundred twenty men ... of the Fifth Cohort.

If the warehouse was filled with waiting gladiators he had no doubt the fight would be bloody and merciless. There could be no other conclusion to this assault. Those within the warehouse knew what their fates would be if captured alive. They already had suffered through the pain and humiliation of becoming slaves. They had often observed what happened to those who rebelled against their slavery. Surrender, therefore, was not an option. Better to die, like a gladiator should, with sword in hand and bleeding foes at one's feet than to endure the pain of torture and the bloody death of crucifixion.

He knew no gladiator would voluntarily surrender. Yet he needed captives. Living captives. He needed information. He had to find and stop Caestus as quickly as possible. Before the man could strike at the Julii. Before the ghosts of wars past again ripped asunder the empire.

In the darkness he peered at the tall shadow that was Quintus Flavius. The young Roman, dressed in the full armor of a Roman centurion, looked every bit like the soldier his father had been. Yes, he had kept the secret. Years ago, in Hispania, he had known Quintus Flavius the Elder. They had shared bread with each other around the embers of a dying campfire. Had fought together in several engagements. A fine soldier. A commanding figure leading his men into battle. He knew the elder Quintus Flavius would have been extremely proud his son had followed in his footsteps.

He had recognized the younger Quintus the moment he reined up his horse and dismounted at the scene where Spurius Lavinus had been murdered. The resemblance had been uncanny. He had refrained from saying anything for fear of possibly shattering any images the boy might have of his heroic father. He had seen it before. A casual remark. An inadvertent word and the feelings a son had for their long deceased relative instantly destroyed. Nevertheless, the dim image towering over him, he could almost feel the pride Quintus Flavius' father would have felt in his place.

"Any word on the origins of the tattoos found on the dead gladiators?"

"None tribune," the centurion answered quietly. "I've sent drawings to every trainer of gladiators in every school I can think of. No one has come forward with any information. It's as if these men had never stepped into an arena and stood before a cheering crowd. At least not a Roman crowd."

"Perhaps you are correct, my son. Perhaps we've been looking at this with preconceived beliefs all along. False beliefs which have led us down the wrong path."

Quintus Flavius stared down at the smaller framed shadow that was Decimus Virilis. The two banks of barge oarsmen slowly pulled on their oars, the sounds of them dipping into the water in unison and rising to begin another stroke came to their ears, and he waited for the tribune to continue. He knew the older man was speaking more to himself than to him. It was how the tribune's mind worked. And, unsurprisingly, it was one way he knew he could learn from his mentor. All he had to do was remain silent and listen.

"All this time we have assumed Caestus brought with him a number of his fellow gladiators to complete some secret mission. A mission which needed strong, ruthless men to complete. How many times have we come across clues referencing gladiators? We discover Spurius Lavinus owns a gladiator school. We are set upon by a group of swordsmen whose leader openly admits he is a gladiator. We find a ship burning on the shore near Ostia with the bodies of what appears to be gladiators lying about after being brutally slaughtered. Our guest back in Rome believes Caestus is a gladiator who won his freedom in the arena. We witness the abduction of Tertius Julius Romanus from his apartment by a gang of gladiators."

"A logical conclusion, tribune. Who else could it be if not gladiators?"

"A ruse, centurion. What if this has all been a ruse skillfully designed for misdirection. What if we are chasing a mirage? A set of ghosts which have never existed. While we run from Rome to Ostia and back chasing ghosts and rumors the real mastermind of this affair slips away and disappears into the night."

A deep scowl of confusion spread across Quintus Flavius' face. As he watched the prow of the flat-bottomed barge edge close to the wooden wharf of the warehouse, his mind flashed back to the last few days and reviewed everything that had happened. His confusion grew. All the evidence suggested the henchmen they faced were gladiators. But apparently the tribune had doubts. What had happened to make the tribune pause and reconsider an alternate route? In the darkness he heard a soft chuckle of amusement beside him. It was as if the tribune was reading his thoughts.

"*Maris secreta tenemus...*" the tribune's voice filled the night softly. "*The sea keeps its secrets from us.* That is the clue, Quintus. The sea... and the predators who dwell in secret upon the sea."

"Pirates! We are not looking for gladiators. We are looking for pirates!"

"Spurius Lavinus owned at least one school for gladiators. But his true wealth came from the profits of his various shipping and trading enterprises. Felix Graccus, Atia's father, the same. The Gracci specialized in importing and exporting from the Levant. Tertius Julius Romanus owns both gladiator schools and shipping. His ships plow the trade from Rome to Greece. You see the connections, Quintus. Most of our conspirators own gladiator schools. But all of them have a direct association with the sea."

"Let's not forget our friend, Caius Septimus. A noted pirate captain himself."

"Now consider Caestus. An ex-gladiator. A pirate. A Greek. The Greek islands are infested with pirates. Hardened men willing to kill anyone if the price is right. With undoubtedly a number of them being ex-gladiators. How difficult would it be to recruit experienced cut throats from this deadly garden? But that leads us to another possibility, Quintus. What if this whole affair is not what it appears to be. What if all the basic assumptions we have, including all the initial information fed to us in the beginning, are false. False clues fed to us in an attempt to mask the true nature of this bloody exercise."

Startled, Quintus Flavius started to say something but stopped when the blunted prow of the barge slammed into the wharf with some force. Ropes were hurled into the night from guardsmen instantly. Men erupted from underneath the canvas tarps as one trained explosion of flesh and armor. Some men leapt for the mooring ropes and expertly secured the barge to the dock. A much larger band of men bent low with one hand holding their rectangular shields high in front of them while the other gripped the handholds attached to a long iron lance. They leapt onto the dock as one, manhandling the large metal ram out of the barge with them. With a single command the iron ram, and the men gripping it between them, flew toward the stout door of the warehouse. With an ear thunderous roar of splintering wood, the ram smashed into the middle of the largest warehouse door, hurling the heavy wood back a good two feet before it finally tore from its hinges and smashed inward and down onto the warehouse floor within.

What followed next was bloody chaos. Hidden in the darkness of the warehouse interior were forty men. Forty hardened, seasoned pirates well versed in sword and shield work. Undoubtedly trained once as gladiators true pirates who, like the gladiators they once were, decided to fight to the death. The clamoring hammer of steel biting into steel, or the flat sound of steel blades being blocked by a heavy *scutum* of a legionnaire, filled the night. The fighting became intense from the first moment a Roman blade crossed the blade of a Grecian pirate. Knowing their fates were sealed, the pirates fought like crazed animals. The screams of men dying violently mingled the screams of men slipping into the blood fury of a berserker.

Twice Decimus found himself facing furious assaults from pirates flinging themselves out of the darkness. But *gladius* and *scutum* were the tribune's oldest companions. Shield and sword work were natural extensions of Decimus' baser instincts. He used both as offensive weapons. With the bottom edge of his shield, he caught one pirate squarely in the throat with a vicious lunge while the hand gripping his *gladius* slit the man's stomach wide open with the weapon's polished steel edge.

The second pirate went down after three strokes from shield and sword. Hot blood from a severed aorta splashed across his shield as he saw from out of the side of his eye two more pirates leaping toward him. This time the opponents caught him unbalanced. One attacked from his front while the other side stepped and attacked from his left. The one in front of him gripped a short sword and a small round shield. The one on his left gripped and Egyptian war axe with a strange spoke wheeled black iron head while defending himself with a heavier looking shield. This man was the one who knew how to fight. With his round shield he smashed Decimus' *scutum* to one side just as he lifted his war axe high over his head to deliver the fatal blow. The pirate plunged it toward the tribune's exposed neck. A vicious blade of Roman steel appeared out of the darkness, sweeping horizontally across the plane and decapitated the pirate's head from his shoulders in one blinding motion.

The remaining pirate, for a brief moment, had an opportunity to slip his short blade toward the throat of the unbalanced tribune. But to his amazement, his last in the brief moment remaining to him, he watched the unbalanced Roman rotate completely around in a circle, lowering himself in the process, and felt the Roman's blade slide just underneath his cuirass and sink deep into his chest cavity. He was dead before his carcass slid off the Roman's stout blade and fell to the floor.

Quintus Flavius, smeared in garish swipes of blood across his cuirass and shield, exhibited a huge grin visible from underneath his helm. He, stepped out of the darkness and saluted the tribune playfully.

"Hot work, eh tribune? I believe, sir, working in your service is going to be very stimulating indeed. Very stimulating!"

The battle raged around them. Praetorian guards, shoulder to shoulder and shield to shield, worked grimly the profession they had trained all their adult lives in. For a few more minutes the din of weapons beating against each other continued. But in time it subsided and then finally ceased. Only the groans of dying men remained and then, eventually, that too subsided. Light from a dozen torches exploded to life all at once, illuminating the immediate area around them in flickering yellow light.

Decimus nodded to the guard's senior officer. A quick command was barked out and men with torches began searching the building. It did not take long to make a grim discovery.

CHAPTER THIRTY-SEVEN

He sat on the stone floor of the warehouse, his back hugging a bare wall, with heavy iron shackles and chains clamped on his wrists keeping him tightly pinned to the wall and floor. In front of him was a tall brazier filled with the cold embers of freshly consumed wood and an assortment of branding irons. The bloody figure propped against the wall had suffered hours of torture. Hours of pain. Blood covered his tunic. His bare shoulders and arms exhibited all the marking of a man who was an expert in inflicting pain onto a helpless prisoner with a white-hot iron.

Caius Septimus looked more dead than alive. His face had been beaten savagely. His left eye was swollen shut. His nose nothing more than a red mass of broken cartilage and dried blood. Yet the man lived. Even smiled, groaning in severe pain for doing so, as tribune and centurion knelt on either side of him.

"Ah. I see the Goddess Fortuna still smiles upon me, tribune. Though, if truth be told, I would judge you to be somewhat late in your timely arrival. I had hopes of an earlier appearance. But we shall not quibble over minor details. You're here and I still live."

"Caestus did this to you?" Decimus asked softly, reaching up to examine one of the heavy shackles.

"Yes, the master himself. An artist at beating a man senseless, I might add. He wanted to know who I worked for. Wanted to know what you knew about him. About his mission. Wanted to know the name of the traitor who betrayed him to Caesar. Wanted to know who gave the order to kill Spurius Lavinus. The man was quite mad. Almost beside himself with rage."

A guardsman stepped up with a pair of heavy shears. Opening its steel jaws, he slipped the chains holding Septimus to the floor and gripped it firmly in its heavy pincer like jaws. It took some time for the sharp edges of the shear's mouth to finally cut through the heavy chains. But they did. First the right hand and then the left.

Decimus and Quintus gripped the pirate's arms and propped him higher up onto the wall as another guardsman handed Quintus a bag of wine to quench the pirate's thirst. Caius Septimus drank deep, wine spilling out of his mouth and soaking his blood caked beard and chest. Finally, thirst quenched, he pushed the wine from his lips and looked at Decimus with his one good eye.

"Tertius Romanus is dead. Caestus worked him over first before he turned his attention to me. I... I was chained to the wall here and had to watch the whole thing. Watch and hear a so-called noble Roman cry out in pain and weep like a child pleading for his life. Humorous, don't you think? How a Roman of noble birth trained from childhood to rule the world with the edge of a sword, becomes in the end, nothing more than a lowly peasant himself when he faces the end of his life filled in pain."

"What did Romanus confess to Caestus? Did he say

anything about who leads this conspiracy? Did he say anything about documents? Secret documents?"

"Ah. The fabled Octavian letters," Caius Septimus said, grunting a pained chuckle of amusement before relapsing into a spasm of throaty coughing.

"Septimus!" barked the tribune angrily, grabbing the man's right bicep and squeezing painfully. "Speak! The documents. What did Romanus say about the documents?"

"There were none!" the pirate almost screamed, twisting his arm out of the tribune's grip and glaring at him. "There never were any documents. Romanus swore no one saw any documents. Only the promise of documents were mentioned. Only a promise!"

"Where is Caestus?" Quintus barked after glancing at the tribune.

"I heard him tell one of the men to prepare for a rapid departure. He was leaving to gather the rest of the men and bring them back here. When they returned all of them were going to board ship in Ostia and depart Italy. Carthage ... they were moving everyone to Carthage and severing all ties with Greece."

Septimus' head dropped down to his chest. His strength was draining rapidly. He fought with himself not to succumb from his pain and wounds. He even chortled in amusement as he raised his head and looked at Decimus again.

"They hate you, tribune. Hate you with a dark passion. They know of your loyalty toward Caesar. Know of your reputation for being Caesar's henchman. Caestus wanted to kill you immediately. In fact, twice sent out teams of assassins to cut you down. He wanted to personally cut your living heart out of your chest with a knife. But his master wouldn't allow it."

"Who are *they*, Septimus? What did they wish to accomplish? Where did Caestus go after he left you here in the warehouse?" the tribune hissed, his anger rising.

"They? Caestus, Romanus, all of them. All of them who came together to buy the mythical letters reported written by the Imperator. All of them. They wanted revenge, tribune. Revenge. No grand plot to destroy the empire. No desire to rule. Just revenge. Simple revenge. Their desire was to strike a blow against the Julii. A blow that would make the Julii suffer as much as their families had suffered. What exactly they were to do I never gleaned. Nor do I know Caestus' plans. He left in a furious rage. That is ... is ... all I know."

The pirate's last few words were no more than a whisper before his head dropped and he slowly slid down the wall to the floor. The centurion reached out and felt the man's neck. A weak pulse still beat within the resilient man's chest.

"Alive," he said to the tribune before standing. "But barely. He needs a physician."

"Order a two man escort to take him and the barge to Ostia. Inform the rest they must stay here, hiding themselves as best as they can, and capture anyone who tries to enter. We must be quick about this, Quintus. The end game is upon us, and we must strike first before our opponents do. So hurry, my son. Hurry!"

CHAPTER THIRTY-EIGHT

What they found in Rome was death and destruction. The small villa he called his own no longer existed. Occupying the dark space on the Palatine Hill where his residence once stood was nothing more than the gutted remains and charred ruins of his home. Along with a dozen or more blackened corpses who had perished in the fire.

Surrounding the house and sifting through the charred ruins were a dozen or more of the city's *Vigiles*, leather water buckets in hand, moving about slowly and deliberately, dousing out hot spots with cold water. Also present were half a dozen men and officers of the Praetorian Guards. Commanding the guardsmen who had set up a perimeter of the disaster was Darius Milinius, the *optio* they had met only the night before.

"My condolences, tribune. When your servant sent word that suspicious men were surrounding your house and requested help, I immediately rounded up as many men as I could find and came hurrying to the call. But when we arrived the house and surrounding buildings were on fire. When we arrived we found a dozen or more men in the streets fighting a pitched battle. But they fled the moment we came upon the scene."

The tribune nodded at the centurion with a mask of silent rage. Gripping a flaming torch in one hand, he turned to inspect the blacked forms pulled from the ashes of the villa. With Quintus Flavius at his side, the tribune went from one corpse to the next, kneeling and holding the torch just over the body's burnt face, and inspected them closely. With each corpse inspected the tribune's face darkened even more in silent fury. When at last he stood after inspecting the last of the dead he turned and faced both centurions, the bubble of illumination from the brightly burning torch engulfing them all.

"Two of the bodies I recognize. My servants and ex-comrades, Hassad and Rufus. The third is a woman. A woman with the signet ring of a Lavinii member half melted on one of her fingers."

"Atia Graccia," Quintus Flavius said, looking down at the grotesque form lying in the charred soil by their feet.

"From the looks of it she was dead before the fire consumed her. There are several deep wounds in her chest and neck. Stab wounds. Someone wished her to die swiftly and painfully. She is of the same height and form of our guest. One would naturally assume it was the wife of Spurius Lavinus lying here dead."

But the centurions heard the odd note in the tribune's voice. Both watched him with interest. For his part, Decimus' eyes roamed over the twisted, blackened form lying in the mud beside him and forced himself to speak in a calm voice.

"Evidence suggests it is Atia Graccia. There is the family signet on her finger. A piece of cloth from her garment untouched by fire which I knew she was wearing the last time I saw her. The only woman in the household. A woman under my protection and guarded by both Hassad and Rufus diligently."

"But something troubles you, tribune," the suddenly smirking Quintus Flavius put in. "There must be something here which bothers you. What do you see that we do not?"

"Look closely at the ring, Quintus," the tribune answered, offering the brightly burning torch to the centurion.

Quintus Flavius took the torch in one hand and knelt beside the body and inspected it closely. Within seconds both Decimus and the Praetorian centurion heard a surprised grunt just before Quintus came to his feet.

"The ring is on the wrong finger. Not only that, but the wrong hand as well. The ring is on her left hand. The woman was right-handed."

"Exactly so," nodded Decimus. "What does that suggest?"

"An innocent woman was murdered," the Praetorian officer chimed in quickly. "Someone was found with the same physical characteristics of your guest and then brutally murdered and then robed in her clothing and jewelry. But for what purpose, tribune?"

"To gain some time from any pursuit, centurion," Quintus Flavius answered. "To throw us off the scent. For some time now the tribune has suspected Atia Graccia as being involved in a conspiracy. But if she is dead, along with the others of her fellow conspirators, the need to pursue the investigation becomes moot. Those who are left are nothing more than the leaderless underlings. They too will be eventually found and detained. Although I would suggest Caestus is yet a burning torch that needs to be extinguished as quickly as possible."

A guard came out of the darkness and saluted his centurion quickly before whispering something into the man's ear. The centurion waited for the man to leave before looking at Decimus.

"We have orders. From the palace. Word has come a large body of men disguised as legionaries are marching toward Brundisium not too far from here. Three cohorts of Praetorian Guards have been ordered to pursue and capture them before any further mischief takes place. We must leave you now. Good hunting, tribune! May you find your prey and run them down swiftly and mercilessly."

The centurion pulled from his belt a small wooden whistle and lifted it to his lips. Two sharp notes filled the night air followed by the quick footsteps of men running to fall into formation. Decimus and Quintus watched the men disappear into the night, leaving only them and the remaining *Vigiles* in the moonlit night.

"What is our next move, tribune?"

"We wait," Decimus answered quietly. He studied the remains of his once small but comfortable home. "Wait for Gnaeus, Hassad, and Rufus to send word to us where we might find Caestus and the woman."

"What?" Quintus shot back, surprise clearly written on his face. "I thought you said Hassad and Rufus were dead? You lied to Darius Milinius?"

Decimus faced the younger man and smiled. The smile on his lips did not match the rage filling the tribune's eyes. Quintus had the distinct feeling he was staring into the face of a pit viper about to strike. It was not a pleasurable experience.

"Quintus Flavius, let me say it once again. Trust no one when it comes to dealing in imperial politics. *No one.* Darius Milinius might be a loyal Roman. He might be aligned with the Julii as faithfully as we are. On the other hand, he may be serving those who are trying to destroy the Imperator and his wife by whatever method is offered to him. We don't know. The best spies employ themselves in positions which allow them to be closest to their intended victims. Until we know more about this Praetorian it would be in our best interest to not trust him."

The handsome centurion sighed and shook his head in frustration. There was no need to argue. He saw the logic in the tribune's words.

"So where is Gnaeus and the others? And why are you sure Atia Graccia is the mastermind behind whatever dangerous game is being played here?"

"To answer your second question first, I do not know for sure if Atia is a friend or a foe. There is not enough evidence to decide the issue in either direction. A factor which, I confess, frankly worries me. We should have some evidence to point to one direction or the other by now. As to your first question, I have a simple answer. I set a trap. My *suspicions* tell me the woman is dangerous. A dangerous prey who is trying desperately to escape from her captivity. Twice she has asked for permission to flee to Carthage as soon as she can. Notice how the city of Carthage keeps popping up in our discussions of late? I find this somewhat telling. Why Carthage? What not Athens? Or Alexandria? Is she fleeing to Carthage to be with her only son? Or is there something more sinister about the city we have yet to fathom?

So. On a hunch I gave orders to Gnaeus to gather Hassad and Rufus and keep an eye on the villa from a discreet distance. We hired loyal ex-legionaries to guard Atia in their absence. I thought perhaps she might try to escape. I had no thought Caestus would come to her aid until too late to warn anyone. The deaths of old friends hired to do a simple task of guarding a lovely house guest rests upon my shoulders. I plan to avenge their deaths as quickly as possible."

"They are tracking Caestus and the woman as we speak?"

"I believe so," said Decimus, turning again to staring at the gutted, charred walls of his home again. "But until we hear from them, I cannot be absolutely sure. All we can do now is wait for the morning light and implement the trap Tiberius and I hatched out to capture our pirate friend days earlier."

"Surely that plan has fallen by the wayside, tribune. Caestus wouldn't dare to attack Tiberius and his royal bodyguard now in open day light. Not after we have gleaned their intentions and have acted to thwart their moves."

"Nay, centurion. A sane man would run for his life knowing the game has been furrowed out. But we are not dealing with sane men. We deal with madmen, Quintus. Madmen filled with the thirst for revenge. Hatred for the Julii has plunged them all in a dark Hades all their own. Hatred and revenge are the only emotions they feel now. Sanity has long since left them. Caestus is consumed with the desire to harm the Julii. He has become even more dangerous than he was earlier. Rest assured. He will attack either Octavius, or Livia, or Tiberius on the morrow. The attack will come as surely as I know the sun will rise shortly. So let us find some place of lodging for the night. We should rest as best as we can for tomorrow's festivities."

Decimus turned and began to walk away but paused.

"What troubles you, centurion?

"The words of Caius Septimus, tribune. Something he said troubles me greatly."

Decimus Virilis waited. He knew exactly what troubled the young man.

"When Caestus tortured Septimus, he demanded answers. One of his demands was the revelation of who killed Spurius Lavinus. That's what troubles me, tribune. If the woman did not kill her husband, and if Caestus himself did not kill Lavinus, then who? *Who* killed Spurius Lavinus?"

"Ah," the tribune echoed, grimly pulling his lips back in a

vicious snarl. "The very question that has haunted me all this time. Who killed Spurius Lavinus?"

Quintus Flavius watched the older man for some moments and then startled, almost jumped in surprise. Decimus Julius Virilis knew! Knew at last who was the harbinger of death ... all these horrible and bloody deaths! In his excitement he took a half step toward the tribune, raising a hand toward the old soldier... But the tribune frowned, shook his head and lifted a finger to his lips in a gesture of silence.

Not here. Not now, Quintus Flavius. Soon all would be revealed. But first, fiends desperate and murderous had yet to be hunted down and throttled before more innocent blood was shed.

CHAPTER THIRTY-NINE

It was as if *Jupiter Invictus* himself set on his horse at the head of the slow moving entourage of horsemen and wagons. Through a crack in the low hanging clouds a shaft of bright sunlight lanced through the dull, early gray morning gloom and bathed Tiberius Caesar in a magical aura of shimmering gold.

Tiberius, atop a black mare of magnificent lines, encased in the armor of a Roman general and a red cape draped over his shoulders, looked every inch the conquering Roman emperor. He was in a good mood today. Laughing and joking with his officers riding just behind him, the wind running through his cropped dark hair carelessly, a quick smile often creasing his lips like the slash of a swift sword stroke. But all was a sham. A show of bravado. A planned theatrical exhibition. Tiberius knew. Danger lurked near and he had to be prepared. Prepared ... yet not in such a way as to alert those who waited for him somewhere further down the road.

The entourage of Tiberius, his staff of twenty young patrician sons, followed by his personal bodyguard of thirty hardened, experienced Roman legionaries, along with six heavy framed wagons with large swaths of canvas draped over the heavy wooden crates within each, moved at a snail's space down the paved road toward Ostia. The road traffic of wagons and pedestrians, already heavily populated this early in the morning, nevertheless parted like ocean waters before Neptune himself for Tiberius and his men.

On their right flowed the slow- moving waters of the Tiber. On the far banks of the river was a swath of dark marsh. Eyeing the river and the marshes, Decimus' lips almost creased into a grim sneer. Sitting on his horse a few rows back from the rear-most ranks of Tiberius' staff officers, he and Quintus Flavius rode side by side. Both were dressed in the armor of *Cohortes Urbani* officers. But their positions in the entourage hid them from view. Flanking each of them were men of Tiberius' guard. Grizzled old veterans loyal to Tiberius who rode beside tribune and centurion of the *Urbani* with orders to protect both at all costs. They had not been told why they had to stay close to the two. But they sensed it. Years of hard service and bloody work had instilled within them that sixth sense. Action was close at hand. So they rode close to their charges, their eyes suspicious of all fellow travelers they swept by as they moved down the road.

Decimus felt amazingly calm. He sat in the saddle of his hardy little steed and quietly waited for the final act of this deadly charade to unfold. As he was certain it would. All the preparations had been carefully set in place. All the actors were present. Caestus would strike. On this road. Just a few miles outside of Ostia at a very specific place where the terrain would give him the best opportunity for success. There was nothing to do now but wait for the action to begin. And, maybe, pray to the gods that the son of Livia Drusilla lived to see the next morning's sunrise.

Glancing at the centurion, Decimus flashed a brief grin of amusement. But for only a second. One look at the troubled face of the young officer told him Quintus Flavius was mentally wrestling with formidable imaginary foes. Imaginary foes which apparently were taxing the young man's abilities to the extreme. Decimus smiled again and leaned toward the centurion casually.

"Tell me what troubles you, my son. Your face is filled with storm clouds. A man struggling with a host of thoughts so near to combat is a man destined to meet an untimely demise. So tell me. What is it about this affair which makes you so ill at ease?"

A flash of irrepressible youth shot across the centurion's expression as he glanced toward the river and then back to the tribune. The man's eyes flashed with a bright light of inquisitiveness shaded by frustration. Yet the dimpled smile of a boundless energy filled the man's face.

"I confess, it is you, tribune. You confound me constantly. I have been by your side since almost the beginning of this affair. I have seen what has taken place. I've heard directly, or from your lips, everything that has been said. We have examined every piece of evidence together. Yet I freely admit the obvious. With each passing hour I become more confused and mystified. These killings beginning with the murder of Spurius Lavinus and then the others. The grisly deaths of all those gladiators on the shoreline above Ostia. Everything ... it simple doesn't add up. It makes no sense. Yet you know. You *know* who killed Spurius Lavinus. How? How is that possible?"

The older man glanced at his young protégé for a moment and then nodded. He could see the lad's eyes were filled with questions. He felt the centurion's need to understand his method on how he had come to his conclusions. A genuine hunger. A driving thirst to drink the cold waters of understanding. And this pleased the tribune. Pleased him more than he cared to admit.

"Consider the whole problem. I admit, solving complex cases like this requires us to break it down into smaller, more pragmatic sub-sets so we can examine all the details more closely. But at some point, usually late in the affair, all the details have to be pulled together and looked at more closely as a whole. When this time comes, any relevant information from out of the past, or from experience, must be added into the cauldron and stirred vigorously in as well. Here is where your confusion comes in, Quintus. You know the present. Your abilities to observe and deduct what is before you have been improving immensely. But you are not familiar with the past. What has happened long before the death of Lavinus, yet oddly directly related to this case as well."

"You speak of the documents now," Quintus uttered after glancing at those riding beside them.

"No," the tribune answered, shaking his head. "Not directly. I'm speaking of the history of Spurius Lavinus. Of his unique qualities which made him the perfect man for such a conspiracy to begin. What I have not told you until now is that Lavinus and I have a past history with each other. We've crossed paths twice. Neither instance generated any lingering fondness for the other."

"Secrets, tribune? You keep secrets from me?"

"As you keep from me, my son. As all men keep from others for one reason or another. The whole world is one gigantic secret. Mysteries abound everywhere. Most of the time these secrets are withheld not for any maleficent purpose. Memories are forgotten. Some memories not shared in order to protect one from any embarrassment. There are numerous reasons why one keeps secrets to himself. It is neither here nor there. But in this case, the two occasions Spurius Lavinus and I crossed paths have only an indirect, but vital, value to our current pursuits.

Ten years ago Lavinus was given the *Legio XXI, Mars Victorious,* to command. The legion was packed up and hastily sent off to Africa to reinforce the legate in Numidia who was facing a minor uprising of desert tribesmen."

"Carthage," the centurion grunted, his voice containing a hint of curiosity.

"Carthage," the tribune repeated. "That is a thread which seems to bind all the various parties of this case together. In itself it may mean nothing. But there, nevertheless. Yet the main point of this history lesson is this. I was a centurion back then in the twentieth. The first spear of the first cohort. So the legate and I got to know each other intimately. I saw how he commanded a legion. How he treated men underneath him. He was not brilliant. There were no flashes of greatness about him. But he was steady. Personally brave. And he treated everyone equal to their station.

What I am saying is this. Of all the supposed members of this conspiracy, Spurius Lavinus was the only one who had any real military experience. On top of that, his family is as old as Rome itself. Old and very rich. He wasn't the sharpest sword on the field. But his name, his experience, and his money would have been exactly what would be needed for the conspiracy to gather others to their cause."

"Yet he was the first one to die," the young centurion said, frowning. "It doesn't make sense."

"Precisely," the tribune agreed. "The first to go. And from the moment of his death the others began to be removed one by one."

"You said you had two encounters with this Lavinus. What was the second?"

"Three years ago," the tribune answered, lifting his head up to peer over the horsemen in front of them curiously. "Just before I retired from the army. Our benefactor asked me to look into the rumor that a certain Roman senator was having dealings, both financially and politically, with a foreign potentate who held no love for Rome. A discreet inquiry, mind you. Our benefactor did not want to reveal to this senator he was under investigation."

Quintus Flavius grinned amusedly. *Our* benefactor was none other than Caesar himself. And now he was being counted among those in the inner sanctum of operatives close to the Imperator himself. He wondered if he should be honored, or more interestingly, *worried*, for the inclusion.

"Your investigations revealed?"

"Nothing," the tribune returned. "There was not a whiff of evidence to suggest any wrongdoing. But there was ample evidence available indicating the Lavinii had no love for the Julii. Now return to the present. A set of incriminating documents are stolen which would seriously jeopardize the authority of our benefactor. Who would be the one family this daring thief would go to, to negotiate a price over?"

"The answer is self-evident."

"Precisely. The patriarch of the Lavinii. But, and here it gets interesting, we've only recently been informed that *no documents were purchased*. No one saw one page of the documents. But soon afterwards, the murders begin. Many victims, some quite logical in some respects. Some quite strange. But all related to each other. Like you, the questions have haunted me. If there is a conspiracy and a number of patrician families are about to join a grand conspiracy, why would anyone begin with the murders of supposed key conspirators now? Why not wait until all the parties involved could be identified?"

"Someone developed cold feet and threatened to reveal to the authorities all that he knew."

"Yes ... we all *assume* that is the likely conclusion. But on closer examination it does not make sense. Spurius Lavinus would never have developed cold feet. Once his mind was committed to complete a task, no force on earth would have changed his mind. And remember. If this whole plan to incite an uprising against the Julii was to succeed, he was the key factor which would lead to success or failure. His death, therefore, severed the cabal's head and stopped it in its tracks."

"So what are you saying, tribune? This Caestus could not take up the mantle and replace a Spurius Lavinus? Or perhaps the beauty and intellect of an Atia Graccia would not have found some other prominent individual to be the face of this opposition?"

"Neither ..." Decimus began but halted as some distance ahead of the column, the screams of terrified men and women began to lift into the air.

The entourage of Tiberius Caesar continued to move slowly down the road, the column of men and wagons entering a small copse of trees lying picturesquely on the banks of the Tiber. Not a particularly large stand of trees. But the tall willows and poplars were densely packed, sending travelers who had been moving down an open road underneath a warm and very bright morning sun into a sudden pit of almost pitch black shadows.

Ahead, women, children and men of all ages and ranks were fleeing back down the road toward the ranks of armed men surrounding Tiberius Caesar. On their faces were the portraits of sheer terror. Far ahead, in the narrow slit of sunlight on the road coming out of the trees, framed the image of fleeing souls in front of two ranks of bare-chested gladiators armed with sword and shield marching in unison toward the opening of the road. Already the bright splash of crimson smeared the blades of several warriors and a few bodies lay scattered across the ground. But the terror did not end there. Behind them more screams cut through the still air.

Gladiators, running hard from the riverbank to form a heavy line of steel and shield, sealed any escape out of the tree line behind them. Sunlight reflecting brightly off bronze helms, both groups of warriors began marching toward the horsed Tiberius and his guard. To their left, in the depth of the darkness and underbrush, men rose from out of the foliage like wraiths and pounded their shields angrily with the flat of their stout blades in an incredible din of terrifying noise.

"Now!" screamed Decimus, viciously twisting the head of his horse to the right and screaming at the horseman beside him. "Now, for the love of the gods! We must move! We must get back to the wagons and deploy our men!"

CHAPTER FORTY

At the head of the column of men, Tiberius, sword in hand, was astride his black steed and screaming orders to his men. From the front and rear the ranks of gladiators continued to march slowly down the narrow channel of the road toward them. But on their flank the gladiators who were making their way through the trees were finding it hard going. Here Tiberius decided to attack first. Leading his personal body guard, along with a dozen or so other horsemen, the next Caesar plunged into the depths of the closely packed trees and straight toward a tiny gap which had naturally opened in the middle of the gladiator's line. The attending crash of horse, legionnaire, and gladiators was a tumultuous clatter of steel upon shield and steel upon steel. Horses screamed in terror and pain. Men screamed in defiance. The noise of tree limbs and shrubs being hacked to pieces mingled with the rest of the usual cries of battle and filled the still air of the small knot of trees. For a few brief moments the clamor of battle seemed to fill the entire world with its horrors. But Tiberius and his horsemen outnumbered the men arrayed against him the trees. Apparently no one had thought of the possibility that the son of Caesar would attack first. Therefore, the two lines of assassins coming down the road were too far away to support their comrades among the trees.

When the last of the bare-chested warriors fell dead into the thick brush, the sudden clap of silence descending onto those yet living was both startling and surreal. Soon broken, however, by Tiberius' commanding voice ordering his men back to the road and toward the wagons.

While Tiberius and his men fought among the trees, Decimus, Quintus Flavius, and the men assigned to protect them had been busy as well. Thundering through heavy underbrush and ducking underneath tree limbs, the tribune and centurion worked together to reach down from their saddles and grab the corners of the heavy canvas sheets which covered the wagons and pull them off in a precise, coordinated effort. As they worked one wagon, the legionnaires with them worked the others. What had appeared to be wagons heavily loaded down with massive wooden crates turned out to be quite different. Thin wooden walls had been built on three sides of each wagon fabricated in such a fashion to appear as if wooden crates were piled high underneath the canvas tarps. In reality each wagon carried twenty heavily armed infantry of Tiberius' own men. In a matter of seconds after the tarps were ripped away a full cohort of legionnaires spilled out onto the road and took up defensive positions around the wagons.

The smiling Tiberius' eyes alit with excitement, and his horsemen clattered down the road shouting encouragement to his men, and in return, accepted a raucous *Hurrah!* of martial spirit from one and all. With an athletic leap from his horse he landed on the ground and strode confidently up to Decimus' side, a wide grin on his handsome features.

"Well tribune, I must say. You certainly know how to organize a fabulous going away party!"

"Yes, well ... I could think of more pleasant experiences to be attending to at this particular moment. But Caesar, I do hope you remember your promise to me on the promise I gave to your mother."

"Yes, yes. I remember," the smiling Caesar answered, his white plumed helmet nodding reluctantly. "I will honor my promises. Like you, I do not enjoy the prospect of disappointing mother."

There was no more time for talk. From their front and rear the lines of gladiators fell upon the compact array of dismounted horsemen and infantry with a ferocity only the condemned can exert. There was no question the outcome of this battle. No one would throw down their shield and sword and beg for mercy. Gladiators, to a man, fought with the certainty they would either triumph or die. In truth, none believed they would live through this day. But they fought. Fought ferociously. Their hatred for all things Roman filled them with a sense of purpose. Knowing that a son of the Julii stood among the ranks of the Romans further enhanced their fighting zeal. If but one of them could carve their way through the standing Romans and cut down none other than Tiberius Caesar, their deaths would be well worth the price! So they fought. Fought like men. Fought like animals. Fought like demons.

The battle raged on. The sun drifted over the stand of trees ever so slowly. The ringing of steel and sword filled the surrounding countryside with maleficent ardor. Men died, both gladiator and Roman. Falling to the blood-soaked ground, bloody sword in hand, never to rise again. In the end, late in the afternoon, the sound of many horses galloping toward the copse of trees could be heard. Horns, farther along, of approaching infantry blared into the late afternoon sky. Reinforcements from Ostia were hurrying to assist in the fight to save Tiberius Caesar. But by this time the fight was over. The last gladiator fell to his knees bleeding from various wounds and died before collapsing into the dust in front of the blood-drenched figures of Decimus and Quintus Flavius.

By late night the carnage along the road and in the trees was cleared. The bodies of the dead were piled high onto a river barge which had been commandeered nearby. But as each body was carried on board and thrown onto the flat deck of the barge, Decimus and Quintus inspected each face. Somehow both knew. Neither was surprised the body of the mysterious, powerful Caestus came up missing altogether.

CHAPTER FORTY-ONE

Rome glowed in the light of a bright yellow sun. From the terrace, the white glare of the many marbled temples surrounding the home of Octavius was bright enough to hurt Decimus' eyes. Standing beside a marbled terrace railing, flanked by two small statues of the Greek god Dionysus standing on dark stone pedestals beside him, the serenity and calm of the old Caesar's home atop the Palatine was a stark contrast to his surroundings the day before. The city in daylight was a spectacle to behold. On any of the seven fabled hills of Rome a spectator would behold breathtaking beauty. But the view from the house of Octavius Caesar was unequalled. Unequalled not so much in the simple surrounding view of the city. But unsurpassed in the knowledge that one stood encapsulated in the aura of absolute power.

He knew he stood in the very center of Roman authority. He knew he should tread carefully. To pick and chose his words wisely. He knew the stakes. One false move. One word uttered inadvertently and he, along with the young Quintus Flavius who accompanied him, might disappear forever from the world of man and never be heard from again. Like so many other enemies of the Julii had suffered before. But hearing the soft shuffle of two sets of feet moving across the terrace, he knew himself as well. He knew Octavius. And Livia Drusilla. The three shared a bond. Shared a set of expectations genuinely unique with each other. Theirs was a relationship forged in battle and strife. Based on absolute trust. And honesty. An honesty that, for a Roman, was an emotion all too costly to possess, or share, with anyone.

"Decimus, my congratulations. You have saved the empire, again I might add, from ruin. I'm sure this must be quite tiring for you by now. But nevertheless, it goes without saying. We are indebted to you and to your young centurion here. The both of you performed magnificently!"

Caesar's voice was that of an old man. Soft and gentle. But holding a trace of humor and sarcasm at the same time. A voice long familiar to Decimus. The Imperator gripped both hands around Decimus' outstretched forearm and shook it fondly. On the old man's face was a wide grin of pleasure. Pleasure and relief. The relief of a man who had, suddenly and unexpectedly, been relieved of an immense weight from his shoulders.

"We must reward you, cousin. We must reward both of you. And I have the perfect gift in mind. You no longer own a house. Until now. On the other side of the Palatine is a house which once belonged to an old friend of mine. A senator by the name of Claudius Apollonius. Long since dead. No heirs. Bequeathed to me for some reason. Empty for some years. Now, however, it will be occupied. It is not ostentations and gaudy. Not a palace in any sense of the word. I know your tastes, Decimus. It is relatively small. Very comfortable. With a splendid set of gardens surrounding it. I will have it refurbished and restored. Plus I will give you a small yearly stipend so that you may hire servants to maintain the estate properly. What do you think of that?"

"I find myself speechless, Caesar. But there is no need for such extravagance. It was my duty to serve. I served without thinking of reward."

"Too many times you have served and suffered at our expense, Decimus. On many occasions serving our needs in matters so delicate I could not take the chance to reward you. But this time I can, and I shall. Take the house and its gardens. Take the stipend I offer. More importantly, accept my heart felt appreciation for such loyal service to us."

The old man's eyes turned to latch onto the face of Quintus Flavius as a jaunty smile of mirth lit up his features.

"You, young centurion, come from a very wealthy family already. What could a rich man give to a rich man that he does not already have? A promotion perhaps? A senior position in a legion? A command of your own?"

"Caesar, forgive me. But I believe I am too young to be given a command of my own. I admit, serving in an active legion has always been a dream of mine. But there is one gift I would cherish the most."

Both husband and wife set eyes upon Quintus Flavius with interest and remained silent. So too did Decimus. In the last few weeks he had found it quite pleasurable to work with this infectiously charming young man. The smiling young centurion was quick witted, unfailingly honest, brave to the point of foolishness, and very adept at commanding men's loyalty. Given the time and the circumstance he knew he could make Quintus Flavius into a very valuable agent. But it appeared as if that was not to be.

"The prize I wish for the most is to remain with the tribune and work for him. The empire, I am sure, is safe for now. But it is an empire. Which means there will always be a crisis to resolve sooner or later. A crisis which, perhaps, would directly appeal to the tribune's interests. I would like to be present when that happens."

"Ah," Livia Drusilla said with an odd, quirky glint in her eyes as she looked up into the face of Quintus Flavius. "Do we have a younger version of a Decimus Virilis morphing before our very eyes, husband?"

"I suspect so, my dear. Uncanny, don't you think?" Caesar answered, lifting an eyebrow and examining the young centurion closely. "If I didn't know better, I would say there was even a slight family resemblance here. But that can't be. What do you say of this, cousin? Are you willing to allow this brash young puppy to stay at your side and haunt you day and night with his incessant questions?"

"Do you have another assignment for me?"

"Perhaps," the old man mused, running a gnarled old hand across his chin thoughtfully. "There is this woman, this Atia Graccia to track down. She seems to have quite mysteriously disappeared. And this creature who calls himself Caestus. Where is he? He too has disappeared into thin air. I do not enjoy leaving anything unresolved in cases like this. Unresolved issues tend to become serious threats sometime in the future."

"Caesar," Livia said, laying a gentle hand on Caesar's arm to collect his full attention. "Perhaps we should send cousin Decimus and his men to Carthage. His reports mention Carthage often. I suspect Carthage might be the key here. Perhaps the destination of both Atia Graccia and this pirate who calls himself Caestus?"

"An excellent idea. Decimus, would you be willing to travel to Carthage in say, two months from now? Two months should give both you and your men time enough to recuperate and relax before going off again. What say you?"

Decimus smiled thinly, glancing at the grinning Quintus before bowing slightly. "We would be delighted, Caesar."

"Then it is settled," the old man said firmly, half turning to look at his wife. "I find myself aching a bit too much, Livia. I need to recline and rest some. Entertain our guests for a few moments longer? Perhaps take an escort of men and show Decimus his new house. I think the three of you would enjoy that."

"A splendid idea, husband. I would enjoy a brisk walk over to his new house. You go and rest, Octavius. You have been far too busy of late. Neither of us are as young and robust as were once were."

Caesar said nothing as he made his way across the terrace toward the large house behind him. The three watched the old man for some time in utter silence before Livia turned to the tribune.

On her face was the look of a lioness eyeing her next prey.

"So, Decimus. I see it in your eyes. You have questions to ask. Feel free to express them. Let us not keep anything hidden between us. Each knows too many of the other's dark secrets already. Let us not be coy with each other. Speak your mind openly and clearly as you have always done."

"The attempt on my life a few weeks ago. While we were at the races. That was you, wasn't it? You ordered my death."

Livia Drusilla lifted her head and laughed in delight. Soft and child-like, it sounded like music to both men's ears.

"Not your death, dear cousin. I needed you in this affair. But I wanted to make sure I activated your keenest senses, your fullest cooperation. You were the only one who had the talent to track down those who planned to harm my son. I knew if I asked, or Octavius asked as he did, you would accept the commission. But it would have been a half-hearted commission on your part. A perfunctory duty you would complete in due fashion. But I wanted more than that. I wanted commitment. Dedication. How not to solicit such a response than by someone trying to kill you?"

"And Caestus," the tribune began, his face an unreadable mask. "He is your man, isn't he."

"He is indeed. The best there is in the things he does for me. A very deadly man who does not know who he works for. He thinks his master is a man who hates the Julii as much as he does. But in truth, he is the magnate which draws those who wish to do harm on our house toward him. When did you suspect the ruse?"

"When we discovered the dead littering the shoreline above Ostia. My suspicions were reinforced with the murder of Felix Gracchus and the return of Atia Graccia."

"Speaking of the witch, I take it you have her in chains somewhere?"

"My men intercepted her just as she was about to board a ship in Ostia bound for Carthage. She is here in Rome. In a wine cellar and guarded day and night."

Quintus Flavius stared at the tribune and the wife of Caesar in open disbelief. He heard the exchange between the old woman and the tribune. But his mind ... his mind was simply too confused to understand. The wife of the Imperator *ordered* a fake assassination on the tribune's life? Caestus was, unknowingly, a spy? A spy working in the service of Livia Drusilla? Impossible! Impossible! But even more astonishing—Atia Graccia was in chains?! How? When? How ... why ... when did the tribune know?

A wave of weakness swept over him. He felt light-headed. His knees threatened to give out. His mouth was dry. He staggered to a slab of carved marble and slumped down, pitching forward so far as to have his head between his knees.

"Poor child," the old woman said gently, stepping over to the stunned centurion and laying a hand on the young man's shoulders. "So much to learn in such a short time.

Decimus, you have a true and faithful servant here. If you are going to trust him, you should not hide so much from him. Do him a kindness and inform him all that has taken place so far. To be honest, I would like to hear it myself. I've always admired how your mind works."

She walked around the back of the marble bench to the other side and gently settled her old frame onto the cold stone before patting Quintus on his shoulder in a motherly fashion again.

"Pay attention, Quintus Flavius. You are about to hear a genius speak. And I mean that most respectfully, Decimus. A true genius."

"Thank you, cousin. But we both know who the true genius is in this family," he answered, bowing slightly toward Livia Drusilla. "Does Octavius know you've been doing something mischievous behind his back again?"

"He is old, Decimus. He is in pain. Constant pain. He is not the man he once was. But he suspects. That I am sure of."

"As he should," said the tribune. "He knows you as well as you know him. It is truly astonishing to contemplate the number of years you two have lived as man and wife and one has not tried to murder the other. Truly astonishing."

A cackle of that child-like laughter escaped the old woman's lips and amused delight flashed across the woman's still handsome face. A crooked, old finger lifted up into the air and waggled back and forth in front of her dark eyes.

"Before your time, Decimus. Long before your time many years ago. But that is behind us now. Continue, old friend. Enlighten us with your deduction."

"Yes, tribune. Tell me what in the name of the gods is going on here!" Quintus Flavius echoed in confusion.

"There was no conspiracy, Quintus. At least not a planned, long nurtured, deeply felt one hatched between old families years ago and hidden deep within family closets for generations, waiting for the right time to emerge."

"Then what was it? Why were so many people murdered? Why were we forced to fight a pitched battle in order to save Tiberius Caesar from assassination?"

"Do you want to answer that, dear cousin?" Decimus retorted, looking at the wife of Caesar.

"No. You are doing nicely, Decimus. Please continue."

The tribune nodded, frowning, and turned his attention back to the centurion.

"It was a witch hunt, Quintus Flavius. A cunning plan to root out anyone who might be an enemy to her son and may threaten his rule once he becomes the new emperor. Livia's determination to see her son become emperor is well known. Her cunning and ruthlessness equally well known."

"I would not say ruthless," the quite calm Livia Drusilla sighed as she crossed one leg over another and smoothed out the folds of her long gown. "Pragmatic is a word I would choose. Yes. Pragmatic. We live in cruel times, child. We all have suffered heavily for our family's past sins. No Roman family escaped from being severely mauled by those who wished to acquire power by any means necessary. I know what power can do to a person. I know what it has done to me. I merely wished to protect my son for as long as possible from such cruelty. Can not a mother strive to protect son from the world's cruelties? Is that not a mother's duty?"

"So ... all of this is your doing?" Quintus uttered, turning to look at the woman sitting beside him in stark wonder. "You planned all of this?"

"Indeed," Decimus sighed. "She knew of Caestus' talents. Knew he was both pirate and gladiator. Over the years I'm sure her spies had warned her repeatedly about the Lavinii and the Gracci. And others within the Julii for that matter. She realized her husband was close to his death. Knowing that Tiberius would be the heir to the empire, she decided to act on her own. She came up with a plan to remove the threats for Tiberius before they became true threats."

"Decimus, you are referring to me as if I have left Rome and sailed to some foreign land. I am here, sitting beside this handsome boy. Be so kind as to refer to me in the first person."

"As you wish, cousin. I suspect your spies informed you of the Lavinii's interest in the Antonian letters. In them you had the perfect bait to draw out those who might want to harm Tiberius. So you had them removed from your husband's private papers and hid them in some place where you knew they would be safe. And then you began spreading the rumors. The rumors that the letters had been stolen and were up for sale. Caestus the pirate was to be the go between. He would negotiate the sale of the letters to interested parties."

"Very good, Decimus. Very good. Spot on detective work. The original plan was to merely offer the letters and then round up and arrest those who might make a bid on them. But plans change, old friend. As you well know."

"The Lavinii, the Graccii, and some minor families of our own came together to form a cabal. You began to suspect the cabal may be even larger than you originally thought. You wanted to plumb the depths to see just how deep the rot within the patrician families went. So you ordered Caestus to suggest to anyone who would listen that he had in his possession evidence which would be the source for an open revolt. I suspect Caestus found evidence to suggest a number of families might be interested in the plot."

"But why kill Spurius Lavinus so early in the investigation?" Quintus asked, still feeling confused.

"Lavinus, that pompous fool, forced my hand. Before we realized it, he had already transported over a hundred trained gladiators from Greece to Ostia and more were on the way. On the night Caestus murdered him he was hurrying to Brundisium to board ship and flee to Greece. His spies told him Octavius had brought Decimus out of retirement to begin an investigation on a possible conspiracy. A move on my husband's part which caught me completely by surprise. Lavinus knew he would be the first of many you would question. I could not allow him to escape with his family fortune and whatever letters of communication he might have on him with his fellow traitors. I also had to find this band of gladiators loyal to the Lavinii and remove them from the scene as quickly as possible. I told Caestus to remove both threats."

"He was partially successful," Decimus continued. "He murdered Lavinus and removed all the letters which would incriminate the others. He found a portion of the gladiators freshly arrived from Greece and slaughtered them. But he did not find them all. Thus another plan had to be quickly slapped together in a desire to eliminate one and all."

"I do so love hearing you speak, old friend," Livia Drusilla exclaimed, clapping softly in appreciation of the tribune's skills. "It is as if you were at my side through all these last few days, hearing my every word and listening to my every thought. Yes. Yes. A new plan was hatched. Can you imagen what that might have been, young Quintus? Have you any idea how absolute power can become so absolutely corruptive to one's soul?"

"I ... you ... ordered Caestus to ingratiate himself into the confidence of Felix Gracchus in an effort pump him for any and all information he might know. And then ... and then after he was successful, you ordered the pirate to brutally murder the old man in his own house."

"Yes!" the hissing cackle of a madwoman retorted excitedly.

"Yes! Felix Gracchus and I are old enemies. He fought with the forces of Marcus Antonius in the wars. His pirate hordes preyed upon my family's ships for generations! When Antonius died, the Gracii saw the writing on the wall and came on their knees to Octavius begging for mercy. I almost strangled my own husband when he pardoned the entire family and welcomed them back into Roman life. So yes! I had Felix Gracchus murdered. He was to have done the same to Atia if she had arrived in time. But she returned home just moments after Caestus vacated the place and just as you and Decimus arrived."

"But Caestus did not learn of the whereabouts of the remaining gladiators, did he Livia? Felix Gracchus did not know. So a massive threat still remained. That meant either Atia Graccia might know or our distant cousin, Tertius Julius Romanus. You could not come and take Atia away from me. To do so would mean informing Octavius you were directly involved in this affair. So that left Tertius Romanus. But then a serendipitous event happened. Tiberius informed you I had spoken to him about the threat that possibly hung over him and of my plans to use him as a magnet to draw the remaining pirates out into the open. But to make sure for yourself that I was fully aware of the dangers and implications in such an endeavor, you asked me to meet you in private. I compliment you, cousin. You were very circumspect in ascertaining my intentions. Apparently I convinced you your son would be well protected in whatever adventure might come."

"You have never broken a promise to me, Decimus. I have never doubted you, either. When you said my son would be protected at all times, I felt very relieved. Your assurance allowed Caestus to go after and find Tertius Romanus."

"But ... but the pirate tortured both Tertius Romanus and Caius Septimus," Quintus said, who all this time had remained fully attentive to every word both of the Julii had said to each other. "Did you not know Caius Septimus was an agent working for your husband's chief spy?"

"She knew," Decimus replied, both men watching a wicked smile of a fox slip across Livia's lips. "The evidence being Caestus did not kill Septimus. By this time Caestus had discovered a smaller band of pirates lying in wait for orders. They being the ones we discovered in the warehouse night before last. In order to maintain control with the pirates he told them there were snitches among them who were about to be turned over to the authorities. To prove his point, he tortured Tertius Julius and Caius Septimus. He found out the hiding place for the main body of pirates and soon left. But not before killing Romanus as ordered."

"Still, why torture Septimus?"

"Information, child. Information," Livia answered gently. Like that of a mother talking softly to a dim-witted child. "Septimus apparently had been with this cabal from the very beginning. I needed to know how much he knew, and how much my husband might know, of my involvement. Fortunately, nothing was said of me. Which, indirectly, possibly saved the man's life."

The wife of Caesar came to her feet, a hand coming up to delicately hide a yawn which overtook her. She smiled at the sitting Quintus and then moved over to Decimus and ever so gently reached up and kissed the tribune on his cheek in a sisterly fashion.

"Darling, you are far too intelligent for your own good. You realize this, don't you? Thank Lady Fortuna you are a loyal and trusted friend and kinsmen. Otherwise you would be an implacable and most dangerous enemy to deal with. That, I confess, would be a tragedy for both of us. But let us think of happier thoughts. Come by sometime tomorrow afternoon, the two of you, and we shall tour your new home together. It should be fun."

She started to walk back to the large house but stopped a few feet away. She turned to look at the two men like the wolf they knew she was.

"Bring Atia to me in chains, dear cousin. To me personally. I will deal with her in my own fashion. Understand?"

"She says she is innocent, Livia. I lean toward believing her," the tribune said calmly.

"Yes, I know. Everyone at one time or another say they are innocent. Perhaps some are, to one degree or another. Sometimes. But this is Rome, Decimus. In Rome there are no innocent bystanders. There are only victims and perpetrators. I will decide which one she might be," she answered, smiling sweetly and waving a hand goodbye. "Good day, my handsome men. Thank you for your loyalty to the Julii. Until tomorrow?"

She left them standing shoulder to shoulder staring at the one Julii who might have been the most powerful of them all. A small woman. Very petite. Very intelligent. Very gentle. But with a spine made of tempered steel.

When she disappeared into the large house it was Quintus who finally broke the silence and forced the two of them back to the present.

"She terrifies me, tribune. I would rather stand before a howling mob of furry Gauls than stand before her when she is filled with anger. Am I wrong, or did I hear her correctly? She did threaten you, didn't she? Saying you might become an implacable and dangerous enemy?"

Decimus took in a deep breath and then exhaled slowly as a sly grin spread across his lips. "Yes, there was a threat given. But fear not. She has said that to me every time I've completed an assignment, either for her or her husband. To date this has been the fifth such warning."

"Not a comforting thought, tribune." Quintus scowled looking back at the house of Caesar Augustus. "Let us leave this place while we still have our heads attached to our shoulders. Where should we go next?"

"To a place that provides good wine. Lots and lots of good wine. Let us drink until we can remember no more and then later on, we shall bathe the alcohol out of us in the finest bath house in the city. We still live, young Quintus. We still live. Let us live to the fullest while we can. For who knows what tomorrow will bring us?"

"Again. Not a comforting thought, tribune," Quintus growled, turning to follow a departing Decimus. "Not a comforting thought at all."

They still lived. Rome still was the city of the Julii. And nobody knew what the morrow would bring.

The End

ABOUT THE AUTHOR

My name is B.R. Stateham. I am a 72 year-old male with a mind still filled with the wonders and excitement one might find in a fourteen year old boy. I write genre fiction. You name the genre, I've probably got a short-story, a novella, or a novel which would fit the description. I've been writing for over 50 years. Which, frankly, means very little in reality. Most writers can say the same thing. For a writer, storytelling is something built into one's psyche. From birth on, a writer was probably telling some kind of story to himself, or anyone close to him. Whether they listened or not.

For the last 37 years I've been married to the same patient woman. A school teacher, now retired, who has this thing of sitting down with me and discussing, or verbally outlining, concepts for stories knocking around in my head. We have three grown adults for children and six (if I got the current number correct) grandchildren. None of the children or grandchildren think that me being a writer is of any particular significance. As it should be.

I like writing dark-noir. Or hardboiled detective/police-procedural novels which border the demarcation line between dark-noir and hard-boiled fiction. In fact, I like mixing up sub-genres in my fiction. Don't be surprised if you read something of mine traditionally found in the dark-noir niche with tinges of Science-Fiction or the Supernatural thrown in to spice up the tale.

That's it. There's nothing else to say. I'm just as writer. But I hope you'll find something of mine to read and find it enjoyable.

To learn more about B.R. Stateham and discover more Next Chapter authors, visit our website at www.nextchapter.pub.

Printed in Great Britain
by Amazon

43683344R00162